INVISIBLE

JAMES PATTERSON is one of the best-known and biggest-selling writers of all time. He is the author of some of the most popular series of the past decade – the Alex Cross, Women's Murder Club, Detective Michael Bennett and Private novels – and he has written many other number one bestsellers including romance novels and stand-alone thrillers. He lives in Florida with his wife and son.

James is passionate about encouraging children to read. Inspired by his own son who was a reluctant reader, he also writes a range of books specifically for young readers. James is a founding partner of Booktrust's Children's Reading Fund in the UK. His books have sold in excess of 300 million copies worldwide and he has been the most borrowed author in UK libraries for the past seven years in a row.

Also by James Patterson

STAND-ALONE THRILLERS

Sail (*with Howard Roughan*)

Swimsuit (*with Maxine Paetro*)

Don't Blink (*with Howard Roughan*)

Postcard Killers (*with Liza Marklund*)

Toys (*with Neil McMahon*)

Now You See Her (*with Michael Ledwidge*)

Kill Me If You Can (*with Marshall Karp*)

Guilty Wives (*with David Ellis*)

Zoo (*with Michael Ledwidge*)

Second Honeymoon (*with Howard Roughan*)

Mistress (*with David Ellis*)

A list of more titles by James Patterson is printed at the back of this book

JAMES PATTERSON
& DAVID ELLIS

INVISIBLE

arrow books

Published by Arrow Books in 2015

1 3 5 7 9 10 8 6 4 2

Copyright © James Patterson, 2014
Excerpt from Burn copyright © James Patterson, 2014

James Patterson has asserted his right under the Copyright,
Designs and Patents Act, 1988 to be identified as the author of this work

This novel is a work of fiction. Names and characters are the product of
the author's imagination and any resemblance to actual persons,
living or dead, is entirely coincidental

This book is sold subject to the condition that it shall not,
by way of trade or otherwise, be lent, resold, hired out,
or otherwise circulated without the publisher's prior
consent in any form of binding or cover other than that
in which it is published and without a similar condition,
including this condition, being imposed on the
subsequent purchaser

First published in Great Britain in 2014 by Century

Arrow Books
Random House, 20 Vauxhall Bridge Road,
London SW1V 2SA

www.randomhouse.co.uk

Addresses for companies within The Random House Group Limited can
be found at: www.randomhouse.co.uk/offices.htm

The Random House Group Limited Reg. No. 954009

A CIP catalogue record for this book
is available from the British Library

ISBN 9780099594529
ISBN 9780099594536 (export edition)

Typeset by SX Composing DTP, Rayleigh, Essex, SS6 7XF
Printed and bound in Great Britain by Clays Ltd, St Ives Plc

MIX
Paper from
responsible sources
FSC® C018179
www.fsc.org

Penguin Random House is committed to a sustainable
future for our business, our readers and our planet.
This book is made from Forest Stewardship Council®
certified paper.

To the Kasper family—Mike, Laura, and the little angel, Sophie Mei-Xiang

Chapter 1

THIS TIME I know it, I know it with a certainty that chokes my throat with panic, that grips and twists my heart until it's ripped from its mooring. This time, I'm too late.

This time, it's too hot. This time, it's too bright, there's too much smoke.

The house alarm is screaming out, not the early-warning beep but the piercing *you're-totally-screwed-if-you-don't-move-now* squeal. I don't know how long it's been going off, but it's too late for me now. The searing oven-blast heat within the four corners of my bedroom. The putrid black smoke that singes my nostril hairs and pollutes my lungs. The orange flames rippling across the ceiling above me, dancing around my bed, almost in rhythm, a taunting staccato, popping and crackling, like it's not a fire but a collection of flames working together; collectively, they want me to know, as they bob up and down and spit and cackle, as they slowly advance, *This time it's too late, Emmy*—

The window. Still a chance to jump off the bed to the left and run for the window, the only part of the bedroom still available. The enemy is cornering me, daring me, *Go ahead, Emmy, go for the window, Emmy*—

This is my last chance, and I know, but don't want to think about, what happens if I fail—that I have to start preparing myself for the pain. It will just hurt for a few minutes, it will be teeth-gnashing, gut-twisting agony, but then the heat will shrivel off my nerve endings and I'll feel nothing, or better yet I'll pass out from carbon monoxide poisoning.

Nothing to lose. No time to waste.

The flames hit my flannel comforter as my legs kick over to the floor, as I bounce up off the mattress and race the one-two-three-four steps to the window. A girlish, panicky squeal escapes my throat, like when Daddy and I used to play chase in the backyard and he was closing in. I lower my shoulder and lunge against the window, a window that was specifically built to *not* shatter, and ringing out over the alarm's squeal and the lapping of the flames is a hideous roar, a hungry growl, as I bounce off the window and fall backward into the raging heat. I tell myself, *Breathe, Emmy, suck in the toxic pollution, don't let the flames kill you, BREATHE*—

Breathe. Take a breath.

"Damn," I say to nobody in my dark, fire-free room. My eyes sting from sweat and I wipe them with my T-shirt. I know better than to move right away; I remain still until my pulse returns to human levels, until my breathing evens out. I look over at the clock radio, where red fluorescent square numbers tell me it's half past two.

Dreams suck. You think you've conquered something, you work on it over and over and tell yourself you're getting better, you *will* yourself to get better, you congratulate yourself on getting better. And then you close your eyes at night, you drift off into another world, and suddenly your own brain is tapping you on the shoulder and saying, *Guess what? You're NOT better!*

I let out one, conclusive exhale and reach for my bedroom light. When I turn it on, the fire is everywhere. It's my wallpaper now, the various photographs and case summaries and inspectors' reports adorning the walls of my bedroom, fires involving deaths in cities throughout the United States: Hawthorne, Florida. Skokie, Illinois. Cedar Rapids, Iowa. Plano, Texas. Piedmont, California.

And, of course, Peoria, Arizona.

Fifty-three of them in all.

I move along the wall and quickly review each one. Then I head to my computer and start opening e-mails.

Fifty-three that I know of. There are undoubtedly more.

This guy isn't going to stop.

Chapter 2

I'M HERE FOR the Dick. That's not what I actually say, but that's what I mean.

"Emmy Dockery for Mr. Dickinson, please."

The woman parked at a wedge of a desk outside Dickinson's office is someone I've never met. Her nameplate says LYDIA and she looks like a Lydia: cropped brown hair and black horn-rimmed glasses and a prim silk blouse. She probably writes sonnets in her spare time. She probably has three cats and likes Indian food, only she would call it *cuisine*.

I shouldn't be so catty, but it annoys me that there's someone new, that something has changed since I left, so I feel like a stranger in an office where I faithfully labored for almost nine years.

"Did you have an appointment with the director, Ms. . . . . Dockery?"

Lydia looks up at me with a satisfied smirk. She

knows I don't have an appointment. She knows because they called up from the lobby to see if I was authorized to enter. She's just reminding me that I've only gotten this far as some kind of courtesy.

"The *director?*" I ask with faux confusion. "You mean the *executive assistant director* for the Criminal, Cyber, Response, and Services Branch?"

Okay, I can be a bitch. But she started it.

I wait Lydia out, because I wouldn't be standing here if the Dick hadn't agreed to see me.

He makes me wait, which is so like him, but twenty minutes later I'm in the office of the Dick. Dark wood walls and trophy photographs on the walls, diplomas, ego stuff. The Dick has a tremendous and entirely undeserved opinion of himself.

Julius Dickinson, he of the ever-present tan and comb-over, the extra ten pounds, the smarmy smile, gestures to a seat for me. "Emmy," he says, thick with false pity in his voice but his eyes bright. Already, he's trying to get a rise out of me.

"You haven't returned any of my e-mails," I say, taking a seat.

"That's right, I haven't," he says, making no attempt to justify the stiff-arm he's given me. He doesn't have to. He's the boss. I'm just an employee. Hell, I'm not even that at the moment; I'm an employee on unpaid leave whose career is hanging by a string, whose career could be destroyed by the man sitting across from me.

"Have you at least read them?" I ask.

Dickinson removes a silk cloth from his drawer and cleans his eyeglasses. "I got far enough to see that you're talking about a series of fires," he says. "Fires that *you* think are the work of a criminal genius who has managed to make them appear unrelated."

Basically, yes.

"What I *did* read in its entirety," he adds with a sour note, "was a recent article from the *Peoria Times,* the local newspaper in a small Arizona town." He lifts up a printout of the article and reads from it. "'Eight months after her sister's death in a house fire, Emmy Dockery is still on a crusade to convince the Peoria Police Department that Marta Dockery's death was not an accident, but murder.' Oh, and this part: 'Doctor Martin Lazerby, a deputy medical examiner with the Maricopa County Medical Examiner's Office, insists that all forensic evidence points to death by an accidental fire.' And this is my favorite, a quote from their police chief: 'She works for the FBI,' he said. 'If she's so sure it's murder, why doesn't she get her own agency to investigate it?'"

I don't respond. The article was crap; they took the police's side and didn't even give a fair airing of my evidence.

"It makes me wonder about you, Emmy." He puts his hands together and collects his thoughts, like he's about to lecture a child. "Have you been getting therapy, Emmy? You badly need help. We'd love to have you return, of course, but only after we've seen some progress in your treatment."

He can hardly suppress a smile as he says this. He and I have history; he was the one who had me brought up on disciplinary charges for *inappropriate conduct* that got me suspended—I'm sorry, in bureaucratic-legal lingo, placed on *unpaid administrative leave*. I've still got seven weeks before I return, and even then, it will be a sixty-day probationary period. If I hadn't had a recent death in the family, I probably would have been canned.

He knows the real reason why I was brought up on charges. We both do. So he's taunting me here. I can't let him get under my skin. That's what he wants. He wants me to blow up, so he can tell the brass that I'm not ready to return.

"Somebody's running around the country killing people," I say. "That should concern you whether I'm in therapy or not."

His eyes narrow. He doesn't have to do anything

here; I'm the one who wants something. So this is his idea of torture, sitting there tight-lipped and stubborn.

"Concentrate on your rehabilitation, Emmy. Leave the law enforcement to us."

He keeps repeating my name. I'd rather he spit on me and called me names. And he knows that. This is the passive-aggressive version of waterboarding. I wasn't sure he'd see me today, unannounced. Now, I realize, he probably couldn't wait to see me, to shut me down, to laugh directly in my face.

He and I have a history, like I said. Here's the short version: he's a pig.

"This isn't about me," I insist. "It's about a guy who—"

"Are you feeling angry right now, Emmy? Do you feel like you're in control of your emotions?" He looks me over with mock concern. "Because your face is getting red. Your hands are balled up in fists. I'm concerned you still can't contain your emotions. We have counselors on staff, Emmy, if you need someone to talk to."

He sounds like a late-night commercial for chemical dependency. *We have counselors waiting to talk to you. Call now!*

There's no point in proceeding further, I realize.

It was dumb of me to come. Dumb of me to expect he'd listen to me in person. I was screwed before I got here. I get up and turn to leave.

"Good luck with your therapy," he calls out. "We're all rooting for you."

I stop at the door and look back at him.

"This man is killing people all over the country," I say, one hand on his office door. "And it's not that we're chasing him and can't catch him. It's that we don't even know there's someone to catch. It's like he doesn't even exist to us."

Nothing from the Dick but his cupped hand, a tiny wave good-bye. I slam the door behind me.

Chapter 3

I WAIT UNTIL I leave the building before I blow off any steam. I won't give Dickinson the satisfaction of seeing me angry, and I won't give him fodder to use against me when I try to return to my job in seven weeks. (The truth is, I probably already have; he can point to my e-mails, and however he chooses to paint the conversation we just had, as proof that I'm "obsessive" and also committing the greatest sin of a research analyst—acting like an agent, forgetting my place in the hierarchy.)

When I settle into the return drive on I-95, I give my steering wheel a couple of good hard smacks, which doesn't make me feel any better and, if I'm not careful, could leave me with broken fingers. "Asshole!" I yell. That makes me feel better; the only thing I might hurt is my vocal cords. "Asshole! Asshole!"

Dickinson owns me now, after the disciplinary hearing; I'll be on probation, and if I make one false step—or if the Dick even *claims* I misstepped—I'm done. Oh, watching him smirk at me back there, pretending that I'm in need of therapy. We both know my only *disciplinary problem* was that I pushed his hand off my knee every time he put it there, I said no to late dinners, and even laughed at the idea of a weekend getaway, just the two of us. It was the laugh, I think, that finally did it. By the next morning, he had concocted some story to the upper brass that *I* was harassing *him,* and becoming more and more aggressive. Add in words like *erratic* and *volatile*—words that are easy to say and hard to disprove—and voilà, you are a discipline problem.

Asshole.

But really, Emmy, get a grip. Solve the problem. I have to do something. I can't give up on this. I know these cases are connected. But I'm stuck. I can't go outside the chain of command, and the Dick is shutting me down, not on merit but out of spite. I'm stuck. What can I do? What else can I possibly—

Wait.

I let my foot off the pedal, for no particular reason, other than pissing off the SUV driver behind me—he *is* following me a little close—while I think it over. No. No. It's the last thing I should do.

But, yes, it might be my only way in. So I have to try it.

Because if I'm right about this guy, he's getting better and better at killing. And nobody even knows he exists.

Chapter 4

Welcome to my world. You can call me Graham, and I'll be your host.

You don't know me. My anonymity is a testament to my success. As I'm sitting here talking to you, I'm not famous. But I will be when these recordings are released, whenever it is that I decide to release them. Then I'll be on the front page of every newspaper and magazine around the world. They will write books about me. They will study me at Quantico. Websites will be devoted to me. Movies made.

You will never know my real identity—"Graham" may or may not be my real name—so whatever you know about me will come from these audio files, my oral diary. You will know what I let you know. I may tell you everything and I may leave

14

some things out. I may tell you the truth and I may lie to you.

A bit about me to start: I was sufficiently athletic to play high school sports but not enough to go beyond. I got good grades in school but not enough for the Ivy League, so it was a state university for me. I absolutely detest onions of any variety, cooked or raw, a vile weed no matter its iteration. I can speak three languages, though my French borders on the embarrassing at this point. But I can say *no onions please*, or the functional equivalent of that phrase, in no less than eleven languages, having recently added Greek and Albanian to my tally. I prefer your basic pop music to classical or adult alternative or heavy metal, but I don't admit that to my friends. I once ran a half marathon in one hour and thirty-seven minutes. I don't exercise regularly now. And I never, ever drink light beer.

Two of the things I just told you aren't true.

But this one is: I've killed a lot of people. More than you'd believe.

And you? I don't even know who you are, the person to whom I'm addressing this narrative: a sentient being, perhaps the spirit of one of my victims? A tiny demon perched on my shoulder, whispering dark thoughts in my ear? An FBI profiler. An enterprising reporter. Or just an ordinary citizen listening to these audio files on the Internet someday, hovering over the computer with lascivious fascination, hungry for any morsel, any kernel of information, any insight whatsoever into The. Mind. Of. A. Madman!

Because, of course, that's what you'll do—you'll try to understand me, diagnose me. It makes you feel comfortable and safe to do that, to assign me to some nice, neat category. You'll ascribe my behavior to a mother who didn't show me love, a traumatic event that redefined me, a mental illness in the *DSM-IV.*

But here is what you'll find instead: I could be chatting you up in a neighborhood bar, or trimming the hedges next door, or sitting next to you on a jet from New York to Los Angeles, and you would never even notice me. Oh, in hindsight, sure, you might pick out something about me that seemed off. But in real time, when I'm standing right in front of you or sharing an armrest or seated across from you, I would make no impression on you. I would be a set of data collected and immediately discarded. I would seem, in a word, normal. And do you know why?

No, you don't know why. But I do. It's why I'm so good at what I do. And why nobody will ever catch me.

[END]

Chapter 5

TWO YEARS AFTER it opened, the bookstore in downtown Alexandria still looks fresh and new, red brick with wood trim painted powder blue. The name THE BOOK MAN is stenciled across the front sidewalk window, which is filled with the latest releases, fiction and nonfiction, but focusing more these days on children's and picture books.

I take a breath before I enter the store, debating yet again the wisdom of this decision. But I've hardly slept the last two nights and I'm out of other ideas.

I push through the door to the *ding!* of a cheerful bell, and I see him before he sees me. He is wearing a plaid shortsleeved shirt untucked, blue jeans, and moccasins. It gives me a start to see him not wearing a suit and tie. It smells like new books and coffee in here. Sedate, peaceful.

He's behind the counter, ringing up a customer, when he sees me. He does a double take, then remembers to smile at the customer and throws a bookmark into a plastic bag. When the customer's on her way, he comes around. He wipes his hands on his jeans and stops short of me.

"Hello, Books." Figure I might as well start.

"Emmy." Just hearing his voice, deep and commanding but somehow gentle, unleashes so many memories from behind the mental dam I've erected. The *gentle* part is a tad more so, I notice, probably because the last time we saw each other, eight months ago, I was burying my sister. He showed up the morning of the visitation to console me. I'm not sure how he even knew about it— maybe my mother called him; I never asked—but there he was, never pushing, just fading into the woodwork, making himself available if I needed him. He always had the capacity to surprise me.

"Thanks for agreeing to see me," I say.

"I didn't. You just showed up."

"Then thanks for not kicking me out."

"I haven't had the chance to kick you out. I still might."

It's the first time I've smiled in weeks. Books looks great. Fit and relaxed. Happy. The jerk. Isn't he supposed to be miserable after our breakup?

"Are you still a coffee snob?" I ask.

Now he smiles, a little, grudgingly. Lots of memories there. Even on a government employee's salary, he always sprang for the good stuff, ordering Italian beans over the Internet. "Of course," he says. "Are you still a neurotic pain in the ass with a big heart?"

That's a fair assessment. Books knows me better than anybody. Still, the small talk between us is awkward, forced. I might as well cut to the chase.

"I need your help," I tell him.

Chapter 6

"NO," BOOKS SAYS, shaking his head furiously. "No way, Em."

"I want you to hear me out on this one, Books."

"No, thanks."

"You've never heard anything like this."

"As I said, or *think* I said out loud, no thank—"

"This one gets my vote as the most evil prick in the entire history of the world. I'm not exaggerating for effect, Books."

"I'm not interested. I'm not. I'm not," he repeats, as if trying to convince himself.

We're in the warehouse next to his store, surrounded by books stacked on tables or sorted on shelves. I found a small space on one of the tables, where I stacked up fifty-three case files for his review. "It's all right there," I say. "Just read it."

Books runs a hand through his sandy hair. It's

longer these days, bangs hanging over his forehead and curls in the back, now that he's a private citizen. He paces in a circle while he collects his thoughts.

"I don't work for the Bureau anymore," he says.

"You could come back for this," I answer. "They never wanted you to leave."

"This is more an ATF assignment, anyway—"

"Then we'll do a joint task force—"

"This is not my *problem,* Em!" He swipes at a table and knocks a stack of paperbacks to the floor. "You know how hard this is for me, to have you suddenly show up like this? And to ask me for help? This isn't fair." He jabs a finger at me. "This is not fair."

He's right. It's not fair. But this isn't about fair.

Books stands there for about two minutes, hands on his hips, shaking his head. Then he looks over at me. "Dickinson shut you down?"

"Yes, but not on merit. He never even read the files. You know the Dick."

Books allows for that. "And did you tell him why you care about this?" he asks.

"It's obvious why I care. A man is killing—"

"That's not what I mean, Em, and you know it." He walks toward me now. "Does Dickinson know that your sister died in a fire of suspicious origin eight months ago in Peoria, Arizona?"

"That has nothing to do with this."

"Ha!" A mock laugh, hands flying up. "This has *nothing* to do with it!"

"It doesn't. Whether my sister was one of the victims or not doesn't change the fact that a serial—"

Books doesn't want to hear it. He waves me off, la-la-la-I'm-not-listening.

"Emmy, I'm sorry about Marta. You know I am. But—"

"If you're sorry, then you'll help me." As soon as I say the words, even I realize I've crossed a line. Books has moved on with his life. He's done being a special agent. He sells books for a living now.

I put up my hands. "Strike that last comment," I say. "I shouldn't have come here, Books. I'm . . . I'm sorry."

I walk out the same way I came in, without a word from my former fiancé.

Chapter 7

"Graham Session"
Recording # 2
August 22, 2012

I love the smell of fresh flowers in the evening. It's such a summer-unique smell, isn't it? It makes this whole bedroom feel . . . what's the word . . . *new*. New and fresh. Fresh paint on the walls, pink with lemon accents. That bed is new, too, a queen-size bed with an old-fashioned canopy—is that like what you had when you were a little girl, Joelle? Was this a congratulatory present from Mom and Dad on the new townhouse, the new start on life?

Oh, never mind. I'm afraid Joelle can't talk right now.

The rest of this is positively quaint. The antique vanity, probably dusted off and hauled up from the parents' basement. A nice reading chair. Best of all, the makeshift nightstand, straight out of a college dorm room, two milk crates stacked, with a small alarm clock and that vase of fresh lilies.

A girl on a budget, with some taste but not yet the money to showcase it. A starter townhouse for a girl starting a professional life.

I wish I could take a picture of this room and show it to you, because this, right here, is the essence of America, the essence of hope, of starting small but dreaming big things. Joelle Swanson had grand plans. She dreamed of taking her criminal justice degree and becoming a big crime-fighter, maybe first a cop but someday the FBI or even the covert world of the CIA. Impressive stuff. Big things!

Anyway, I'd *like* to take a photograph for you, but I don't see how that will work later, how it would fit in with my narrative. I'd be too afraid you'd look at the pictures and ignore my words. I'm sure a psychiatrist would say that I limit these sessions to my oral testimony because I want to control every aspect of it; I only want you to know what I let you know, to see what I let you see.

It's true that this mode of communication has its limitations. You can't smell what I smell, that palpable odor pumped out through the glistening sweat on their skin. You can't see that desperate terror, the dilated pupils, quivering lips, the sheet-white color their skin turns when they realize that their worst nightmare has come true. You can't hear the sounds of a plaintive cry, a weepy, panicked, breathless plea forced out through a full throat. You simply cannot experience what I'm feeling.

So I will do my best to help you. I will do my best to teach you.

[Editor's note: sounds of a woman coughing in the background.]

Oh, look who's waking up. I guess that means I have to bid you adieu.

Hmmm. I wonder if this is too much, too fast with you. Maybe you need to get to know me better first, before I let you see what I do up close like this. Maybe I need to dance cheek to cheek with you first, wine-and-dine you, tell you some anecdotes, show you what I find funny and scary, my likes and dislikes.

Maybe I should tell you why I do what I do.

Why I pick who I pick.

Why I'm so damn good at it.

I have so many things to tell you. But let's take this slowly. We'll get there. By the time I'm done, you're going to understand me. You're going to find common ground with me.

Heck, you may even like me.

And some of you will want to *be* me.

[END]

Chapter 8

I POP AWAKE, gasping for air, the dancing flames on the ceiling receding to a dark, quiet room. I wipe sweat from my eyes with the comforter and shake away the remnants of the familiar nightmare, only this time with a twist: this time, the person in the bed wasn't me. This time, the person in the bed was prettier than me, smarter than me, braver than me. This time, the person in the bed was Marta.

My sister has made the occasional cameo in the dream, basically the same dream as when I'm the one about to be burned alive, only she doesn't scramble for the window like I do. She sucks in her breath and lets the flames race along the comforter until they lick her and swallow her whole.

I'm sure I won't be able to go back to sleep. I never can. I've taken to an early bedtime, early for me, anyway—ten o'clock usually—knowing that sometime between two and four in the morning, I'll be engulfed in flames, then up for the day.

So I put on some coffee and boot up my laptop. The breaking-news e-mails come at all hours of the night, so I'll have plenty to keep me busy.

I make the mistake of passing a mirror and looking at my reflection. Not a pretty sight. The first signs of gray in my locks, and I'm too stubborn to color my hair, too proud to succumb to modern technology's answer to female aging, which is to change yourself in every way possible, to hide your flaws. I put on minimal makeup and shower most days and brush my hair and figure I've done enough. No wrinkle creams or hair coloring or push-up bras for this gal. I'm supposed to be impressing someone with this attitude, aren't I? So far, no line has formed to congratulate me.

You're your own worst enemy, Marta always said to me. *You don't need anyone to torment you because you do it to yourself.* Marta was, in many ways, the polar opposite of me. Fun-loving when I was brooding. Glamorous when I was granola. Waving pom-poms and cheering on the football team while I was joining the PETA protest of the slaughterhouse outside of town. Partying on Friday nights with the popular crowd while I had my nose in one of the classics or some book on statistics.

She was two inches shorter than me, had darker and silkier hair, and wore a cup size larger than me. How two girls born within the space of eight minutes could be so different was anyone's guess.

"Damn, I miss you, girl," I say to nobody in the kitchen. I can't even say that line without an acknowledgment to her; it was what she always said to me at the end of our phone calls, her patented sign-off, when we were across the country from each other during college, or when she went off to grad school in Arizona while I, for some reason nobody could figure out, joined the G, the Federal Bureau of Investigation.

I still remember her reaction to the news that I was signing up with the FBI. Her face read stunned, confused, like she'd heard it wrong, a left-wing protester joining the establishment, but her words came out softer. *If it makes you happy, it makes me happy.* That was the other thing she always harped on with me, happiness. *Just be happy, Em. Are you happy? It's okay to want to be happy.*

Coffee's done. I carry a mug into the second bedroom and start scrolling through the usual websites and checking e-mail. Nothing I see immediately raises the hair on my neck. A single-family home up in flames in Palo Alto, no casualties. A fire in a subsidized-housing complex in Detroit, several believed dead. A chemical plant ablaze outside Dallas. No, no, and no.

But this one might be interesting, a fire that happened only hours ago in a place called Lisle, Illinois. A stand-alone townhouse. A single victim.

Her name is Joelle Swanson.

Chapter 9

The day after. Not unlike a hangover, the comedown after an overly indulgent night. I'm lying in bed, talking to you with this handheld digital voice recorder, staring at the photograph of Joelle Swanson I took last night after we ended things, and which I printed out on my color printer. She was a fighter, I'll give her that. All that blood, all that pain, and yet she still fought for her life at the end. Sometimes, I just don't understand people.

I know, I know, I told you I don't take photographs—but I do take one of each victim at the end of the encounter. Can't a fellow keep a souvenir?

Anyway—good morning! I try to start each day with the sunrise roundup at five in the morning. No better source for

30

car crashes, murders, other incidents of ill tidings. Especially on a day like today, the quote, unquote Day After, the news is required viewing. Here, I'm pulling up the video clip on the website right now . . . here it is:

"A house fire claimed the life of a woman in suburban Lisle overnight. Twenty-three-year-old Joelle Swanson, a recent graduate of Benedictine University, was killed when a fire erupted in her townhouse bedroom in the early hours of Wednesday morning. Authorities say the cause of the blaze was a lit candle that tipped over by her bedside. They do not suspect foul play.

"Well, coming up next in sports, the NFL season is just around the corner, but a labor dispute will keep the referees—"

Enough. Click that right off. I wish you could have seen the footage of the ink-black smoke billowing out of the rooftop of Joelle's townhouse. I love that word, *billowing*, one of those words that really only applies in one context. Does anything else besides smoke ever *billow?* They also had a sanitized photograph of Joelle that must have come from her recent graduation yearbook, posed and airbrushed. I prefer my photo of her; it has more character, more scars, more life.

By the way, I'm aware that it's strategically indefensible to retain photographs of my victims. Yes, I know, if I were caught, this would be a blow-by-blow tour of what I've done, better than a signed confession. What can I say? I need these photographs. I'm willing to be reckless on this one point. If it makes you feel better, I stash my collage between pages

232 and 233 of my mother's old *Betty Crocker Cookbook*, right next to the recipe for ground-beef lasagna. (Yes, it was a deliberate, if gory, choice.)

Ooooh, you're thinking. *His mother. The first mention of his mother occurs during the third session, at three minutes and seventeen seconds. Is there some significance to the time? Is 317 their street address growing up? Was her birthday March 17? Did she sexually abuse him 3 + 17 times?*

Okay, I might as well tell you: my mother made me dress up like Little Bo Peep when I was a child, and it's haunted me ever since. After I killed her with a machete, I vowed to mutilate all beautiful young blond women with whom I came into contact to rid myself of that horror. But it DOESN'T MAKE THE NIGHTMARES GO AWAY!

Just kidding. I know, I didn't sell that very well. Didn't have my heart in it. Maybe I'll tell you about my mother sometime. Maybe I won't.

I need to get ready for work now. Big day planned. I have one more adventure planned, at least, before Labor Day.

[END]

Chapter 10

I SPEND THE morning like I've spent every morning the last several months, sitting in my office (also known as my mother's second bedroom), combing through research and data. Because I'm on suspension, I don't have access to NIBRS—the National Incident-Based Reporting System. But NIBRS is useless to me, anyway; it only collects information on fires classified as arson. If they're deemed accidental, or even "suspicious" in origin, they never make it to NIBRS. And my guy is making the fires look accidental.

Which means he's staying totally off the radar. The locals aren't reporting these fires to the Feds, and they aren't talking to each other.

Which leaves me with the utterly unscientific method of setting up alerts on sites like Google and YouTube, then monitoring websites and message boards devoted to fire-fighting and arson, and getting breaking-news reports from local news websites. There are fires involving the loss of human life every day in this country, intentional or accidental, and whether they are reported to federal law enforcement or not, they at least make the local news in that area. So I'm inundated on a daily basis with news of fires, 99 percent of which is irrelevant, but all of which I have to review to make sure one of them isn't the needle in the haystack.

It's late afternoon now. I've spent hours huddled over this laptop and chasing down leads. I made one inquiry about the fire in Lisle, Illinois, but the cop there hasn't called me back yet.

My smartphone buzzes. Speak of the devil. I assume it's the cop, but after a day of solitary confinement, I'd happily chat up a telemarketer selling me life insurance.

I set my cell to speakerphone and call out a hello.

"Ms. Dockery, it's Lieutenant Adam Ressler, Lisle PD."

"Yes, Lieutenant. Thanks for the return call."

"Ms. Dockery, could you clarify for me your status? Are you with the FBI?"

This is my problem. I'm not. It would be bad

enough that I'm a research analyst, not a special agent—some locals will only talk to agents—but I'm not even a research analyst right now. When they look up my authorization code, they always find mine, so they know I am who I say I am, but the problem is that there's no clearance level next to that code.

"I'm on temporary leave with the Bureau," I answer, "working on a special assignment."

A lawyer would call that a *technically accurate statement*. It just so happens that the FBI has nothing to do with this "special assignment," which in fact I have "assigned" to myself. Basically, I'm a girl on suspension who is doing something completely on her own. But I made it sound a little better than that without lying.

Usually this works—to a point. I manage to fall on the spectrum somewhere between a random citizen or nosy reporter and an actual law enforcement officer. So I get answers to generally harmless questions, minimally sufficient for my purposes but not enough to give me the full picture I would prefer.

"Well, okay, why don't we see what you need," he says, meaning he'll answer some questions and not others. "You were calling about Joelle Swanson?"

"That's right, Lieutenant. The fire from three nights ago."

This is all I know so far: Joelle Swanson, age twenty-three, resided at a new townhouse at 2141 Carthage Court in Lisle, Illinois, a suburb roughly twenty-five miles outside Chicago. She lived alone. She was a recent graduate of Benedictine University and was working in their admissions office. She was single, no kids, not even a boyfriend. She died in the fire overnight, in the early hours of August twenty-second. No sign of foul play, according to the local fire chief.

"What was the cause?" I ask the lieutenant.

"A burning candle," he says. "Looks like it was on a desk and fell over onto the carpet. Between the carpet and some newspapers lying around and the polyurethane mattress, the whole bedroom went up real fast. The victim was burnt to toast right there on the bed."

I remain quiet, hoping he'll keep going.

"Chief said there was no evidence of an accelerant used. He said it looks like—well, he said, 'One of those stupid things people do,' falling asleep with a lit candle."

And with some stray newspapers conveniently lying around. "You're sure the fire originated in the bedroom?"

"Yeah, fire chief said no question. No question of cause or origin."

"What about the candle?" I ask.

"What about it?"

"Any theory as to how it fell over?"

He doesn't answer. It probably seems like a minor point to him, but really, how likely is it that a candle sitting on a desk would just fall over? It was indoors, after all. It's not like a harsh wind blew it over.

"If you don't mind me asking," says the lieutenant, "why does the FBI care about this?"

"Wish I could answer that, Lieutenant. You know how it goes."

"Well . . . okay, then."

"Will there be an autopsy?"

"I don't think so, no."

"Why not?"

"Well, for one thing, I'm not sure there's a body left to autopsy. And the better question is why? The chief says there's no sign of foul play. We don't know of any reason anyone would want to hurt her, and we don't have any evidence that anyone did hurt her."

"That's why you perform an autopsy, Lieutenant. To find the evidence."

There is a pause in the action. Over the

speakerphone it is dead silence, as if he's hung up. Maybe he did. Cops don't like being told their business by anyone, but especially not by the Feebs. "I know why you perform an autopsy, Ms. Dockery, but you don't autopsy every death. There's nothing at all suspicious about this, according to the experts—"

"You guys have an arson task force out there, don't you?" I ask. "Can you refer it to the task force?"

"We have a countywide arson task force, yes, ma'am, but we don't refer every fire to the task force or they'd never have time to work on the real arsons. Now, do you have some information to give me about Joelle Swanson that would make us believe that foul play was involved?"

"I don't know the first thing about Joelle Swanson," I concede.

"Well, then, I think we're done, ma'am. I'm busy."

"I know you are, Lieutenant, and I sure do appreciate your time. Can I ask for one more favor?"

An audible sigh, loud enough to make sure I hear it. "What?"

"The bedroom," I say. "What can you tell me about the layout of her bedroom?"

Chapter 11

LIEUTENANT RESSLER PROMISES to send me that information on Joelle Swanson's bedroom as soon as he can. That could mean ten minutes, and it could mean never. I probably could have managed his ego a little better; it tends to facilitate co-operation. But I'm getting tired of hearing about firefighters who know a lot about suppressing fires but precious little about starting them, closing up files before a thorough investigation has taken place. If this were a warehouse with millions of dollars' worth of damage, they'd dig through the ash and investigate the shit out of this. But a relatively small fire, with an obvious cause staring them in the face, is enough to make them shut down the investigation before it's started.

Needing a break from the computer, and having no appetite for microwaved mac and cheese, I start scrubbing the kitchen floor. I'm kind of a neat freak, and it's what the real estate agent wants, anyway; he was glad to hear that I was moving into the place after my mom moved to Florida and put it up for sale. It's easier to sell a house that someone is occupying. It was convenient for me, too, when I got suspended from the FBI. My condo in Georgetown was well beyond my financial capacity without a monthly salary.

So this is my life: I'm living in my mother's house in Urbanna, Virginia, for now, while Mom heads for sunnier skies in Naples. Living at home, unemployed, and not in a relationship. Emmy at thirty-five!

When the kitchen floor is clean, I sit on my haunches and stretch my arms. I'm tired in every way, physically and mentally. I got my hopes up with Books, I have to admit. He has the FBI director's ear, and if anyone would believe in me, it would be Books. But I can't blame him. He had every right to react the way he did. That's probably what bothers me the most.

I mean, what did I expect? I broke up with him three months before the wedding. I freaked out, basically, and broke the heart of a wonderful man. Now, two years later, I come waltzing back into his life and expect him to say *How high?* when I say *Jump*.

So now I'm back to a one-woman show, the Emily Jean Dockery Task Force, combing through data in the most amateurish way possible and calling local law enforcement all around the country, most of whom think I'm a lunatic.

And they might be right.

A knock at my door. A cold wave runs through me. I don't have many acquaintances here, much less friends. And it's past eight o'clock now.

I don't have a weapon, either. I have my sponge and bucket. I could threaten to clean the guy to death.

"Who is it?" I yell from the hallway.

The voice that comes back is familiar.

I exhale and open the door.

Harrison Bookman is wearing a different shirt but the same blue jeans as the other day. Under one arm, like school homework, is the stack of files I left him.

"He never kills on Sundays," he says.

"Never."

Neither of us speaks for a long beat.

"You better have good coffee," he says.

"I do."

"Sure, *now* you say 'I do.'"

That's twice I've smiled this week.

Chapter 12

WE ARE WALKING, Books and I, along Pennsylvania Avenue Northwest, past where D'Acqua used to be—our place, if any place was *our place*, selecting dinner from the fresh catch of the day on the iced display in the dining room and sipping white wine, or sitting outside and looking over the fountains of the Navy Memorial. A bit froufrou for both of our tastes, but it was our indulgence. It was our Friday night date.

But things change. The restaurant's business lost steam, and so did our relationship.

"This is only happening because you're a man," I say to Books.

Books appears to consider that seriously and gives a curt nod. "That's one possibility," he concedes, his brow furrowed. "Or maybe . . ." He strokes his chin like he's Sherlock Holmes puzzling over a riddle. "Maybe it's because I'm considered to be sane by a few people in the building, and you aren't." He snaps his fingers, like that sounds right to him.

"No, it's a gender thing. It's because I'm a woman."

"A woman with *sanity* issues."

"Books," I say, but then he stops cold just outside of FBI headquarters.

"You wanted this, not me," he snaps. "I'm trying to get you something you want. Why can't you just be happy about it without analyzing it to death?"

Yowza. That's a little more hostility than I would have expected.

He brushes past me. We give our names in the lobby. There was a time when each of us could flash a badge and walk on through. Now we're visitors, Books by design and me against my will.

"Just a moment," says the woman at reception. Books clasps his hands behind his back. It's always little things that bring back the memories. He always held himself that way when he was on the job, always the formality. Get him alone and he could have me in stitches, but to work with him, you'd think he was a typical humorless agent, Joe Friday, *just the facts, ma'am.* I used to make fun of him, in happier days, clasping my hands like him, walking like a robot and saying, *Yes, ma'am, no, sir.*

"Remember, Emmy, this is my meeting." Books turns and looks at me.

"I'll be good. Pinkie promise."

"I'm not a girl. So I don't know what the hell that means."

"But you do have a pinkie, don't you?"

He sighs. "It better mean that we do this my way."

"That's what it means. I wouldn't have it any other way, Books."

He lets out an exasperated grunt that tells me he doesn't believe me. He knows how high-maintenance I can be.

"You're the big man," I tell him. "I'm the little girl carrying your bag."

"You're not carrying my bag."

"But I will, if you want."

We get visitor badges from the receptionist, our bags are thoroughly checked, and we head to the elevators.

"You're full of vinegar today," Books says.

He's right. I'm hyped up, anxious, and this is how I'm compensating. This is the most important meeting I've ever had, so much is at stake, and here I am, cracking wise.

"You understand that even getting this meeting is a favor," Books says.

"I do."

Books shoots me a look before we step into the elevator. He won't speak, not a word, as we rise. It's one of his rules, his super-secret-spy mind-set. No discussing business in front of strangers.

But I know what he wants to say. I strung those two words together again: *I do*.

In my defense, I did break it off three months in advance. We got back the deposit on the banquet hall and the invitations hadn't gone out yet. I wonder if Books would consider that consolation? I'm guessing . . . not.

We give our name to some woman, and she shows us down the hall to one of the big conference rooms used by FBI director William Moriarty.

I can see Books tense up as we approach the room. This is the first time he's returned since he handed in his papers—over the director's objection—the first time he's roamed these halls with the thin carpeting and cheap artwork and the air of intensity, the thrilling whiff of the chase, hunting bad guys and keeping the nation safe. This can't be easy for him. I've asked for a lot from him, not that I deserve any courtesy from him whatsoever after what I did to him. Mental note: Books is good people.

I mean, he not only got a meeting, he got one

with the top dog. He managed to bypass my boss, the Dick, who clearly would have shot it down if he had the chance. I'm glad he won't be in this meeting.

The door opens. Standing at the end of a long table is Director Moriarty, flanked on his left by his chief of staff, Nancy Parmaggiore.

And to his right, the executive assistant director for the Criminal, Cyber, Response, and Services Branch. Also known as Julius Dickinson. Also known as the Dick.

"Shit," I whisper, as Books gently shoves an elbow into me.

Chapter 13

WILLIAM MORIARTY, FORMER FBI agent, federal prosecutor, congressman from New York, and federal judge in Washington, DC, now the director of the FBI for the last three years, lights up when he sees Books. Books worked under Moriarty during Moriarty's previous stint with the Bureau, and Moriarty didn't get where he is by forgetting people. "I took credit for a lot of this guy's good work," he tells his chief of staff and the Dick, both of whom smile and nod with appreciation like good little soldiers. "Didn't want to let this one go. Now he's selling books!"

The director takes a seat and motions for everyone else to do the same. Then he makes a point of checking his watch. "I have to brief the president at three, so I only have about ten minutes," he says.

Ten minutes? To talk about the worst serial killer in our nation?

"Assistant Director Dickinson has briefed me on the particulars," he says, "and I have to agree with him that if this is the work of one man, it's the most incredible story I've ever heard."

The Dick nods eagerly. After a moment, his eyes make their way over to mine. The dirty little bastard. But I promised Books I would behave. And anyway, the point is to get the Bureau to investigate, whoever gets the credit.

But for the record: fuck him.

"Now," says the director, raising a hand, "I don't know the details like Julius does, but from what he's told me, I agree with him on something else, too."

That he's a conniving, backstabbing, brownnosing ass?

"It's very, very premature to believe that this is one man's work. Or that these are even crimes in the first place." Moriarty looks over at the Dick. "Julius suggests that we take this slowly, before we commit too many of our precious resources to this issue. Julius is recommending that we open a preliminary investigation."

Is that what Julius recommends after his careful review of the evidence? How great of Julius!

"Books, do you want in on the Bureau's team?"

"Yes, Mr. Director," says Books.

"Sir." The Dick raises a hand. "With Agent Bookman retired, we'd have to iron out some details for reinstate—"

"Then iron them out." The director looks at the Dick. "You can iron them out, can't you, Julius?"

"Yes, sir, of course."

The director nods in Books's direction. "Maybe he'll have so much fun, we'll get him back for good."

Books clears his throat. "Mr. Director, will I be running the team, then?"

Moriarty jabs a finger to his right. "Assistant Director Dickinson will run it and report to me."

"You gotta be kidding," I say, before I can stop myself.

All eyes turn to me. I've just violated the one rule of behavior laid down by Books before we came in, but really—the Dick is going to run this operation? Are you freakin' *kidding* me?

Books puts a hand on my arm. "Very good, Mr. Director. But will I have a say in the staffing of the team?"

Moriarty looks surprised, like he can't understand why something like that would require his attention. "I'm sure you and Julius can work that out."

"Very good, sir, but specifically—Emmy Dockery here, one of your research analysts, the one who put together all of this . . ."

Books stops talking because the director is no longer listening. The Dick has leaned in to whisper something to the director, and the chief of staff is now huddling with them as well. While his underlings are chatting in his ear, the director looks up at me. I try to look like a stable and composed research analyst, not someone whose head is about to spontaneously combust.

Finally, Director Moriarty waves them both off. "Ms. Dock—Dockery?"

"Yes, sir," I say.

"Give us the room, if you would."

Give them the room? What the heck does that mean? I look at Books.

"He wants you to step outside so we can talk about you," says Books.

"Oh." I get to my feet and don't even look down the table at the big shots, for fear that daggers will spring from my eyes and pin back their ears.

"Thank you," I say, not sure why I've chosen those words. I close the door behind me, so people more important than I am can decide my fate.

Chapter 14

A RECEPTIONIST OR some lackey meets me when I step out of the conference room—nobody's allowed to just wander around up here—and I find myself in a small waiting area reading a *Time* magazine story about how our nation is getting really fat. No shit—just discovering that now, are we?

Once I've been let in on the shocking revelation that the reason for childhood obesity is that kids are sitting around playing video games and eating lard-filled fast food and sugar-coated, chemically enriched sodas and snacks, Books appears and sits across from me. I raise my eyebrows with expectation.

He smiles and shakes his head, then claps his hands. "Tomorrow at five o'clock sharp, we're meeting in Dickinson's office, and he's going to give us our marching orders," he says. "And we're going to follow them, Emmy."

"So that means I'm going to be a part of this *team?*"

"That's what it means. The director agreed—over Dickinson's objection, of course—that you can assist the team. Under my supervision."

"I don't like how any of that sounds."

"I don't, either, Emmy. I'm questioning whether I should be doing this at all."

I can see from his pained expression that he means it. He probably had to fight for me in there, and I should be grateful. I am, I guess. I just don't like being treated like someone who has to be babysat. This whole stupid, male-dominated place—

"Smile, Emmy," he says. "Because if you don't like this, I'll just go back to Alexandria and sell books. And without me, you're back on suspension."

"You don't get to order me to smile, Books."

He actually laughs, but not because he finds me humorous or because he's in a good mood. I know that laugh. It's a laugh of exasperation, his other emotions—frustration, anger—depleted.

"You have a personal interest in this investigation," he says. "No agent would ever be allowed on a team with a personal interest. No agent would *ever* be allowed to investigate her own sister's death—"

"I'm not an agent," I say, batting my eyes like a schoolgirl. "I'm just a mere research analyst."

"And lucky for you," he replies. "Because the only reason you get a pass is that, as a technical matter, you're merely assisting in the investigation. You get to be a part of the team."

He's right. I know he's right. I'm supposed to be happy right now. I throw my head back, swallow hard—very, very hard—and take a deep breath.

"You got this meeting with Moriarty and it worked," I say. "And you fought to have me be a part of this team. I appreciate all of that, Harrison. I do."

Shit, I said "I do" again.

His index finger waves at me, a *tsk-tsk* motion. "Don't call me Harrison. I came back because it's possible—possible—that we have a serial killer on the warpath, and I don't like serial killers as a rule. And you're the reason we even know about him. If this person is real, if this is a real thing, then he's not like anybody I've ever seen."

"And we're going to catch him," I add.

"Yes, if he's real, we're going to catch him, and Julius Dickinson is going to take all the credit. And you're going to be okay with that."

I raise my hands in surrender. "As long as we catch him," I say.

Books eyes me carefully, then pushes himself out of his chair.

"If he even exists," he says.

Chapter 15

Hello, class. Do you mind if I call you "class"? I assume you're listening to this because you want to learn, and when I say learn, I don't just mean learn *about* me—background, motivations, etc.—but learn *from* me, too. Maybe not every one of you. Some of you just have plain ol' morbid curiosity, looking for a peek at a "day in the life," in the same way you slow your vehicle at the site of an accident, hoping for a glimpse of a split forehead gushing blood or a limp body on a gurney, a dead hand dangling down. But at least some of you out there, I'm sure, want to know more than *how* I do it and *why* I do it.

You want to know if you could do it, too.

Here's the good news: you can! And I'm going to show you how.

I'm going to walk inside now. It looks like it might rain. I'll talk a little louder inside, and I hope you can hear me over the crowd noise, because this place is really starting to fill up.

Just for your information, if you're wondering how I'm talking to you while I'm in a crowd of people: my audio recorder looks like a smartphone, so I just hold it up to my ear and talk into the end with the microphone as if I'm on the phone with some friend. As long as I do the necessary things to sell it—pause occasionally while my phantom person-on-the-other-end speaks, sprinkle in some interrupted sentences, occasionally throw in a *What?* or *Can you hear me now?* or the like, scrunch my face and put my hand over my ear and concentrate now and again—no one will doubt I'm on the phone.

For example, here I am, threading my way through the crowd forming in this bar, and I'm not three feet away from a guy who looks pretty intense, muscle-bound with a tight haircut, his T-shirt two sizes too small, that kind of thing, and I know that I can say whatever it is I want to say about him and he won't so much as bat an eye because I'm speaking in a conversational tone with an electronic device against my ear. Here, I'll show you. I'd like to have a few minutes alone with this fine gentleman so I could stick an ice pick through his ear and keep pushing until I hear a crunch, and then I'd like to set his body on fire with some kerosene and a blowtorch, and you have no idea at all that I'm talking about you, do you, my friend?

Invisible

What's that? Can you—can you hear me now? Is that—is that better? Can you hear me okay?

See, it's a piece of cake. And this is one of the points I want to make to you, that I'll keep returning to: whatever it is that you're doing to further your goal, you have to sell it. I mean, sell it all the way, from start to finish, go all out, everything you have. It can be a big thing or a minor detail. Actually, it's usually the minor details that derail you, when you have to be the most careful.

So, for example, with me on the phone right now: when I'm done visiting with you, I could just drop the recorder-posing-as-a-phone into my pocket without doing the things you normally do when you end a call—say good-bye and punch a button or, if a call is dropped, shout into the phone, then look perplexed or disgusted and shake your head. I could give up the ruse, in other words, and just stuff the recorder in my pocket.

But what if someone *is* watching me, for some reason? Or what if someone with a badge clipped to his jacket is watching the security video of this establishment later, looking for signs of something amiss? It's not very likely, I'll grant you, but what if that happened? Then they'd see me walking through the bar, appearing to talk on the phone, but then ultimately just slipping it into my pocket. They'd know I was engaged in deception. I would stand out to them. And standing out to people is not what you want to do. It is — pay attention now — the very *last* thing you want to do.

So I'll make sure, whenever I pick up this recorder to speak to you in any place where anybody could possibly see me, that I say, "Hello? Hey, how's it going?" or some such salutation. And when I'm done with my session with you, it will be, "Talk to you later," "See ya," whatever, and then I'll touch a button to indicate hanging up. Just so you understand, so I don't confuse you.

This matters because I expect that the police might—just might—be reviewing the video footage from this bar tonight when they learn that this was the last place that Curtis Valentine was seen alive. That's him, over there in the corner, the guy with the ponytail and some extra weight in his midsection, the black shirt and blue jeans, his head down in a glass of foamy beer, awkwardly shifting his weight from one side to the other. He runs a website maintenance business out of his home called Picture Perfect Designs. I learned that from Facebook. He seems like a nice enough guy. I learned *that* from talking to him on the phone yesterday, when I set up this appointment, meeting for a beer at a local pub.

Okay, he sees me now. We've never met in person but he's guessing I'm his appointment, the way I'm looking around for somebody.

Curtis? Hey, how are you? Nice to meet you in person. Hey, one second, let me finish up this call!

Okay, class, I gotta run now. Talk soon. Bye!

Sorry, Curtis. It's great to finally meet you in person . . .

[END]

Chapter 16

BOOKS COMES TO my place—my mother's place, technically—to do more research and then spends the night. It's the first night we've spent under the same roof since I broke off our engagement. Yeah, it's weird. It's Alice-in-Wonderland weird. But it's a long drive back home for him from here, so it made sense for him to stay.

But it's kinda weird.

We're in the kitchen. I'm at the table with my laptop, checking e-mails and my familiar websites, while Books is cooking some pasta. He's a better cook than I am, which isn't saying a whole lot. Actually, we used to cook together all the time, opening a bottle of wine and nibbling each other's necks while we chopped vegetables and stirred sauces. Good memories. I have a lot of good memories with Books. He's the only person in the world besides Marta who ever truly got me, which, *ahem,* is probably why things didn't work out.

"You have any red pepper flakes?" Books asks.

"I have no idea," I say absently, combing through my e-mails of recent fires, eliminating the easy ones, flagging for follow-up anything that raises my hackles. "Look around."

"That's great advice. I thought if I stood here, closed my eyes, and opened my hand, it would magically appear. You say I should look around?"

My smartphone buzzes on the table. It's Dorian. I'd called her earlier today and left a message.

"Hi, Mom."

"You said you had good news," she tells me. There is a faint slur to her words, a problem she's had since my dad passed away five years ago. She never gets falling-down drunk, just likes to lubricate the edges with Tanq-and-tonics before dinner. It got worse for a short time after Marta's death. Marta, I always thought, had been her favorite, their shared features and cheerleader-happiness thing. When I was growing up, Dorian was wont to say things to me like, *I just don't understand you, Emmy,* when she really meant, *Why are you so different from me? Why aren't you more like Marta?*

"I do. I'm gainfully employed again."

"With who?"

"What do you mean, 'with who'? With the Bureau, Mom. I have my job back."

"Oh, that's great. They brought you back early?"

"Yeah. I showed them my research on the fires, and they agreed to open an investigation. With me on the team."

Silence. Mom was always ambivalent about this obsession I had with all these fires. She thought that I was looking for something positive out of Marta's death, that if I could tie it to a crime that I could solve, I could make it all mean something—*Marta died so we could catch this killer,* something like that. She has never believed that Marta was murdered.

"This is where the mother says to the daughter, 'That's great, honey!'"

"If I thought it was great, Emily Jean, I'd say it was great."

"Books is on the team, too," I add, thinking that might perk up her attitude. She always liked Books. Everyone likes Books.

I glance over at him, stirring penne noodles while the steam hits his face.

"*Harrison?* I thought he quit the FBI after you broke up with him."

Lovely how she put that. "He did quit the Bureau, Mom, but not because I broke up with him. He quit because he'd done what he wanted to do, and he was looking for other challenges."

"I don't believe that," Mom says. "He quit because it was too painful for him to be in the same building as you."

"Well, he's right here, so let's ask him," I say, feeling a little testy. "Books, come here and tell my mother why you quit the FBI."

Books puts down the wooden spoon he was using to taste the pasta sauce, wipes his hands with a towel, and walks over to the table. He takes my phone. "Hi, Dorian, how are you? I'm fine, thanks. Yeah, the book business is tough these days but we're doing okay. How's Naples? Good to hear, great . . . Anyway, the reason I left the FBI was because Emmy broke up with me."

He hands me back the phone. I've never seen so wide a smile on his face.

"That's not true," I protest to my mother. "He's just saying that."

"I'm not just saying that!" he calls out, his hand cupped over his mouth.

"He's not just saying that," Mom joins in.

"Mom, I gotta run. This has been one of our more enjoyable chats."

I punch out the phone.

"That was real sweet, Books."

"Pasta's almost ready. You about done with that research?"

"Just about. I don't think there were any arson victims last night."

"Well, that's too bad. Actually—that's good, right?"

Books plates the food—penne with red sauce, steamed broccoli with garlic, a little salad. I notice for the first time some small flecks of gray at his temples, more noticeable with the longer hair. He catches me looking at him and I break my eyes away. If evading intimate moments were an Olympic event, I'd have a gold medal.

By the time he's opened the bottle of wine, I'm done with my breaking-news e-mails and regular websites. For now. They come in like avalanches throughout the day.

"You work too much," he says to me as he sits down.

I make a face. "Coming from you?" The wine, something Books bought in town, has a coppery taste to it, too pungent.

"Well, that was something I realized about myself when I left the Bureau," he says. "Life isn't all about work."

"No? What are you, taking up mountain climbing all of a sudden? Parcheesi?"

"Don't put down what I'm saying," he says.

"I'm not putting you down. I would never put you down."

Books takes a long drink from the wine, savors it in his mouth, swooshes it, swallows, then lets out a pleasurable sigh. "Leaving me at the altar was kind of a put-down."

"That wasn't a put-down."

"No? What was it? A compliment? A ringing endorsement?"

I kind of like Books like this, looser, more sarcastic, more relaxed.

"It was a . . . life decision," I say.

"Oooh, I feel better already." He winks at me. "Forget it, kid. I'm over it. Eat your food now, understand? You have to impress our team tomorrow."

Chapter 17

Hello? Hey, honey! I'm great. What did . . . oh, really? Great. What? It's hard to get reception down here—oh, I'm in Champaign, Illinois. Remember that website maintenance company I was telling you about, Picture Perfect Designs? Curtis Valentine? Well, I'm in his basement office right now and I gotta tell ya, this place is a-*mazing!* No, even *better* than we thought!

Curtis, I'm sorry, I hope you don't mind me taking this call—we've been talking about this appointment all week.

[Editor's note: sounds of a man's voice, inaudible.]

Okay, so I'm walking away from Curtis for a moment and I want to tell you, my audience, something. I said I wasn't going to let you see or hear what I do up close for a while and

I'm not. I'm going to shut this off before I do it, but you have to see how good I am at this, how completely I've gained his trust, that I can just walk up behind him and steal his life away, how effortless it can be if you have discipline and focus, and yeah, I guess, I also want you to see how exciting this is for me. It's still exciting. It never gets old. I wish you could feel this rush I'm feeling, the joyous pump of my heart and the electricity that fills my veins, this euphoria that overcomes me. I mean, you get it, don't you? This isn't about hate. This is about love.

Okay, let's do this. Walking back to Curtis in 3 . . . 2 . . . 1 . . .

Anyway, honey, you should see what Curtis can do with a website. I think we can do some crazy-cool business with this guy. Curtis is sitting at his workstation, and he's got, like, what is it, Curtis, how many do you have, four?—four different computers working together, and he's in this zone, like he's consumed with what he's doing, like—

Like he has no idea what I'm about to do to him.

[END]

Chapter 18

BOOKS AND I show up at the Dick's office at 5:00 p.m. as instructed, but we are redirected to a conference room down the hall. Scheduling this meeting at the close of the business day is a message in itself; the Dick is not planning on devoting much time to us. But then he makes matters worse by making us wait for more than two hours. Finally, at 7:15, he saunters into the conference room, munching on something (the jerk probably had dinner while we waited), and drops into a chair without acknowledging us. He spends ten minutes wiping his eyeglasses with that same silk cloth, which is his way of making it clear how important we are to him. Glasses, first. Investigation, second.

He has brought two people with him, contract consultant and former agent Dennis Sasser and a research analyst named Sophie Talamas. This, apparently, is our team.

Denny Sasser has a forehead of age spots, only wisps of white hair on top, sunken eyes, and narrow, crooked shoulders. He got mandatory at age fifty-seven and, after a couple of waivers from the director, retired. But he was retained as an outside consultant and has worked in several areas since then, the latest of which is asset forfeitures, an assignment that is about as desirable as a goiter. Usually that assignment means, *We're not going to be renewing your contract, pal.* So he's not exactly climbing the ladder, which is good because I don't think he could climb a ladder if you held your hand under his fanny and pushed. He's been with the Bureau since before the invention of electricity. The Dick tells us that Denny once worked on some arson cases, but I'd wager a mortgage payment that those cases took place back when you created fire by rubbing two sticks together so you could cook the stegosaurus you killed with a spear and dragged back to the cave.

Sophie Talamas, I don't know. She must be new. She's younger than I am (which, unfortunately, isn't saying a lot) and a lot prettier (see previous comment). Whether she's good at her job or not, I have no idea, but she's probably still wet behind the ears and will need some grooming, which I don't have time for.

So this is not what you'd call the A-Team. The Dick made sure of that.

We've been set up to fail.

"All . . . right," Dickinson says, as he wipes the last specks off his eyeglasses. "I am not . . . going to waste precious resources . . . on a fishing expedition." He dons his glasses and looks us over with disdain. "I've reviewed the so-called *research* that Emmy has put together, and so far what I've concluded is that there is nothing here. There are a bunch of fires, of course. But there are fires every day in this country. There are fatalities in fires every day. All that I see here is that our Emmy has compiled a list of fires, all of which have been determined by fire investigators to be accidental." The Dick shakes his head. "I don't see a single case here where the United States could get a conviction in court beyond a reasonable doubt."

"That's true," I chime in. "He's that good."

"He's that good," the Dick replies, "or there *is* no master criminal. These accidental fires really *were* accidental."

"If I may say," says Denny Sasser, lifting his hand off the table, indicating that he is, in fact, capable of movement, "Ms. Dockery, I don't see a pattern here. The cities are different. The victims come in all shapes and sizes—men, women, black, white, Latino, Asian, old, young, wealthy, middle-class, poor. What's the unifying theme?"

"These fires have taken place on every day of the week except for Sunday," says Books. "So we have to consider a religious angle. Maybe a religious connection between the victims. Maybe they were all sinners, and this is a religious zealot casting the heathens into the fire. Or maybe a Satanic thing."

I have to admit, I'd noticed the never-on-Sunday thing but never attached any significance to it. Books did, though. It was the first thing he noted. Which is why I need him.

"Satanic," Sasser says. "Because of the fire?"

Books shrugs. "Could be. We should consider a numerology analysis. Maybe the dates, or the addresses of the victims, or the ages. A connection to six-six-six, the number of the beast and all that. Sophie, that would be a good assignment for you."

Sophie, she of the large brown eyes, silky blond hair, and cute little figure, perks up. "Okay, Agent Bookman."

"It's Books," he says. "Everyone calls me Books."

"Okay, Books." She smiles at him. He smiles at her.

Even Dickinson is smiling. At me. A gloating, toothy grin.

Oh, Dickinson, you little weasel—that's why you added Sophie to the team. Because you knew Books would be attracted to her.

Enough. Get a grip, Em. This is the chance you've been waiting for. This is showtime.

It's time to explain a few things to these folks.

Chapter 19

"THESE CASES HAVEN'T been investigated properly," I say. "The locals are taking the easy answer, which is precisely what our subject has given them—an easily explainable accidental cause. Arsons are very easy to cover up, because the evidence goes up in flames. Sometimes the arsonist makes it easy on you by splashing accelerant around the place—gasoline or kerosene—which can be detected in the aftermath. But otherwise, arsons are usually detected in very nonscientific ways, like a gas can or bottle-bomb found at the scene; a knife found next to a cut gas line; eyewitness reports of someone fleeing the scene in the middle of the night; maybe even a strong motive, either a financial one or some personal dispute. The point being, if an arsonist is careful and meticulous, he can usually hide any evidence of his crime.

"And our subject, I believe, is very careful. He doesn't leave anything behind that would arouse suspicion, he picks victims with whom he has no connection, and on top of that, he hands investigators an easy explanation on a silver platter. What are investigators going to pick? The easy explanation, every time."

Denny, who has listened attentively to my monologue, dutifully nods, but I see I haven't won him over. "Ms. Dockery," he says.

"Call me Emmy." If Sophie gets to address Books informally, Denny gets to do the same with me. Somehow, this doesn't make me feel like I've evened the score. He gets Malibu Barbie, I get Grandpa Walton.

"Emmy, we have to consider the possibility that the easy answer is the right answer," says Denny. "If there's one thing I've learned in over thirty years on the job, it's that the simplest answer is usually the correct one. You're asking us to believe that a genius arsonist is at work based on the fact that there's no evidence of arson."

That's understandable. That, in fact, is why our subject is so good at what he does, because the proof that he's a good arsonist is the *lack* of proof of arson.

"I don't have all the answers," I concede. "We

need autopsies, forensic analyses of the crime scenes, witness interviews, everything."

"We don't have the resources for that," says the Dick.

"Then we have to convince the locals to do it for us."

"Based on what?" Denny Sasser asks. "I just don't see the evidence."

"Neither do I," the Dick chimes in.

I look at Books, who gives me a curt nod.

"Show them," he says.

Chapter 20

I PLACE a poster-size map of the United States on an easel near the end of the conference table. All around the country, little stars have been placed where one of our fires has occurred. Fifty-four stars in all—thirty-two of them red, twenty-two of them blue.

"Here are fifty-four fires," I say. "Fifty-four fires since basically Labor Day of last year until the present. So that's a one-year period. As you can see, the fires occurred all over the country, from California to New York, from Texas to Minnesota, from Washington state to the Florida panhandle. Fifty-four fires, all determined to be of accidental origin. Fifty-four casualties."

The room is silent. There is something about death, even for law enforcement professionals, even if I'm totally and completely wrong about my theory—either way, fifty-four is a big number, a lot of dead people, and there's no room for mirth or wisecracks.

"These fifty-four fires, I believe, are linked. Why are they different from the hundreds, if not thousands, of other fires that occur in homes across this country on an annual basis? They are unique because they all have four things in common. First, they were determined to be accidental. Second, there was always one, and *only* one, casualty. Third, in each of these fires, the victim was found at the point of origin of the fire—in other words, the victim was found dead in the same room where the fire started. And fourth, that room, that point of origin, was always the bedroom."

"That's unusual?" asks Denny Sasser.

"Very," I say. "Fires don't usually start in bedrooms. The vast majority of house fires start in kitchens. Others are caused by faulty gas lines in basements or laundry rooms. Some start with electrical wires that arc, often near heat sources, behind stereos and things like that. But bedrooms? It's actually quite unusual."

Denny allows for that. "I haven't studied recent statistics."

I smile at him. "I have. But regardless of the room where it started, most people don't die at the source of the fire. People run from a fire. They don't run *to* the fire. What commonly happens in fires involving death is that while people are sleeping, the fire originates somewhere else in the house— the kitchen, the laundry room—and starts to spread. If there are deaths, it's usually because the victims died of smoke inhalation after their path to safety was cut off. They don't usually just get burned to a crisp while lying in their beds. In each of these fifty-four cases, the victim died in the same room where the fire was determined to have begun, and in many of these cases, they were found dead lying on or near their beds."

"Certainly, though, it could happen innocently," says Sasser.

"Certainly, Denny. In fact, you've just articulated the feelings of fifty-four different sets of fire investigators, each of whom have determined that their single fire was accidental. Just looking at a single incident, sure, it's possible—especially when they find an obvious, so-called accidental, cause of the fire, which our subject always hands them. They go with the easy answer rather than dreaming up some diabolical plot. But we're not looking at one incident. We're looking at this nationally, and we're seeing fifty-four incidents in a one-year period. This, I submit, is a pattern."

I have the room's attention. I'm not great at reading faces, but I think I've cleared a preliminary hurdle with them; maybe nobody is convinced yet, but I'm not way out of bounds, either.

"But let's break it down further," I continue. "Let's start with a four-month period beginning a year ago—approximately Labor Day of last year—and continuing until year's end, or January second, to be specific. Focus now on the red stars on the map. These represent thirty-two fires that occurred during that four-month period. Note the scattered nature of these fires, hitting all corners of the country but not the Midwest. These thirty-two fires killed thirty-two people."

The last fire in that period, the January 2 fire, was Peoria, Arizona. I still remember the phone call from Mom, the panic in her voice, her inability to even get the words out to me. *Marta,* she said, *Marta was—your sister was—.* It took me over five minutes to get her to finish the sentence, though after a few attempts my own panic had begun to rise, as it became clear that the news she was delivering was the worst possible. *Marta was what, Mom?* I cried, my voice cracking, my knees buckling, the ground beneath me splitting open. *What happened to Marta?*

"So that's thirty-two fires in four months,"

Books says, coaxing me along, helping me, sensing that I'd locked up from the memory. I give him a nod of gratitude and snap back to focus.

"That's right," I say. "So that's approximately two fires a week. And as you can see from the map, the fires tended to be in clusters of two. Two in California—Piedmont and Novato—in the same week in September. Two in Minnesota—Edina and Saint Cloud—in the same week in October. So our subject was a traveler. From Labor Day to basically New Year's Day, our subject traveled. Why, I don't know."

Everyone is paying attention, at least. The lovely Sophie is even taking notes, indicating that she does, in fact, know how to spell, or at least doodle.

"But then we get to the second time period, the beginning of this year through the present," I say. "And this is when we start to learn more about our subject."

Chapter 21

"THE SECOND PHASE of our subject's crime spree," I say, "is the roughly eight-month stretch from January of this year to today. These are the blue stars on the map. During this stretch, we have twenty-two fires, and exactly twenty-two casualties. Exactly one death per fire. Rather meticulous, wouldn't you agree?"

Denny Sasser and Sophie Talamas nod. Books does so emphatically, though he's already heard my spiel. The Dick sits passively, revealing no sign of his thoughts.

With my pointer, I outline a circle around the blue stars. "But our subject wasn't such a traveler during this second phase, was he?"

Books shakes his head. "All twenty-two of those fires took place in the greater Midwest."

"That's right. Illinois, Wisconsin, Iowa, Indiana,

Missouri, and Kansas. And this took place beginning in mid-January and through last week in Lisle, Illinois. So that's almost eight months, and only twenty-two arsons. Instead of a pace of two a *week*, he's closer to three a *month*. Why?"

I look over the team like a teacher quizzing her students.

When they don't answer, I do it for them.

"He's taking longer to choose his victims," I say.

Again, nobody answers. It occurs to me I might be annoying them with my question-and-answer routine, but in fact they seem to enjoy it. Everyone in this room, at least in part, entered law enforcement because they like solving puzzles.

"And why is he doing that?" asks the Dick, the first time he's participated at all. I don't know whether to take that as a good sign or bad.

"Because he lives in the Midwest, I believe," I say. "So the rest of his life intrudes—work, friends, whatever he does. When he's traveling, he skips out and commits his crimes. But at home? He has a job to go to. He has friends, family."

"He'd also have to be more careful," Books notes. "If he's killing closer to home, he stands a greater chance of being caught. Heightened caution means more time between victims."

"Exactly," I say. "Note that every murder he commits in the Midwest is in a different jurisdiction of law enforcement. Different cities, different counties. He's making sure he doesn't commit the same crime in the same jurisdiction twice, for fear that people will start looking at these things as a group, instead of one-off fires."

"And you said the victims are always found at the point of origin, where the fire started," says Denny Sasser. "Is there some reason the subject would do that?"

"Sure," I say. "The point of origin is the point where the fire burns the longest, and therefore the hardest. Where the most damage occurs. Where the evidence is most likely to be destroyed."

"Ah. So you think he's using the fire merely to destroy evidence."

"I do. Whatever he's doing to the victims, he wants to make sure we don't find out. He doesn't want us to autopsy them. He wants to make sure that there isn't—"

I think of Marta and my throat shuts down.

"That there isn't a body left to autopsy," says Sophie.

I nod, unable to speak. I still remember my mother screaming at the mortician, at the police detective, at anyone who would listen: *I can't even bury my baby? I can't even give her a proper Christian burial?*

I clear my throat. Books wasn't wrong about the perils of investigating a crime involving a loved one. I don't want to become a cautionary tale.

"So the fire is secondary," says Denny Sasser. "He's not setting fires for some thrill. He's covering up crimes. Is that what you're saying?"

I clear my throat again. "That's what I'm saying. And what he's doing takes time. That's why he seeks out people who live alone. So he can subdue them and take his time with them. Then, when he's finished, he torches their bedroom. He knows that these days, firefighters can arrive within minutes of a fire. He doesn't care if they save the rest of the house. But the victims will be charred before they arrive."

Everyone digests that. I'm not sure I've convinced anybody that we have a killer, but I've convinced everybody that there's good reason to investigate further.

"So where do we start?" asks Denny Sasser.

"We start where he lives," I say. "It's somewhere in the Midwest. If I were to bet, I'd go with the Windy City. So pack your bags, everyone. We're going to Chicago."

Chapter 22

Well, I guess this can technically count as a separate session. It's past midnight, officially Thursday now. What a day it's been, wouldn't you agree?

No? Nothing? Well, folks, since I'm in a good mood, I'm going to answer questions from the mailbag.

I wish there really *was* a mailbag, because I'm sure you have lots of questions for me. You'll try to answer as many of them as you can from these recordings, to read between the lines and study my word choices and voice patterns and all that jazz, but it would be nice for you if I just outright answered some FAQs.

So from time to time, I'll just go ahead and guess what those questions might be and answer them for you.

Invisible

Thus, here is episode one of Graham's Mailbag. Cue the theme music, please. What's that? I'm being told that we don't have any theme music. Sorry, I'll have to work on that.

Question: how do you choose your victims?

The simplest answer I can give you is that I go with what inspires me. What inspires me at a given moment will vary, and thus my victims vary as well. You wouldn't expect Beethoven to write the same symphony twice, would you? Or Tolstoy to pen the identical novel a second time?

Sometimes I seek them out, and sometimes they come to me. Sometimes I must grapple for a time with what I'm looking for, and on other occasions, it simply comes to me like an exotic perfume wafting under my nose.

I am, in a word, a connoisseur.

Sometimes I prefer a nice piece of lamb with a Shiraz. Sometimes lobster with a chilled Chablis. Other times, an Italian beef sandwich with peppers and salt-and-vinegar potato chips. I don't know what I'll be in the mood for the next time. I just know that my stomach will start growling sooner or later.

Question: what is your favorite color?

I'll bet you think my favorite color is red, don't you? Well, close. It's purple. Purple is such a twisted, complex color—it conveys the passion of red, the sadness of blue, the depravity of black. Purple is neither happy nor sad. It is pain and despair but longing, too—fiery desire, beaten and bruised but struggling onward, determined to overcome, to move forward rather than retreat.

Plus, it looks nice with my hair.

We have time for one more question: why set fire to your victims?

Well, let's see. Curtis, have I set fire to you?

[Editor's note: sounds of man moaning.]

No, I haven't. I've done a lot of things to you, Curtis, but I haven't set you on fire. Now, don't lose your head over this, Curtis—I will burn you up when this is over. But that's just so our fun is kept a secret.

Sorry, everyone, that was a little inside joke between Curtis and me, about losing his head. And if it's any consolation, Curtis, you have one of the nicest-looking brains I've ever seen. *Is* that consolation? Do you feel consoled?

You'd probably feel a lot more consoled if I got rid of this mirror, wouldn't you?

[END]

Chapter 23

LIEUTENANT ADAM RESSLER is not happy to see us. Not that I can blame him. A week ago, he had this case all wrapped up, and now we're here to ruin his Labor Day weekend. His thoroughly starched uniform looks stiff and hot in the sweltering August sauna that assaults me as I slide out of the Jeep Cherokee we got from the Chicago field office's fleet.

Ressler wears the uniform well, though. He is handsome, well built, clean-shaven with a just-right angular cut of the jaw, and he carries himself like a man who has spent time in the military. If it weren't for the rivulets of sweat escaping from his perfectly combed hair down to his precisely creased collar, I'd hardly be able to tell he noticed the heat.

"Lieutenant Ressler, I assume?" I ask, trying to

sound breezy, cool, and confident as my hair begins to stick to my neck and forehead. He grunts his assent without offering a handshake.

Denny, looking wilted, clambers out of his car and joins Books, Sophie, and me on the sidewalk. I do quick introductions. Ressler is quick to shake Books's hand, presuming him to be the leader—which happens to be true, but he doesn't know that, typical sexism, but it's no time for my feminist side to show. He looks over Denny Sasser with a you-gotta-be-kidding-me expression; Denny looks like a half-melted ice cream cone, but I'm beginning to suspect he's got more going on behind his hooded eyes than he lets on. Ressler seems awfully impressed with Sophie, as would any heterosexual male with a pulse.

"Ms. Dockery," Ressler starts, "like I said on the phone, this fire was clearly not incendiary in origin. I don't see why you need to see the scene. If you could just tell me what you're looking for, I'm sure we could get this wrapped up."

"You've been such a help already, Lieutenant," I say. "We just need to take a look around. That's all."

He glares at me for a moment, then turns abruptly and stalks toward the house. I guess he didn't like being told to babysit the FBI for the afternoon.

I pause for a moment to examine Joelle Swanson's first and last home-of-her-own. It's a modest two-story freestanding townhome with a brick facade and round pillars at the top of the cement stairs leading up to the entryway. It's new. The whole neighborhood is pretty new, with tiny, hopeful trees and postage-stamp lawns still striped with new sod. There is plywood over some of her windows, and the power is probably off, but there is little other evidence of the devastation of a week ago.

Except for that smell.

Burnt tar, melted plastic, and an undercurrent of something unidentifiable but clearly chemical, all bundled with the jarringly pleasant smell of damp, charred wood, like campfires in the autumn.

"The fire primarily affected the back of the house, as you can see," says Ressler. "The back bedroom was completely involved, as were the master bathroom and the hallway. The rest of the house suffered smoke damage, and of course everything is still damp from the fire suppression, even a week later."

I stop for a moment to take it all in. For all the research I've been doing, this is the first torched house I've been in since Marta's. The house is completely different, of course, but it throws me back anyway. Marta's was a typical Southwestern home: rounded entryways, lots of tile, and adobe-colored everything, with an open floor plan. This one is a more standard midwestern layout, with a living room, half bath, and kitchen on the first floor, two bedrooms and a full bath on the second floor.

I pause at the base of the stairs to brace myself. The walls are blackened starting halfway up the stairs, in sharp angles and lines clearly defining the path of the flames before they were extinguished. The "char patterns," as I learned at Marta's house.

I reach the landing and pause again. Closing my eyes, I can see the licking flames from my dreams—"angel fingers," the firefighters call them—snaking across the ceiling. The boiling smoke ripples like the surface of the ocean just moments before the second story erupts in flashover, simultaneously igniting every flammable surface and turning the cozy home into a convection oven.

Ressler continues, thankfully unaware of my moment of hesitation. "The point of origin was back here, in the master bedroom," he says. "Now be careful, here—this fire burned really hot and fast, and didn't make it through the floor joists, but I don't want to discover structural damage by dropping an FBI agent through the floor."

He laughs, rapid-fire *ha-ha-ha*, to emphasize he's kidding. I'm not sure he is.

We get to the bedroom—*Joelle's bedroom, not Marta's,* I remind myself—and I suck in my breath. The bed, or what remains of it, is positioned directly across from the bedroom door. Not terribly unusual but not that common, either—but it's like she and Marta read the same home design magazine and picked the same bedroom layout. And Marta's room hadn't been laid out that way the last time I'd visited her. She reorganized her room before she died. Or so I thought.

Queen-size mattress with a bedside table on one side (or, at least, what remains of it). Overstuffed reading chair, no doubt once made of highly flammable polyurethane, with comfortable, equally flammable throw pillows and blankets, by the window. Ruined piles of wet ash that were probably piles of books.

The ceiling is gaping open to the sky, where the firemen had vented the fire to prevent smoke explosions. *It should be raining,* I think. *It rained for Marta, even in Arizona, even in January.*

The four of us begin our examination. Joelle's body had been removed, of course, but we knew her remains were found among the ruins of the left side of the bed. The photos had shown her body curled into the characteristic burn-victim posture—legs bowing outward, wrists curled in, arms bent—caused, I knew, by the heating and drying of muscles and tendons as they pulled bones like postmortem marionettes.

The char patterns, where they can be seen, show a narrow V shape right to the side of the window, ending near the floor amid the blackened remains of the desk Ressler had indicated was the origin point of the fire. The carpet is melted and burned nearly completely, though a few places in the farthest corners still show the original color.

After two hours of scouring every inch of the room, the four of us smell like incinerators. There is absolutely no evidence of an accelerant, or of any intentional method of setting the fire that seems to have killed Ms. Swanson. Lieutenant Ressler and the Lisle Police Department had every reason to reach the conclusion they reached.

But I'm surer than ever that this was the work of our subject.

Chapter 24

"SO HERE'S WHAT we know," I say to my team, as we settle into a conference room at the FBI's Chicago field office.

"One: there was a candle, which likely was the point of origin, one way or another.

"Two: the fire spread very quickly up the curtains and around the room until it reached the point of flashover, when everything in the room simultaneously combusted.

"Three: there was an alarm system on the house, but it was not activated at the time of the fire.

"Four: there was one window open in the spare bedroom across the hall from Joelle's bedroom. It was eighty-two degrees at one-thirty a.m. the day of the fire, and her central air-conditioning was on. Her AC was on, but she left a window open.

"Five: we were unable to locate any other

candles in the house. Joelle does not seem to have been a big candle user.

"Six: there is very little smoke staining on the unbroken windows or other glass surfaces, and the char patterns are consistent with a very hot and fast-burning fire. Those qualities are often indicative of a fire assisted by an accelerant. However, we found no evidence of accelerant near the origin of the fire, or anywhere else.

"Seven: the 'fire triangle.' Fires need oxygen, fuel, and heat to burn. There were books spread around her room, many of them open, and papers on the floor. That's fuel. A candle was left burning on a desk too close to a curtain—that's heat. And a window was left open across the hall—that's oxygen. And not only is that oxygen, but the path of the air being sucked in through that window would have ended on the wall directly opposite the door—which is the precise location of Ms. Swanson's body on the bed. And, because the fire will burn hottest where it has ventilation, Ms. Swanson's body was in the hottest-burning fire in the room, and was almost completely consumed in a relatively short period of time, including her skin, fat layers, and much of her muscle.

"Eight: the DuPage County arson task force

has not been called. This fire was determined to be accidental by the fire investigator, and they have no interest in reopening the case. There will be no autopsy performed unless we can convince someone that there is a reason to do so. Or unless we take over the investigation.

"Nine: there are fifty-three other fires that share nearly all of these characteristics. With my limited means over the last several months, I haven't been able to determine the positioning of the beds in each of the other fifty-three bedrooms, but I have obtained information on eighteen of them. And they are all . . . the . . . same."

I look at Books, piercing him with my eyes, so that he understands: *including the one in Peoria.*

Sophie speaks up. "I think all of these people moving their bedroom furniture around into the same position and then burning to death would be a reason for some autopsies. Don't you?"

Maybe Sophie isn't so bad after all. I'd like her even more if she gained thirty pounds and got some acne.

"So we start right there," says Books. "Let's find out about the positioning of those beds in the bedrooms. Let's finish the work Emmy started."

I nod at Books. "And time's a-wastin', folks," I say. "Because two days from now is Labor Day. And if our subject keeps to form, that means he's about to take his show on the road. And start killing two people a week."

Chapter 25

Good evening, class. Tonight, I won't be taking questions from the audience. I want to say a few words about lying, a key ingredient in any respectable artist's portfolio. Lies are fascinating because they expose the paradoxes of our society.

What is a lie? It's a distortion of reality, presented as reality. We say it's a bad thing. We teach kids not to lie. We even put people in prison for lying. And yet there are lies all around us, and half the time we don't even really try to disguise it.

The TV commercial with the bubbly family ecstatically stuffing French fries and burgers in their mouths with the fun-loving clown looking on? We all know those are actors who are paid to play a fun-loving family. They're not having fun. They probably had to reshoot that scene twenty times and they're tired and nauseated and the last thing they want to do is stick another French fry in their mouths. And what about those thick, scrumptious burgers in the ad—are those the ones you get when you go to the restaurant? None of that's real, and we know it but don't care.

Women wear clothes that hide their flaws. Men suck in their guts when those women walk by. Office workers turn the screen away from their game of solitaire when the boss strolls in. Lies, lies, lies.

You're taught not to call someone who's fat *fat,* or someone who's stupid *stupid.* That's wrong, we tell our kids. Don't tell the truth if it's going to hurt someone's feelings. Those lies are okay, too—desirable, in fact.

I'm not complaining, mind you, just commenting. It gives me perspective. And that perspective is: embrace it! Because if everyone else is lying, then you better, too, or you'll get caught in the crosscurrent, spinning and flailing. You don't want to spin and flail, do you?

As you can imagine, I'm a master liar. How else do I woo all these unsuspecting people into letting me into their lives, and usually their homes? Lying is easy, but being good at it is hard. Here is *Graham's Handbook on Lying:*

First: lie no more than you have to. Because for that duration of time you're with a target—be it two hours or two weeks—you're going to have to live with that lie. If you want to get close to a target who happens to be a smoker by saying *you* smoke, too—which works, by the way, there's an unspoken brotherhood between all tobacco users—then you better be prepared to light up every few hours or so. What I do, when I use that ruse, is claim to be a *former* smoker, so of course I love to smoke and maybe just this once I'll partake, so I can have the bonding experience with my target, but I have an excuse not to smoke again if I have to spend a longer time with the target.

Second: be no more specific in your lie than is absolutely necessary. The vaguer you are, the more rope you give yourself.

Let me give you an example of what I'm talking about. This last guy, Curtis Valentine. I found him easily because he runs a website-design business out of his house in Champaign and he's on Facebook, too. To get into his house, I told him two lies:

1. I was starting a consulting business that needed a website; and

2. I hired someone else first, but they scammed me and stole my money.

I couldn't have gotten a meeting with Curtis if I didn't need his services, thus the consulting company. But I said I was *starting* one, instead of operating one already, so Curtis wouldn't be suspicious if he looked up my company on the Internet and didn't find anything.

Why the second lie? Several reasons. Most website designers never meet their clients; they just communicate by phone and e-mail. But if I got burned once by a scammer, it would make sense that I'd want to see this guy's operation for myself, to make sure he was the real deal. Also, it would allow me to appear reluctant when he asked me questions like, *What kind of consulting will you be doing?* That's the last question I wanted to answer, because if I said I was a private detective or mechanical engineer, it might turn out that Curtis studied mechanical engineering in college, or his best friend or brother is a private eye, and then suddenly I'd have to actually know something about private detection or mechanical engineering. But with lie number two, I could just say, *I'd rather not say until I've hired you.* You know, because I've been burned once before, etc.

I lied no more than I had to, and I locked myself down as little as possible. A couple beers at a bar, Curtis talking about how he can expand my business's potential, me looking impressed but also gun-shy after being burned once, and next thing I know it's *his* idea that we go to his house so I can see his operation firsthand.

Any questions? Good. Class dismissed for now. But don't go away—we have a lot of fun right around the corner!

[END]

Chapter 26

THE FBI BUILDING on Roosevelt Road in Chicago never really closes, because the FBI never really does, either. But it's Labor Day, and after business hours at that, so the building is about as empty as it will ever get. The eighth floor, where our temporary digs are located, is positively barren.

Our four-person team, believing as we do (or at least, as I do) that time is of the essence, has been doing its best to make progress, but we arrived on the Saturday of the three-day weekend and haven't had a regular business day yet. Still, we're trying to do the person-to-person stuff, calling local cops or county sheriffs in all the jurisdictions where our subject has killed, asking them to dust off the files on that "accidental" fire so they can tell us the position of the bed in the bedroom where the victim was found. Sometimes there are insurance company investigators involved, too, who often take more photographs than the cops because their money is at stake, so we'll be tracking them down when normal business resumes tomorrow.

The good news is that computers know no business hours, so Sophie and I, the research analysts, have been trying to work cross-references, looking for any number of things that might indicate a pattern. We know (as much as we can say we *know* anything at this point) that he chooses people who live alone and that each of these victims engages, to some extent, in social media, be it Facebook, Twitter, LinkedIn, whatever. But there has to be more. Something has to be connecting these people. Nobody acts completely at random.

At seven o'clock, I get up to stretch my legs and peek into the office next to mine, where Books is stationed. "Thanks, Sheriff, that would be much appreciated," he says, rolling his eyes when he sees me. "Call me anytime, day or night. You have a good night, too."

He hangs up and makes a face. He's been making calls to the upper brass in the local jurisdictions, trying to persuade them to reopen their investigations or, at a bare minimum, conduct an autopsy on the body. The problem is that even if the FBI takes over the investigation from the locals, all of these victims have been buried, so an autopsy would first require us to petition the court for an order of exhumation.

"He said he'd talk to the family about an exhumation," he says to me.

"You don't need the family's permission."

He nods. "But you start there, because you can avoid having to go to court if you get consent. Anyway, I think he's just looking for a reason to turn us down." He blows out a sigh. "Emmy, these departments have closed these cases, in some instances several months ago. If we want to get autopsies, we're going to have to go into each jurisdiction's local court to get the grave opened. And that assumes the local U.S. attorney is even willing to go to bat for us, which is no small thing."

"Then we'll try."

"Right, but you know how long that's going to take? A few weeks would be the minimum. Dickinson—he just hasn't given us the manpower."

"Can you get more agents assigned?"

"That's the catch-twenty-two, lady."

"Right," I agree. We can't get more agents until we show him some hard proof. And we can't get hard proof, any time soon, without more agents.

And all the while, our subject just keeps on killing.

Which is why I'm pinning so much on the two most recent deaths, Joelle Swanson in Lisle, Illinois, and the latest one, a man named Curtis Valentine in Champaign, Illinois. We haven't been down to the Champaign site, but a detective down there with Champaign's police department was kind enough to have a video done of the entire house and e-mail it to me. It was a single-family house, not a townhouse, but otherwise the death of Curtis Valentine bore a startling resemblance to that of Joelle Swanson—a fire that started in the bedroom; the victim found in that same bedroom; a candle as the likely source; char patterns and minimal smoke staining, indicating a fast-burning fire, yet no evidence of accelerant; the bed positioned directly opposite the bedroom door.

God, our subject is smart. I have to admit, even I would think this looks accidental if I only knew of this one fire. None of these investigators know that this nearly exact same pattern has been taking place all around the country.

"You look exhausted, Em," he says.

"I am."

"Let's get everyone together and get something to eat at the hotel bar," he says.

I sigh. "I suppose if we get a change of scenery,

we get away from phones and computers and just talk, maybe an idea shakes loose."

Maybe that's the problem. Maybe we need to take a breath and think big-picture, brainstorm. Maybe the trees are blocking us from seeing the forest.

I look back at Books, who is smiling at me.

"What?" I ask.

"The only way you'll join us for dinner is if we agree to talk about the case, isn't it?"

I raise my hands. "Is there anything else to talk about?"

He shrugs. "We could talk about the Chiefs," he says. "They kick off this weekend."

Books is a die-hard football fan. It's one of his only flaws.

"Okay, fine." Books raises his hands in surrender. "We'll talk about the case. Maybe something will shake loose."

Chapter 27

OUR HUMBLE TEAM hits the bistro located within the Chicago Marriott where we're staying, a place called Rooks Corner that Books has been all excited about because they serve Chicago-area microbrews on tap. Books always liked to take in the local favorites when he traveled, which, as an FBI agent, was often.

The place is dimly lit with dark oak, yellow-cushioned seats, and a hardwood floor. Booths line the walls, with tables scattered near a wraparound bar. A football game plays on the projection screens mounted on the walls. Books orders a Domaine DuPage, whatever that is (beer, I assume; I recognize "DuPage" as the county in which Joelle Swanson was killed), while Denny orders a soft drink and Sophie a berry mojito.

Everyone is happy to have food. For Books it's

a burger, for Denny a club sandwich. I order some French onion soup, and Sophie chooses a pear and pecan salad. Are pretty young women genetically programmed to order fruit-flavored drinks and nibble on rabbit food like salads with low-fat vinaigrette dressing? I mean, couldn't Sophie just break from type this one time and guzzle a Guinness while devouring some nachos with cheese sauce dripping down her chin?

The aforementioned Sophie, I note, has the seat next to Books at our square table and has scooted her chair closer. She is hanging on his every word as he regales everyone with some war story. Special agents have lots of tantalizing tales about their exploits—quirky witnesses, silly miscues, charismatic criminals they've captured. I've heard most of those stories by now. My favorite is from a dozen years ago, when Books was assisting U.S. marshals on a fugitive recapture. He broke through the front door of a Maryland house, tripped over the coatrack, and was knocked unconscious when the rack came down on his head. The other agents had to step over him to get in. They later told him, *At least you blocked the exit really well.*

Sophie asks him, "Have you ever hunted a serial killer?"

"Oh," he says, blowing out air, "I've worked on a few investigations, yeah."

He was working on one when we ended our engagement. He caught his killer, then resigned from the FBI. Reginald Trager, who raped and murdered a number of young women in Portland, then sealed the deal by lopping off their heads.

"Freddy the Machete," I say, because I know Books won't.

Denny Sasser touches his chin. "You worked on 'Freddy the Machete'?"

"It's not as impressive as it sounds, believe me." As much as Books likes to tell stories, they usually involve him in embarrassing situations. Books isn't one to play up his own accomplishments. It was one of the first things I noticed about him when we met four years ago. He figured out the pattern of a crew of bank robbers in Virginia to the point that his team was waiting for them when they hit the federal credit union in Arlington. All the research analysts on the team knew that it was Books's brainpower that got the solve, but he spread the credit around, even walked through the office and left a card for each of the RAs, thanking them individually for their help and noting their specific contributions. RAs notice that kind of stuff. Most of the special agents forget all about us once they've solved their puzzles.

Reginald Trager, dubbed "Freddy the Machete" by the press in Portland, was an unemployed union painter who had recently lost his condominium to foreclosure and apparently snapped. He went on a rampage that included five or six victims—I don't recall the exact number. It came out later that he had a history of mental illness and a previous conviction for attempted rape.

"Did he come up with that name himself?" Sophie asks. "Did he, like, leave notes or anything? Did he want to be famous?" I can't tell if she's flirting with Books or is professionally curious, trying to sponge up all the experience and wisdom she can. Here's a question: why do I care?

Books shakes his head. "Reggie Trager wasn't capable of leaving notes or wanting notoriety. He was mentally ill, a classic sadistic sexual psychopath. He beat women, decapitated them, and performed sex acts on them."

Sophie recoils. "In that order?"

"Oh, yeah. He performed sex acts on headless corpses. Yeah, this guy was a real monster."

"What kind of sex—never mind," Sophie says, "I don't want to know."

"No, you definitely don't want to know."

But I know. I'm probably the only person who knows, outside the team that caught the monster. The detail was never made public, and Reggie Trager hasn't even had his trial yet, so it's basically classified information at the moment.

The sex act was vaginal rape. But he didn't use his penis. He used the machete. The blade penetrated clean through the uterus and colon until it came out their buttocks. The only minor consolation is that they were already dead, already decapitated.

Books enjoys a sip from his pint of caramel-colored beer. He probably can't help enjoying the attention. I can't blame him. If you're going to leave the Bureau, it's a nice case on which to exit.

I take a gulp of my water, not being in the frame of mind for alcohol, and let Books bask in the glow a minute. But he's not much for basking, and I catch him eyeing me when I look his way.

"Emmy wants to talk about our case," he says. "So where do we start?"

"With your profile," I say. "I want to hear your profile of our subject."

Chapter 28

BOOKS SMACKS his lips after another sip from his pint. "Can't do it," he says, which he's already said to me several times. By *several times,* I mean every single day since I dragged him onto this case. He turns to Sophie, the pupil. "Before you can work up any kind of a meaningful profile, you first, obviously, have to establish the commission—"

"Of a crime," I interrupt. "But Books, let's assume these are murders. Murders covered up by arsons. What's your profile? I know you have one."

He allows for that and gestures to Sophie again. "Profiles are an art, not a science," he says. "It's not like you can plug facts into a machine and crank out your profile. You have to thoroughly evaluate the crime scene, interview victims if you can—all things we haven't done here. And even *then,* you can be pretty far off."

"Were you far off in your profile of Reggie Trager? 'Freddy the Machete'?" Sophie asks, practically cooing. If she gets any closer to Books, I might have to find a machete of my own.

"Well, now that's a good example, Sophie," he says, as if he's about to pat her on the head. He's not blind. He can admire her Barbie-doll looks, and he can see the way she's looking at him. "We were able to analyze the crime scenes and the victims. It was clear to us that he didn't plan the crimes much at all; he wasn't careful or logical about his victim selection; he made no attempt to cover up his crimes or modify the crime scene in any way. His victims were violently mutilated, sexually assaulted, and decapitated. They were all white, early twenties, and blond.

"From that, we drew our profile. We believed he was a classically disorganized killer suffering from mental illness. He was a white male in his twenties or thirties. He was socially withdrawn. He had no friends, didn't talk to neighbors, showed no interest in socialization whatsoever. He grew up in a family where he was disciplined severely, probably by a mother. He was likely a high-school dropout. He had no meaningful relationships with women and was quite possibly impotent. He was either unemployed or engaged in manual labor.

He had recently experienced something rather stressful, something like being fired from a job or a breakup with a woman. He had violent fantasies against women and was unable to control them. He lived somewhere within a one-mile radius of the victims. And his first name was probably not Freddy."

Sophie gives him a full-wattage smile. Oh, that Books, he's a real jokester these days. "Why did you think he lived close by?" she asks.

"Disorganized killers usually don't travel by car. They're too caught up in their fantasies. It's not like they carefully select a victim, drive there, commit the crime, and drive home. No, they act on pure impulse."

"Okay, yeah." Sophie is transfixed by the professor. "So how were you wrong?"

"Well, for one thing, he took his murder weapon with him. Most disorganized killers use whatever's on hand; they aren't capable of planning to walk around with a weapon, ready to pounce. But Reggie carried that machete under his long black coat and took it with him after every murder. Also, he kept a souvenir from each victim. That's atypical of disorganized killers, who usually just commit the crime and leave.

"But the biggest thing of all," Books continues,

"is that his last victim wasn't random at all. His last victim was the same woman he'd attacked years before, when he was convicted of attempted rape. So he had definitely planned that out. In fact, those things that distinguished him from the typical disorganized killer are the reasons we caught him. Once that last victim was attacked, a simple background check took us to the guy who'd attacked her previously, who just happened to live seven blocks away from her. And once we rousted him, we discovered he had a machete and all those souvenirs."

"What were the souvenirs?" Sophie asks, beaming.

"Another thing you don't want to know," says Books.

"I do. C'mon."

"He took their tongues," I say. "He cut them out and kept them in a shoe box under his bed." I hate to spoil her appetite. She could use a good meal.

"Anyway," Books says, clearing his throat, "my point is, it's not like we drew up some perfect profile and nailed Reggie Trager. It was dumb luck. He made a big mistake attacking his previous victim again. He might as well have sent us an engraved invitation."

"That doesn't mean profiles can't help," I say.

"And it doesn't mean you don't have one for our subject."

"I don't, Emmy. I need to know more."

"Tell me one thing about our subject, Books," I say. "Just one. And don't say he's highly organized, because I think we all get that much."

Books shakes his head, bemused.

"One thing," I say.

"He's getting better," says Books. "Organized killers improve and hone their methodology with each murder. Our subject was probably pretty good all along. But if he's real, if there really is a man going around murdering people and torching the scenes and making it look accidental, then he's turned this hobby of his into a well-oiled machine." Books blows out air. "He's not going to hand himself over like Reggie Trager did," he says. "We're going to need good police work, yes, but we're also going to need all kinds of luck."

"Oh, my God," I say, pushing my chair away from the table. "That's it, Books."

"*What's* it? You found inspiration in 'we're going to need all kinds of luck'? Wow, I knew I was good but not *that*—"

I've already left the table. I move from a brisk walk to a jog until I've jumped into the first taxi I can find.

Chapter 29

I'M BACK AT the office on Roosevelt, banging on my keyboard, poring over data, when Books pops his head into the office. "Emmy, always with the flair for the dramatic," he says. "You mind telling me what bee got into your bonnet? It can't be anything I said. All I said was our subject was getting better."

"That's all you needed to say."

My eyes move to the large map of the United States, the stars now numbering fifty-five, indicating the various sites of the fires. Thirty-two are red, showing the fires that began about a year ago and ended at the beginning of January with Marta's fire.

"Where was the first fire?" I ask.

"The first . . . I'm not sure I remember," he admits. He doesn't have the data burned into his brain like I do.

"Atlantic Beach, Florida," I say. "September eighth, two thousand eleven." That was part of our subject's cross-country September-to-January spree before he came back to the Midwest."

"Okay, so?" Books says.

"So, how do we really know this was his first kill?"

"We don't," Books concedes. "Not for sure. But you kept going back in time and you didn't find any more fires that fit the unique characteristics. The single victim, found at the point of the fire's origin in the bedroom, determined to be an accidental cause . . ."

"Exactly," I say. "The accidental cause. Anything that *wasn't* determined to be accidental, I didn't analyze, I just totally skipped over. Because it didn't fit into the pattern."

"Okay—so?"

I'm still typing along, using the NIBRS now, the database to which I didn't have access while I was suspended and doing this from home. The data is almost dancing off the screen; I have to be careful I'm not going too fast. When the juices are flowing and the data is voluminous, it's like a treasure hunt, one gigantic puzzle, the answer somewhere out there for me to find.

"So," I say, "you were right when you said he's

probably getting better. Maybe he wasn't so good at the beginning of his murder spree."

"Oh. Oh, I see. Maybe the first fire, he didn't cover it up so well. Maybe it was determined to be an *arson*."

"Exactly, Books." Which is why it's nice to have NIBRS, which reports arsons and suspicious fires.

"I'll bet he screwed up the first one," I say. "Maybe more than just the first one."

"So you're—what? Casting a net across the country for arsons set before that first Atlantic Beach fire?"

"Not across the country. We think he lives here in the Midwest, right? So I'm starting there."

Books is silent behind me. I finally look back at him.

"That's a lot of work, Em. Even narrowing it down to the Midwest, that's a ton of data to process. You're going to start now? It's eleven o'clock at night."

"I'll sleep when I'm dead," I say. "Or when we catch this guy."

Chapter 30

BOOKS IS STILL lingering at the doorway as I type.

"What?" I say.

"We were—we were going to head out for a drink."

I feel something swim around in my stomach. This is different about Books. Back when he was full-time with the Bureau, when he was hot on a chase—a time-sensitive, lives-at-risk chase—the last thing you'd ever catch him doing was drinking alcohol. He was constantly on edge, always rethinking the evidence. There would be times, when we were together, that he would be sitting next to me or across the table at dinner, but I could tell he was miles away, trying to find his way inside a monster's head, challenging assumptions, reexamining angles, closing this eye, then that eye, wondering if it changed the picture at all. I recall being in a movie theater with Books once when, for some reason, I turned to him in the middle of the show, the light playing on his face as the scene on the screen changed, his eyes open wide and glossy, and I could tell that if you saw behind those eyes, they wouldn't be looking at the movie screen at all, they would be replaying some crime scene in Alameda or New Orleans or Terre Haute.

And now we're in the middle of a chase, and he wants to go out for a drink. It's not hard to see what's changed.

We are heading out for a drink, he said. *We.* But *we* doesn't include me. And as much as I've come to like Denny Sasser, I don't think he's up for painting the town at eleven o'clock at night.

Books has every right to do this, I remind myself. *He's a single man and Sophie's a single woman.*

You dumped him. You're the last person on Earth who has the right to comment.

And don't you have a job to do? Aren't you here to stop a killer? Even if you're the only one who really believes that this killer exists?

"You should go out, then," I say, not breaking stride in my typing. "I'm going to keep at this."

"You sure you don't want to come along? Or I could join you here—"

"No, I'm fine," I say. "Sometimes I'm better when

I'm just alone, focusing on this stuff, anyway."

If ever I uttered a true statement, it is that one. I'm better alone. I'm more comfortable alone. I'm supposed to be alone. These numbers and statistics, these patterns and cross-references and data, this hunt is all the company I need.

I turn and listen to Books's footfalls along the carpeted hallway, until he's out of earshot. Then I get back to work.

Chapter **31**

Good day, all. I'm enjoying a burger—rare, of course—and a plate of fries while I watch an old football game on ESPN Classic. I'm using my recorder as a fake cell phone, as I always do in public places like this tavern. I wasn't planning on lecturing you tonight, but it occurs to me as I watch this football game that we have, as they say, a teachable moment.

I've been thinking about how much my artistry resembles that of a quarterback. I know, I know—you're picturing one of these steel-jawed poster boys like Peyton Manning or Tom Brady and thinking, *What the hell do they have in common with a homicidal artist like Graham?*

Anyone can play quarterback badly, just like anyone can

122

stick a knife into a couple of people or pull a trigger or hold someone down under water. But to be the best, to reach the pinnacle, requires self-denial, sacrifice, discipline, humility, and preparation. You have to hurt yourself, scold yourself, analyze yourself, recognize your weaknesses at the same time you try to eliminate them. And those weaknesses you *can't* eliminate must be minimized. You must create a plan that highlights your strengths and hides your flaws. You have to do more than simply want to win. Everybody wants to win, for goodness' sake. But precious few of us are willing to *prepare* to win. You must do things that are difficult, unpleasant, painful.

You must do today what nobody else will do, so tomorrow you can accomplish what others can't.

And then, of course, there is the ultimate test of the quarterback: the audible. Going off plan. Looking over the landscape and making an on-the-spot decision to change up what you're doing. That's what I'm about to do.

Because I've just had the pleasure of meeting Luther. Luther Feagley, seated just two stools down from me at the bar, with a lovely gal named Tammy. Luther isn't going to win any prizes for intelligence or class. Or for his wardrobe, which consists of a gray T-shirt that says "Don't Fuck with the Huskers" and baggy shorts. But, oh, he's full of talk with his lady friend, Tammy, about the fundamentals of football, and she seems not to know very much about the sport, which means she is taking everything he says as gospel, even when discerning lads like myself know that Luther is falling short in his discussion.

Mind you, my only goal tonight was to enjoy a burger and a ball game while on the road to my next project. I had no designs on Luther or Tammy or anyone else in this bar. But a good quarterback calls an audible when the opportunity presents itself. When the cornerbacks are creeping up and there's no deep safety, the quarterback calls a fly pattern and goes for the touchdown, does he not?

Of course he does. And Luther and Tammy may be too good for me to pass up. Luther, because he won't shut the hell up about stuff he doesn't understand nearly as well as he thinks he does, and he has nice big kneecaps that are probably very sensitive to the touch. And Tammy, because underneath those red locks, she has a nice round head. And she has a big, throaty voice that is going to sound nothing short of delicious when she starts begging.

Yes, an audible, then.

Gotta run, folks. Time to be sociable.

[END]

Chapter 32

THE KITCHEN IN which I'm sitting in Aurora, Illinois, is so quiet you can hear the refrigerator humming, the water dripping from the sink. Gretchen Swanson is a petite woman, with a slump to her shoulders and a lined face, a thick head of curly hair, Santa Claus white, combed neatly. Her eyes are scanning something off in the distance, out a window and over a quarter-acre backyard. I don't know if she is pondering everything I've said to her or if she's thinking about her daughter, who probably played back there on that now-dilapidated swing set, or swung in the tire that still hangs from the big oak tree.

The kitchen is lit brightly, but a dark pall hangs over everything here, as if something rotten has infested this once-vibrant house, coloring the egg-yellow walls a dingy beige, turning Gretchen's warm radiance into a despairing reserve. I recall experiencing that sensation after Marta died, how obscene any object of beauty seemed. *How dare something be luminous and pretty,* I would think, *in the midst of such pain and suffering. How dare those people walking down the street laugh and smile. How dare the sky be such a magnificent periwinkle blue.*

I look back down at the kitchen table and jump at the sight of a large cockroach. It's only after I've scooted back my chair that I realize it isn't real; it's just an ornamental piece, a porcelain figurine. Who would have a porcelain cockroach?

"Sorry," says Gretchen. "We've had that thing for years. Joelle loved it. She . . ." Gretchen looks off into space again. "When she was a child, she heard that song, 'La Cucaracha'? You know that song? *La cucara-CHA, La cucara-CHA?*"

"Sure, of course," I say with a smile.

"Oh, she heard that on the radio one time when she was just a little one, maybe three or four years old. She started dancing and trying to snap her fingers along with the music. Her little blond curls were bouncing everywhere." Gretchen allows a smile at the memory. "After that, my husband, Earl, always called her 'my little *cucaracha*.' When she was little, she couldn't pronounce it. She'd say she was his little cuckoo-clock-ah."

Gretchen grimaces at the thought, comforting and painful all at once. I stifle my own memories—hours after I received the news, my mother and I waiting for the flight to Phoenix, my mother drinking one Bloody Mary after another at the airport bar while our plane was delayed. All that time, I wondered if there had been some mistake, that infinitesimal possibility that some signal was crossed, that my sister was traveling somewhere overnight and had someone house-sitting for her, that the burned body in her house was not her, that we'd show up at her house in Peoria that night and Marta would walk up in some athletic outfit and backpack and say, *What are you guys doing here? Did something happen?*

I don't dare move now, don't so much as rattle the ice in the glass of lemonade sitting before me. Don't so much as breathe.

Gretchen closes her eyes and gives a quiet shake of her head—the appropriate response, I came to learn, for such bereavement. It's so overpowering, so incomprehensible, that trying to make any sense of it whatsoever is futile. You just shake your head and cry.

"All right, Emmy," she says. I don't even see her lips move.

I close my eyes, too, and say a quiet prayer.

Then I push the paperwork in front of her and hand her a pen. I thank her with a long, warm hug that devolves into tears from both of us.

When I get outside, I click on my smartphone and call the assistant state's attorney in DuPage County with whom I've made contact, a man named Feller.

"Joelle Swanson's mother just consented to the exhumation," I say, somewhat alarmed at the enthusiasm in my voice. I've been working this guy Feller for the last two days, finally extracting from him, at close of business yesterday, this promise: *if you can get the mother to exhume, we'll get our ME to autopsy her.*

As soon as I end that call, I make another one, to a prosecutor in Champaign County, a woman named Lois Rose, who welcomes my call like she'd welcome a kidney stone.

"DuPage County is exhuming Joelle Swanson for an autopsy," I say to her. "And your guy, Curtis Valentine, isn't even in the ground yet."

"Thanks to you, Emmy," she reminds me. The Valentine family held a memorial service for Curtis in Champaign yesterday—closed casket, obviously—but, at my urging, agreed to hold off on the actual burial for a few days.

"C'mon, Lois. If they're convinced enough in

DuPage to unearth a body, why can't you guys just move a body from a funeral home to a morgue?"

I pause, alarmed at my callous reference to *a body*. My sister was *a body*, too.

Lois Rose makes a noise on her end of the phone, a harsh exhale of air. "Did anyone ever tell you you're persistent?"

"Once or twice, yes."

"If I get our ME to do this autopsy, will you stop calling me?"

I actually laugh. And when the call is over, I pause at my rental car and squeeze my fists so tight I fear I might break a bone in my fingers.

"Finally," I whisper.

Finally, an autopsy—two, in fact—to get the proof we need for the boys at the Hoover Building to give us a team, an army to hunt this monster.

Chapter 33

Okay, I have something very important to discuss with you tonight. I thought it could wait but it can't. So when we last visited yesterday evening, I was at a bar in Grand Island and they were playing a college football game on ESPN Classic with the Houston Cougars from two years ago. You may recall I mentioned a man named Luther, Luther Feagley, sitting two stools down with this woman he was trying to impress, a real beauty named Tammy Duffy? Anyway, after I ended our session, Luther starts prattling on to the fair Tammy about this fancy offense that Houston runs called the run-and-shoot. And Luther, he's sounding like quite the professor, a real academician he is, a man of letters, telling her how the run-and-shoot features four wide receivers, with the quarterback throwing the ball on every down.

So you can imagine, it got me a little hot under the collar.

Houston did *not* run a run-and-shoot offense. It was a spread offense. There's a difference. There are many differences, actually.

The run-and-shoot was developed to maximize the quarterback's options, which include running—thus, *run* and shoot. Typically, the QB does a half roll or a sprint out from the pocket, attacking the corner, enabling him to run if necessary. And the receivers usually call their own route based on the defense they see. So it's a very dynamic offense, with a fair amount of running.

[Editor's note: sounds of a man's voice, muted, as if gagged, attempting to speak in a high-pitched voice.]

Quiet now, Luther. I'm not talking to you. Does it look like I'm talking to you? I'm talking *about* you. That's not the same as talking *to* you. Do you understand there's a difference, Luther?

My apologies; my friend has to learn some manners. Now, the spread offense, there's nothing magical about it. You just place your receivers all across the field to spread out the defense and create better passing lanes. It's not as improvisational.

So I tried to be polite about it. I tried to make the point to Mr. Luther Feagley that Houston ran the spread offense, and this Rhodes Scholar here, this highly cultured member of the intelligentsia, this venerable sage who roams the earth espousing great wisdom, he decides to talk down to me like I'm some single-cell organism. Do you know what your mistake was, Luther? Do you? If you guess correctly, I'll give you back your teeth. Some of them, at least. The top ones.

No? Flustered, are we? Your mistake was insulting someone you don't know. I looked like a nice, normal, harmless guy, didn't I?

I'm going to have to put down the recorder—no, wait, I'll clip it to my Windbreaker . . . okay, good, you can still hear me . . . come here now, my love . . .

[Editor's note: sounds of a woman's muffled cries continue throughout the remainder of this recording.]

You're . . . heavier than . . . I thought . . . there. Phew!

Okay, Miss Tammy Duffy, we're going to have some fun. Let me . . . get you . . . more comfortable first. Come on, now, don't fight me . . . *[Inaudible]* making this any easier . . .

I wasn't expecting this detour, I can tell you that, Luther. I was going to have a burger at the bar last night and watch some classic football and be on my merry way. But I called an audible because you're such a horse's ass.

And I'm going to give you a choice, Professor Run-and-Shoot. I can kill you first, or you can have a front-row seat to what I do to Tammy before I deal with you.

Tough decision? Okay, then the front row it is. I suppose on the plus side for you, it will be an extra thirty minutes of life. That's what you guys all desperately cling to, right? Every last breath?

Well, when you're done watching what I do to Tammy, you'll be rethinking that decision.

[END]

Chapter 34

I PUSH MYSELF away from my computer and stare at the clock. It's past five o'clock now. Where are they? My feet drum the floor. My brain is having trouble focusing. I'm supposed to be swimming through the sea of data in NIBRS for unsolved arsons or suspicious fires but I can't concentrate, not when we're this close now. Each of them, Champaign and DuPage counties, promised me autopsy results by five o'clock. Well, it's past five, people—where are you?

I walk over to Books's office. Sophie Talamas is in the chair on the other side of his desk, scooted forward so that she and Books can speak to each other quietly, each of them with their elbows on the desktop, their heads only inches apart. There's a familiarity between them, a subtle intimacy in their body language. I don't need to be hit over the head to see it. A blind monkey could see the chemistry between them.

When they spot me, they withdraw from each other. Each of them leans back instead of forward, opening up to me with looks on their faces that tell me I wasn't expected. I wish I could just backpedal out of the room, but that would make everything even more awkward.

"Did you get the forensics yet?" Books asks, recovering.

I shake my head and raise my smartphone. "Any minute, I assume."

"Come in. Sit down."

Sophie moves her chair back and makes the seat next to her available.

"Did you work through last night's fires?" I ask her. I've given her the assignment that I've been doing for the last year, monitoring websites and signing up for breaking-news e-mails to monitor all the fires that occur throughout the day, hunting for the next kill committed by our subject.

"Yes," she says. "Nothing from yesterday or last night."

I nod reluctantly. I can't be sure she's good at this yet. I'd double-check her work if I had the time. We're a four-person operation doing the work of a dozen.

"I was just explaining to Sophie about our jurisdictional issue," Books says without prompting, probably reading my facial expression.

I nod, as if I believe him. The way they were huddled together, the way they drew back when they saw me—I don't think a jurisdictional issue was the topic of conversation.

The FBI doesn't have jurisdiction over this case until it crosses state lines, and even if we can establish murders in Champaign and Lisle, Illinois, no state line has been crossed. So unless the locals ask for our help, we are out of luck. It's a hurdle for us, but all we have right now are hurdles, so it has to get in line.

"I didn't mean to interrupt," I say.

"Don't be silly," says Books with too much enthusiasm. "Come in."

Saved by the bell. The bell on my phone, for incoming e-mails. I look to see what the message is.

"Joelle Swanson's autopsy," I say.

Chapter 35

I PULL UP the e-mail on my desktop, where the report from the DuPage County Coroner's Office will be easier to read. I've only read one forensic pathology report in my life and it was from a different jurisdiction, so this isn't my bread and butter. But like the last one I read—probably like all of them—there is a summary conclusion at the end that wraps up, in as close to layman's terms as possible, what the coroner found with regard to the death of Joelle Swanson of Lisle, Illinois. I flip to it and hold my breath.

Fire investigators have found no evidence of deliberate cause in the fire itself, concluding that the fire was caused by a burning candle in the decedent's bedroom that ignited the curtains and spread throughout the upper story of her townhouse.

"Right," I mumble. We always knew that. He made it look like an accidental fire. That's no surprise. Now for the forensics.

The presence of clear soot deposition on tracheal mucosa and the dorsum of the tongue is consistent with the decedent being alive at the time of the fire and inhaling smoke and other toxic chemicals. The soft tissue and blood in the recoverable organs was cherry red, which is typically evident with carboxyhemoglobin levels above 30 percent and is therefore indicative of inhalation of toxic levels of carbon monoxide and cyanide.

"That can't be right," I say. She breathed in the smoke, they're saying. Joelle was alive when the fire started?

These findings are compared against a lack of any evidence of injuries on the decedent's body caused by blunt trauma or other

external force besides the heat generated by
the fire.

No evidence of stab wounds or gunshots
or anything like that. Nothing that couldn't be
explained by flames or the intense heat generated
by them.

"No," I say.

Based on the findings above, it is concluded
that the manner of death was ACCIDENTAL,
and the cause of death was asphyxiation as a
result of smoke inhalation during a fire.

"No!" I shout, pounding the keyboard on one
side, causing it to flip in the air and fall off the side
of the desk, dangling from its plug connector.

"Bad news?" Books has appeared in the doorway.

"It's wrong," I say. "It can't be right. This can't
be right."

I stagger out of my chair and put my head against
the wall, staring at the floor. Books walks over to
my desk and reads the report on my computer.

"Jeez, I'm sorry, Emmy."

My phone beeps again, another e-mail. I don't
move. My head stays against the wall, my eyes
focused on the floor.

"There should be another e-mail in my in-box," I say. "My guess is, it's the report from the Champaign County coroner."

"Hang on." Books gathers the keyboard back up and works the mouse. "Yep. It's right here."

"Read it for me, would you, Books?" I close my eyes as time passes, as the memories slap me in the face, the argument with my mother after Marta's death.

Something's not right, I said to her. *We should have them perform an autopsy.*

Why, Emmy? Because you think her bed was in a different spot than it was a month ago when you visited?

I don't think it, I know it. Whatever, Mom—I'm suspicious. I think we should—

You think we should let them cut up my baby and pull out all her organs? You don't think she's suffered enough from the burning? You want them to chop her up like some science experiment? I won't do it.

"Damn," Books says quietly. "Damn."

"Don't say it," I tell him.

"I'm sorry, Em. It's almost the exact same report as from DuPage. The Champaign County coroner finds Curtis Valentine's manner of death to be accidental, caused by smoke inhalation."

I feel him upon me now. He puts his hands on my shoulders.

"Don't. Don't touch me." I wiggle free, walk to the other side of the room. "They're wrong. Don't you see that? They're both wrong!"

Books breaks eye contact with me, stuffs his hands in the pockets of his suit pants. He *doesn't* see that, of course. What he sees is a woman stubbornly clinging to a truth that isn't true at all, a little girl insisting that the Tooth Fairy is real.

"I'm sorry," he says again. "I'm really sorry."

Chapter 36

I'm looking at this boy. He's five, maybe six. He has brown eyes and messy, unwashed hair and blue jeans. He's shoeless, but they all are; it's a requirement for the kids' play area, the Rocky Mountain Play Park, inside this shopping mall. The parents are sitting around the perimeter, chatting with one another or sipping their Starbucks lattes or shouting at their kids to play nice or slow down or keep an eye on your little sister.

There's probably fifty kids running along the foam-padded flooring, climbing the jungle gym or gliding down the slide with Porky Pig or riding on the river raft with Sylvester and Tweety Bird. Most of them don't seem to know one another, but they're interacting regardless, in that clumsy way that kids will do, sometimes being nice, sometimes being impolite or even rough, sometimes requiring a referee and sometimes being gentle. Some of them form groups and travel from one play station to another, and some go solo and join up with whoever's at the spot they've descended upon.

But not this boy. He is sitting on the floor at one end, not playing with anyone but watching the other kids as they speed past him, ignoring him. A minute ago, a foam ball rolled toward him and he handed it back to a girl, who took it without acknowledging him.

He wants to be a part of what they're doing. I can tell. I can see the longing in his eyes as he watches these breathless children run and shout and laugh. He wants to run and shout and laugh, too. But something is holding him back, keeping him planted in the corner. He feels like he doesn't belong.

But he wants to belong. He really does. If only they'd give him a chance, they'd see that he's just like them, a kid who just wants to feel secure, to understand his place, to be part of a community. He wants the same things they want. He's afraid of the same things they fear.

Get up, little boy. Don't be afraid. They'll like you, they really will.

Someone, please, give him a chance. Extend a hand or call out to him. It won't take much. Just one small act of kindness and he'll happily join in. He doesn't need much, I promise you—he doesn't need much. He just needs one person, just one single person, to show him the slightest bit of kindness before it's too—

[Editor's note: pause of seventeen seconds.]

Get up, little boy. Get up and go play.

[END]

Chapter 37

BOOKS HOLDS THE door open for me, gentleman that he is, so that I am the first to see the smug expression of the man sitting in the leather chair, none other than Assistant Director Julius A. Dickinson.

(The *A* is for *Asshole*. Even his parents knew he was going to be a prick.)

"Well, well." The Dick always manages to be doing something else when you walk into the room, all for the purpose of highlighting your lack of importance and elevating his own. Today, he is reading something, some kind of pamphlet or brochure.

"There's no need for you two to sit," he says, stopping Books and me in our tracks, just short of his desk. "This won't take long."

After making us wait while leafing through the

brochure in front of him, he looks over his glasses at us both. "It sounds like you had an eventful week in Chicago," he says. "Let me see if I have all of this straight. Emmy here assured us that a killer was in the midst of a cross-country crime spree and was brilliantly evading detection through a clever arson scheme. And apparently, this scheme includes rearranging the positioning of the bed in the bedroom to maximize the inflow of oxygen in the room and, thus, the strength of the fire."

He's taking that almost verbatim from the report we issued yesterday, a report that the Dick demanded from us. So at least he read it.

"And during your eventful week," he goes on, "you've been able to determine that, of the fifty-five fires that make up this so-called crime spree, about half can be confirmed as having crime scenes where the bed was positioned across from an open door." He flips a page of whatever he's reading. "But you don't know if the beds were in that position all along, or whether our phantom serial killer moved them there."

Except for Marta, I want to say. *Marta's bed was definitely moved.*

"As for the other half of the fires, you have no idea *where* the bed was positioned. The information has gone too cold. Is all of this true?"

"That's correct," Books says.

"Well, then," Dickinson continues. "About half of these bedrooms had beds directly across from an open door? I would consider that to be a *very* significant fact—"

He looks at me, the trace of a smile.

"—if I were the editor of *Better Homes and Gardens,*" he adds. "But I'm not. I'm an assistant director with the FBI, and I find that piece of information to be staggeringly minor and insignificant. But do you know what I find *very* significant?"

I bite my lower lip, fuming.

"What I find exceedingly significant are the findings of two independent forensic pathologists, studying two different victims in your subset, who have concluded that these victims' deaths were accidental. Not homicides."

He picks up his phone and raises the brochure in front of him. It's only then that I realize it's a menu. This jerk is picking out his lunch. "Lydia," he says into the phone, "I'll have the roast pork sandwich and some potato salad. And I want two pickles on the side. Not one. Two."

The Dick places the phone against his chest and looks at us. "This investigation is now officially closed. Books, your temporary appointment is rescinded as of right now."

Books remains quiet, his arms behind his back.

"And Emmy," Dickinson adds, his expression changing, "come back at six o'clock tonight, so we can discuss the status of your suspension."

I stand my ground, but Books takes my arm and leads me out, while the Dick completes his lunch order.

Chapter 38

"YOU COULD HAVE at least fought for us," I say in the elevator to Books. "You have a lot more sway than I do."

"Not with Julius." Books shakes his head. "And probably not with the director, either. Not anymore."

"You still could have fought for what's right," I say.

"Yeah?" He turns on me. "And what *is* right? Please tell me, Emmy."

It's only then that it hits me, Books's relative silence over the last thirty-six hours, since we got the autopsy reports. I made an assumption that we were on the same page, that my anger and frustration and stubborn certainty spoke for us both.

"You don't believe me anymore," I say. "You don't think these are murders."

"Well"—he coughs, raising his hands—"Emmy, there *are* certain facts we have to face here."

I step back from him. "I don't believe this."

"Hey," he says, reaching for me.

"Don't *hey* me, Books. Just say what you're going to say."

He takes a breath. "Emmy, it's not a question of whether I believe *you. You* don't know these are murders any more than *I* do. It's a question of believing the data. And the *data* says there are no crimes here."

"No," I counter, "the data says our subject is brilliant at covering them up."

"Oh, I'm sorry!" Books throws up his hands. "That's right. First, the complete lack of any proof of arson means he's a brilliant arsonist. And now, the complete lack of any evidence of murder proves that he's a brilliant murderer, too. What's next? The complete lack of evidence that he's an assassin from the planet Mars proves that he's a *brilliant* Martian assassin. The lack of proof that he's the Easter Bunny proves that the Easter Bunny is the most brilliant homicidal arsonist the world has ever seen!"

"Fine!" I yell. "You're just like Dickinson, you know that? I'm really sorry I wasted your time, Books."

Books swats his hand against the elevator panel, smacking the emergency stop button and halting the elevator so abruptly that I almost lose my balance. His neck is a dark crimson, his eyebrows twitching wildly.

"Don't you put me in the same category with Julius," he says, pointing a finger at me. "I gave you every benefit of the doubt. I wanted you to be right. I know how important this is to you. But you're *not* right, Emmy. And it's time you let this go. Remember Marta for the great person she was and do what everyone else does when they lose someone they love—mourn. And then slowly get over it. This crusade of yours is threatening your sanity and it's going to be the end of your career here, if you're not careful. Speaking of which."

He hits the button, resetting the elevator in motion. He pushes a button for the next floor, though it isn't ours.

"You better be very nice to Dickinson at six o'clock," he says, "or you'll never work here again."

Chapter 39

I WALK WITHOUT purpose, killing time until my fateful six o'clock meeting with the Dick. On Pennsylvania Avenue Northwest, I pass the National Archives buildings. I remember coming here as a kid, a summer vacation. My father was most excited about the tour of the FBI building, cops-and-robbers stuff from his own childhood, relics from famous cases involving "Machine Gun" Kelly and "Pretty Boy" Floyd and "Baby Face" Nelson, machine-gun umbrellas, John Dillinger's Colt, the numerous ransom notes from the Lindbergh kidnapping. Marta and my mother enjoyed the Smithsonian's many offerings; the Air and Space Museum was their favorite.

Me, I liked it here best, the archives, the records dating back centuries, the idea of re-creating the past to better understand and even predict the future, the sense of an intertwined history, a community between present and past. When I was a kid, my father predicted I'd be an archaeologist, but I didn't want to dig back that far. I was never interested in hieroglyphics or pyramids or dinosaur bones. It was numbers I craved, numbers and facts easily categorized. Run the numbers, divine a formula, and predict an outcome. Mathematics was my first love. I used to play with numbers in my head. A teacher once told me that if you add any number's digits and get a sum that is divisible by three, then that original number is divisible by three, too. Never again did I look at a number without running that equation in my head. The address 1535 Linscott became $1 + 5 + 3 + 5 = 14$, which is not divisible by three, thus 1535 is not, either. License plate KLT 438 became $4 + 3 + 8 = 15$, which is divisible by three, and thus so was 438.

Life's not just numbers and formulas, Marta used to say to me, her bookish twin sister. *You have to live, Emmy. You have to meet people, let them inside.*

Right. Well, I did that with Books. I let him inside. But that's over now, and that fire won't be rekindled, not for lack of spark but because I'm not capable of sustaining that fire forever. I knew I'd disappoint him sooner or later. It was inevitable. He'd settle into a life with me and then he'd realize that I wasn't the person he'd thought, wasn't the person he *wanted*. He'd be too noble to say so; he wouldn't leave me, but he'd be banished to a lifetime of mediocrity, imprisoned by a wife who was more a friend, a companion, than a lover. He'll probably never realize what I saved him from, the bullet he dodged. He'll never understand that I did him a favor when I ended things between us.

Was he right, what he said in that elevator? Is this just some crusade of mine, divorced from reality? Is this how I've chosen to cope with Marta's death? A girl who grew up adoring statistics and relying on them, suddenly turning her back on all the facts and believing in scary monsters in the closet?

Maybe it's time I grew up.

Maybe it's time I tried to salvage my career with the FBI.

I check my watch. It's five o'clock. I better head back. Don't want to be late for my meeting.

Time to swallow my pride and see if I can keep my job.

Before I reach the Hoover Building, my cell phone rings. Caller ID says it's Sophie Talamas.

"You were right, Emmy," she says to me, breathless. "You were totally right!"

Chapter 40

I STOP IN the shade of some trees along Pennsylvania Avenue Northwest, the breeze tickling my hair, tourists lazily strolling the sidewalks while workers knife through them on their way home. I stick a knuckle against my right ear to better listen with my left to the words of Sophie Talamas as she races through her discovery.

"It happened on Friday," she says. "The victim's name is Charles Daley. He was a shoe salesman who lived in a suburb of Denver called Lakewood. He was found dead in his bedroom, which was the origin of the fire. I know you're going to ask me where the bed was located in the room, but I don't have that yet."

I nod along with her, though she can't see me. "That sounds like our subject," I agree. "But . . ."

"But what?"

"But usually he kills two people in each place he travels," I say. "You just have the one in Lakewood?"

"Well . . . here's the thing," she says. "The short answer is yes, just the one. But I was expecting to find a second fire, too, as you said, in the surrounding area. So I expanded my search a little. And I think I found a second one. It's a little different, though."

"Different how?"

"There were *two* victims in the fire, not one," says Sophie. "Everything else is the same. Fire in the bedroom, accidental cause—but two victims. Luther Feagley and Tammy Duffy. They lived together in a house in Grand Island, Nebraska."

"Nebraska? How far away is that from Lakewood, Colorado?"

"About four hundred miles. A six-hour car ride. But it makes sense, Emmy. Luther and Tammy were found dead in Nebraska two days before the Denver murder—Wednesday, September fifth. If your hypothesis is correct that our subject lives in the Midwest, well, then he could have taken Interstate Eighty west to Denver. Grand Island, Nebraska, is right on the way, off I-Eighty."

I work it through. "So he drove from, say, Illinois or wherever he lives, along I-Eighty. On

Wednesday, he stops at Grand Island, Nebraska, and kills those two people, Luther and Tammy. That gives him plenty of time to hit Denver by Friday and kill the shoe salesman."

"Exactly. You were right, Emmy. He's taken his show on the road after Labor Day. You were totally right."

Maybe so, but nobody in a position of authority believes me. I've just been told by two independent forensic pathologists and an assistant director of the FBI that I'm dead wrong. My entire search has just been kiboshed, my authority revoked.

"How did it go with Dickinson today?" she asks.

I try to think of the right words. "It's still a work in progress."

"Well, we can't stop now, Emmy. We have to catch this guy."

From her lips to God's ears. Or Dickinson's ears. She's right, of course. I can't stop now. Because *he* isn't stopping. But how do I do it?

How am I going to keep this investigation alive?

Chapter 41

I STOP AT my work cubicle before I go up for my meeting with Dickinson. I see Books in the office down the hall, the one they gave him when he came on board for his temporary assignment. That's the Bureau's strict hierarchy for you. A man who isn't even a full-time employee gets an office just because he used to have the title of "special agent."

The few items that Books brought with him to make himself feel at home—a photo of his parents, a football signed by the 1995 Kansas City Chiefs, his Bureau certificate—are in a box now, ready to be transported back to Alexandria. Books looks washed out. His eyes are tired and heavy. His tie is pulled down. Maybe he's glad to be done with this brief stint; maybe he's excited to return to his bookshop.

I walk down to his office. "I was a little rough on you before," I tell him. "I know you did a lot to even get me this far."

He gives a half smile and waves off the issue.

"There have been two more murders," I say. "One in Nebraska, one in Colorado, within a two-day period. He's on the road now. Same profile, same m.o."

Books shakes his head. "Same autopsy findings, too, I'll bet, if it ever got that far. Death from smoke inhalation, caused by accidental fire."

He's probably right about that. You can't solve a crime if nobody is willing to say it's a crime in the first place.

He nods at me. "Y'know, they say you haven't really earned your scars around here until you have one of those."

"One of what?"

"One that gets away. An unsolved case."

Right. Books has one of those. He used to talk about it all the time.

"The Cowgirl Killer," I say.

He tucks his lips inside his mouth and nods. Seven murders over a six-year period in the Southwest—Texas, New Mexico, and Arizona. Each of the victims was an attractive woman that hailed from a ranching family. The killer cut off their arms and legs before raping them. The lurid details were all over the press down there.

But this detail wasn't: he cut off their toes and stuffed them in their mouths.

Books came into the investigation late, but as he's related it to me, the case consumed him. He worked it for years with no result. Informally among the FBI—which likes to give names to its operations—they called the subject the "Cowgirl Killer." The last murder was, like, five years ago or something. Books has been holding his breath ever since.

"You hope he got picked up on some other crime, or maybe died," says Books. "Every day, you ask yourself, is he still alive and well, free to continue his spree? Will today be the day he kills someone else, another person dead because you couldn't do your job well enough?"

And that, in a nutshell, is exactly what I don't want. I don't want our subject to be my cautionary tale. I don't want him to become my "Cowgirl Killer."

Books pushes himself out of his chair and walks over to me. "Whatever happens in there with Dickinson, keep your job, Emmy. He's going to insult you and demean you and have himself a grand time. Just eat it, okay? Just take his shit, if that's what it takes to stay with the Bureau. Because you can be more effective from the inside."

"More effective . . ."

He puts his hand on my shoulder. "More effective finding your arsonist-murderer, kiddo. If you really think this guy exists, and these things are happening, then don't listen to what anyone else says. Not me, not Dickinson, and not some county coroner. Even if you have to do it all by yourself, don't give up."

Our eyes meet for just one small, meaningful moment, before each of us breaks eye contact. He's right, of course. And that's always been my plan. I have absolutely no intention of giving up this investigation.

The only question is what I'll have to sacrifice to keep going.

Chapter 42

"EMMY, DO COME in," says Dickinson. His assistant, Lydia, has left for the day. This floor, where the executives work, is half-empty and very quiet. The room, Dickinson's office, feels smaller to me now.

For the first time, Dickinson is not pretending to be doing something else, to make me wait while he reviews a report or scans a lunch menu or chats on the phone to highlight my insignificance. This time, Dickinson has been eager to see me, eyeing me with that feral expression, a predator smelling blood in the water. He owns me now. I'm his. We both know it. I've lost. He's won.

I walk up to the chair by his desk but remain standing.

"You can sit if you like," he says.

"I'll stand."

He clucks his tongue. "Emmy, Emmy, Emmy. Always choosing the more difficult path when an easier path is available."

We both know what he means by the *easier path*. I knew it more than a year ago, the first time he put his hand on the small of my back in a familiar way, how he used to hover over my shoulder under the guise of reviewing something on my computer screen. Then the roundabout references to a drink or dinner after work, and then, finally, that day he asked me to go away with him for a weekend in Manhattan. I remember that it didn't click with me at first—I was so far from considering a romantic relationship with this guy that it didn't occur to me he was talking about a lover's getaway; I assumed it was business-related. *Why are we going to Manhattan?* I asked. He double-blinked his eyes, stared at me as if the answer were obvious. *To have some privacy,* he said.

That's when I laughed. It was a small hiccup, a chuckle, nothing more, but enough to tell him that the mere thought of us rolling around in the sack together was downright comical.

At the time it happened, I felt kind of bad about it. I had every intention of discussing it with the Dick the next morning. But it never got that far. Because the next morning, I was told that I had been written up by Assistant Director Julius Dickinson for sexual harassment and erratic behavior.

"What's the easier path?" I ask.

Dickinson actually winks at me, causing my stomach to do a flip. Then he gets out of his chair and comes around to my side of the desk. He shows me a small handheld device that looks like an old walkie-talkie, with lights and a small antenna.

"This is what you'd call a bug detector," he says. He pushes a button, and it hums to life, one light turning orange, a small screen with a line bouncing up and down in jagged fashion, measuring radio frequency waves like a heart monitor. "It will detect any sort of eavesdropping device, phone tap, GPS transmitter, spy-cam." He waves it over me and walks behind me. The humming noise continues unabated but steady.

"No recording devices," he concludes, his breath tickling my ear, raising the hair on my neck. "Now I must frisk you. Raise your arms."

"Why?"

"Because my little gadget won't pick up a standard, old-fashioned tape recorder. Or maybe just because I want to."

I raise my arms. He pats me down. He takes his time doing so, probing my various body parts so thoroughly that he knows what kind of underwear

I'm wearing. After he's examined every contour of my body, he takes my smartphone—a basic iPhone—and looks it over before handing it back to me.

"Very good," he says, clicking off his bug detector, the humming abruptly ceasing.

"Why the cloak-and-dagger?" I ask.

"Why?" He leans against the desk, his eyes fully on me. "Because I want to have a conversation with you, Emmy, and I want it to be just the two of us."

Chapter 43

STILL LEANING AGAINST the desk, Dickinson crosses his arms, shaking his head at me like he would at an insolent child.

"A private conversation," I repeat. "You're going to explain what the 'easier path' is that I should be following?"

"You know what the easy path is," says Julius. He opens his hands. "Would it be so bad, Emmy?"

Would it be so bad, having a sexual relationship with him? I'd rather have a tooth removed with a pair of pliers and no anesthesia. I'd rather bathe in volcanic lava.

My cell phone rings. I look at the iPhone's screen. My caller ID says "Mom."

"Ah, Mommy's calling," says Dickinson, glancing down at my phone.

This is about the time of day my mother likes

to call, after happy hour has ended, offering slurry words of love to her only remaining child. The alcohol unlocks emotions that nothing else can, that she's bottled up over the years, that pour out as syrupy expressions of love and regret and then recede to their hidden chamber when she's sobered up.

"I'll get rid of it," I say. I push a couple of buttons and the ringing ceases. Then I place the phone on the chair next to me.

"As we were saying." A smile appears in one corner of Dickinson's mouth.

"I'm not attracted to you," I say. "No offense."

Dickinson lets out a small laugh. "None taken, Emmy. None taken." He looks at me and cocks his head. "You don't get it, do you? That would just make it more enjoyable for me."

It's like an ice cube down the back of my neck. It's all I can do to even stay in this room. It would actually be more arousing to him if I slept with him against my will. My revulsion would be his turn-on.

What am I willing to sacrifice?

Keep your job, Books said. *You can be more effective on the inside.*

"And . . . if I say yes?" I ask, my head turned away from him, unable to make eye contact.

"If you say yes, Emmy, then you get your job back. Starting now."

I close my eyes. "What about this task force? Can we keep investigating these fires?"

Dickinson doesn't answer. His eyes have glazed over. His tongue peeks out and wets his lips. He's imagining it, I realize. He's picturing us having sex right now.

A wave of nausea surges to my throat. I mentally block any image of this pudgy, tanning bed–bronzed man with the bad comb-over in a state of undress, me along with him.

"So," I say, "if I sleep with you—"

"Or whatever *else* I want. I'm a man of many appetites."

I drop my head, pinch the bridge of my nose, and let silence hang between us. Then I look up and say, "No, I can't do it."

Dickinson, he with the upper hand that he so cherishes, tries not to give me the pleasure of seeing his disappointment. Instead, he just shrugs. "Then you've just worked your last day with the Bureau."

"You can't fire me because I won't sleep with you."

"I'm not. I'm firing you because I still consider you mentally unstable. What is this you're saying about my demanding sex?" He leans into me. "That sounds like something that would be your word against mine, doesn't it, Emmy?"

"Maybe so," I say. "Maybe not."

"I think I heard it the same way as Emmy," says Books, booming through the speakerphone.

Dickinson jumps from his spot on the desk, his face ashen, like he just spotted a rat scurrying across the floor. "What is . . . what is this?"

"That's Books," I say. "I guess instead of shutting off my phone, I must have answered it. He must have been listening this whole time."

Still stricken from this turn of events, the blood draining from his face (and presumably his scrotum, too), Dickinson says, "The call from . . . your *mother*?"

Oh, maybe I changed the caller ID for Books on my phone to "Mom." That could have happened in, say, the last thirty minutes or so, before I came up here.

"You look unwell, Julius," I say. "Maybe you should have a seat."

Dickinson staggers backward, away from the phone and me, until he hits the wall. His mind is working overtime, trying to replay our conversation, recalling what he said that Books would have overheard, whether he can spin it a certain way, whether he can get away with an outright denial.

Finally, with a slump to his shoulders, he seems to recognize that he's lost this round. He said plenty to incriminate himself. And while he could get away with a denial when it was his word against a lowly research analyst, he knows that Books is a favorite of the director. All things considered, he seems to have decided it's not a fight worth waging.

"You can't do this," he mumbles, but his heart isn't in it.

"We just did," I say. "Now sit down, Julius, while I explain to you what's going to happen next."

Chapter 44

BOOKS AND I leave the Hoover Building together, a light mist spraying us. We head for his car in silence, still buzzing from our little escapade. Books was not completely at ease with it, the surreptitious eavesdropping of an assistant director's conversation, but I prevailed on him that if Dickinson was going to make a move on me—and I was pretty sure he was, calling me in for a meeting after the close of business—then the only recourse was to fight fire with fire. (Pardon the pun.)

"What an asshole," he says, once we are far removed from Hoover. "I mean, I knew the guy was a jerk, but . . . wow."

"We probably should have asked for more," I say. "We probably could have gotten more."

We turn into the parking garage on Tenth Street Northwest, happy to be out of the escalating rainfall. Books doesn't like rain. Never has. Snow, no problem. Blistering heat or teeth-chattering cold, he can handle. But he hates getting rained on. He doesn't like wet clothes and damp hair, the messiness of it all. I, on the other hand, love the smell and feel and taste of rain on my face, the musty odor afterward, the feel of slick grass between my toes. Maybe Mother Nature was trying to tell us something about our compatibility.

"We're the good guys, remember?" he says. "What we asked for is what we deserve, at this stage. Nothing more. I don't want to waste the Bureau's resources any more than Dickinson does, Emmy. Your investigation's going to have to stand on its own two feet, and if it can't, then we can't force Dickinson to keep supporting it."

He's right. Still . . . it was kind of fun to place the noose around Dickinson's neck and watch him squirm. There was a part of me that wanted to demand all kinds of things from him—a new office, a higher salary, a stipend—but I had Books, the voice of reason, tempering my excesses.

He's always done that, I remind myself. *He's always smoothed over your rough edges. He was the anchor in the water, while you rocked up and down on the waves.*

Invisible

"It's probably your last chance," Books says to me. "So let's hope it works."

We reach his car, a new Honda sedan, and drive to Reagan National for our flight back to Chicago.

Chapter 45

I'm driving tonight, on my way back home. It's a long, lonely drive with endless stretches of nothingness, just a well-lit highway and blackness on each side. It can mess with your mind, I can tell you.

Do you . . . do you know why I'm doing this? Why I'm recording these thoughts for you? I'm doing it because you think you know me, but you don't. You don't know anybody, really. And I can prove it to you.

Just use yourself as an example. You have thoughts that nobody else knows about, don't you? Thoughts that you haven't shared with a single human being, not your best friend or sibling—nobody. And sometimes it's more than thoughts. It's actions, things you do.

174

Invisible

You could be the most generous and loving father, the most charitable of men, but if your buddies knew about those photographs of barely legal Asian girls you've downloaded to your computer, they'd remember that above all else—you'd be the pervert, first and foremost—so you keep it a secret. You could be a faithful wife who would never cheat on your husband, but if he knew that you touched yourself in the shower while thinking of the grade-school principal or some movie star, his opinion of you would change, so you hide it.

You don't share those thoughts because you're afraid your extremes will define you, that people will let those little nuggets overpower everything else they know about you, that finely honed image you've constructed. So you hide. You put on a mask. But don't you see? Nobody can really know you *unless* they know your extremes. If all they know is the gooey, creamy center and not the ragged edges, the outer reaches of your personality, then they have an incomplete picture, a series of snapshots.

And do you think you're special? Do you think you're the only one who hides things about themselves? Of course not. Everyone does. Everyone around you has a sexual proclivity or a sadistic streak or some surrender to temptation that they bottle up inside, that they hide behind their Armani suits or fancy makeup or warm smiles or polite laughter. You don't really know anybody in this world except, maybe, yourself.

So that's why I'm telling you everything about myself. I want you to know me. I want you to know everything.

Because you definitely know my extremes, don't you? You know my secrets. Should that define me? It probably will, but it shouldn't. I'm more than just these things you know about. That's not all me.

For example, did you know that I would never, ever hurt an animal? Did you know that I sponsor one of those children in a Third World country for thirty dollars a month? Did you know that I once paid for a neighbor's funeral and tombstone because his widow couldn't afford it?

Yeah, that really fucks with your head, doesn't it? You want me to be some evil person because that's easy to understand. You don't want to know that I can be generous and compassionate. That doesn't fit into your nice, comfortable construct. That doesn't make sense to you, because you've painted me with one brush, one color, and there's no room for any others on your mental palette.

I just don't think it's fair, that's all. I don't expect anyone to canonize me, but at least recognize that I'm a complex person like anyone else. I mean, at least I've taken off my mask for you. That's more than you can say, isn't it?

[END]

Chapter 46

THE COOK COUNTY Medical Examiner's Office is a great beige cement block with windows that some architect tried to pretty up with an angle or two at the edges. The blast of cold air as we enter is downright delightful. I never thought I'd be this happy to arrive at a morgue; the rental car's air-conditioning had coughed tepid air at the four of us on the short drive from the FBI's Chicago office. While Sophie Talamas may be dewy and rosy-cheeked, Denny Sasser, Books, and I just look like blotchy, irritable suits.

The harried-looking receptionist shows us to a tiny, windowless conference room. We all sink into the somewhat battered chairs, and I pick up a *Vogue* magazine, as if there's any chance I'll read it.

"So he killed a couple in Nebraska," says Books. "And then a shoe salesman in Denver."

"Right."

"Where's he going this week, Emmy?"

Like I know. Seattle? Austin, Texas? Burlington, Vermont?

Dr. Olympia Janus finally enters the conference room. She is a handsome woman, tall and straight and strong-looking. Her hair is short and black with strands of soft gray, and she wears simple, square black glasses attached to a beaded chain around her neck. She is wearing sensible shoes—Dansko?—and classic-cut gray pants with a blue cotton blouse.

"Hi, Lia," says Books. Denny Sasser stands to greet her as well.

"Books and Denny! Nice to see both of you."

Introductions all around, everyone shaking hands with her. Dr. Olympia Janus is an FBI special agent and forensic pathologist. The Bureau doesn't often conduct its own autopsies, but when it does, it's usually Lia Janus who performs them. She was at the Twin Towers, she was at the Waco and Ruby Ridge standoffs—she's been everywhere that mattered to the Bureau.

This was my one final chance, the one concession I got from Dickinson—that he would let Lia Janus autopsy our two Illinois victims, Joelle Swanson and Curtis Valentine. *If she says there's no foul play,*

I said to Dickinson, *I'll go away quietly.*

My heart speeds up as she takes her place at the head of the table and lays two thick case files in the center of the table. She is all business. Professional. Guarded. But not at all aggressive.

"I appreciate all of the background information you got for me, Denny, on the two victims," she says. "It was helpful."

"That's what I'm here for." Denny has been doing the fieldwork, gathering whatever information he could about Curtis Valentine and Joelle Swanson while delicately tiptoeing around the local authorities.

Lia Janus looks around the room and releases a heavy sigh.

"Well," she says, "you have certainly gone and confused things for some perfectly good coroners."

Is that good or bad? It sounds good . . . right?

"I've conducted more than a thousand autopsies in my career," she says. "I've seen people maimed and butchered and tortured, crushed and beaten and cut and burned. I've seen everything, guys. It's impossible to surprise me."

And? And?

"After examining the bodies of Joelle Swanson and Curtis Valentine, you can put me down as surprised," she says.

"They didn't die of smoke inhalation?" I ask, jumping the gun, unable to help myself.

"Actually, they did," she says, turning to me.

That's the last thing I wanted to hear, of course, but there is something in her tone, something to the glint in her eyes, that tells me I'm still in the game.

"But their deaths were no accident," she says. "These were homicides. And these were the most ingenious, meticulous, and cold-blooded murders I've ever seen."

Chapter 47

"I WANT TO make sure I'm on record telling you this," says Dr. Janus. "If I'd received these bodies in a routine fashion, without having spoken with you about them first, I likely would have come to the same conclusion as these local MEs did—that the manner of death was accidental."

She opens the first file and passes around copies of photos and forms. "We have Curtis Valentine of Champaign, Illinois, male, age thirty-nine. And Joelle Swanson of Lisle, Illinois, female, age twenty-three." Dr. Janus continues in a dry, raspy voice, as if she is reading something she's read a thousand times before. "In each decedent, there is clear soot deposition on tracheal mucosa and the dorsum of the tongue. The soft tissue and blood in the organs was cherry red, which is usually evident with carboxyhemoglobin levels above thirty percent and is therefore indicative of inhalation of toxic levels of carbon monoxide and cyanide.

"All of this evidence, as you know, is consistent with the decedents being alive at the time of the fire and inhaling smoke and other toxic chemicals—which is exactly the conclusion reached by the medical examiners in Champaign and DuPage counties."

We all nod in agreement.

She pauses, looking at each of us for just a beat longer than is comfortable. It's pretty hard to make the four of us uncomfortable, after the week we've had. It seems as though she's assessing us.

"But you told me to dig deeper," she says. "So I did things medical examiners wouldn't ordinarily do. For example, I examined the soot in their mouths and throats and lungs more closely. I analyzed the toxic gases present. It's usually carbon monoxide and hydrogen cyanide, of course. Those are usually the main culprits, and any damage caused by other gases is difficult to separate from direct particulate injury. That's the logical assumption. But when I dug deeper, guess what I found?"

"What?" I ask, like an eager student, wanting the gory details to justify my original hypothesis—but *not* wanting them, at the same time, knowing that my sister was one of his victims. I don't know which emotion is causing the buzz in my head, the tremble in my limbs.

"The chemical residue in their lungs and throat—it's not what I would have expected, based on someone lying in their bed, surrounded by fabric and polyurethane and carpeting and books. What I found was an unusually high presence of sulfur dioxide," she says. "Much higher than you'd ever expect from a normal house fire. It's like . . . well." She laughs, as if apologizing.

"It's like what?" I ask.

She shakes her head. "It's like they inhaled the smoke coming off a tire fire."

"A tire fire?" I repeat.

"Correct." She gives me a grim smile. "And I saw nothing in the reports or background information that suggested any burned rubber at the scenes."

"No, of course not," says Denny Sasser.

"And that's not all," says Janus. "There isn't evidence of burning inside the trachea and lungs. The smoke they inhaled wasn't hot." She taps the table with a manicured fingernail. "If they'd inhaled smoke from the fire, it would have scalded their trachea and lungs."

"So—what are you saying?" asks Books.

Dr. Janus shrugs. "Off the record, I would say that someone must have created this kind of smoke and forced them to inhale it, to make it appear that they were alive at the time of the fire—so that a medical examiner would conclude that smoke inhalation caused their death. But these individuals didn't inhale the smoke from their house fires. The smoke came from a different source. By the time their houses were burning, they were already dead."

It's as if the entire room collectively releases a tightly held breath. The composition of the smoke, and the lack of heat, eliminate any possibility that Curtis Valentine and Joelle Swanson breathed the fire smoke. That, alone, refutes the findings of the coroners in Champaign and DuPage.

I note, for the first time, the drumming of my fingers on the tabletop—not idle, distracted tapping, but quaking spasms. *Hold steady,* I warn myself. *You need to hear this. Don't think about her. This isn't about Marta. It's about catching a killer.*

"I assume that's not all you have to tell us," says Books.

Lia Janus lets out a nervous chuckle. "No, that's not all," she agrees. "If that were all, then last night I wouldn't have had nightmares about my work for the first time in twenty years."

Chapter 48

WE LISTEN WITH anticipation to the next phase of Dr. Olympia Janus's findings. But make no mistake, we have already scored a major victory. The conclusions reached by the local coroners have been tossed out the window.

So why don't I feel like celebrating? Because, under the category of careful-what-you-wish-for, Dr. Janus is about to give us some very specific details about how Curtis Valentine and Joelle Swanson died—and thus, how my sister was murdered, too.

Each of the four members of our team, in his or her own way—eyes downcast, shoulders closed in, feet tapping—is reacting the same way right now, even without the personal connection I have. We already know the heights of his brilliance. Now we're going to learn about the depths of his depravity.

Janus passes around glossy photographs that, she explains, are close-up photos of the upper thigh of Curtis Valentine and of the areas immediately surrounding the elbows and knees of Joelle Swanson.

"Look, here, at the splits in the tissue," she says. "Splits, in and of themselves, are normal in a death like this. Heat from a fire will cause splits in the skin as the flames cause the outer layers to fry and peel off. After that, the thicker dermal layer begins to dehydrate, shrink, and split. This splitting occurs parallel to the muscle fibers, do you see that?"

I guess I do. It's hard for someone like me to make sense of these photos. But it looks like the skin has split open vertically to reveal muscle in the same direction, like the husk stripped down to reveal the corn.

"That's the key," Janus continues. "The skin splits caused from a fire's heat will be *parallel* to the muscle fibers. When the splits are caused by lacerations—a knife, some kind of slashing wound, what have you—the lacerations will typically be across muscle fibers. That is a key way that an autopsy will reveal foul play, by comparing the laceration's direction to the muscle fibers. Do you follow?"

"Yes," Books says. "So these skin splits are

parallel to the muscle. They look like they resulted naturally from the heat of the fire."

"Correct. But upon closer scrutiny, these lacerations are quite precise. And by precise, I mean of surgical quality. They are even and symmetrical. They are simply too perfect to be natural.

"And he was clever," she adds. "He chose his spots wisely. These lacerations occur in areas of the body that were nearly completely consumed by fire, leaving little but a greasy layer of flesh over charred bone, or in areas riddled with natural splits in the skin. Whoever did this had solid medical knowledge and a steady hand. Your subject sliced them up, and he did so right where he knew we wouldn't discover it."

I catch my hands trembling again and lace my fingers together to calm them. The slow buzz between my ears, the gentle hum, rises in volume, like the charge off a high-voltage battery.

"I'm sure you've heard of the pugilistic attitude that bodies assume when burned, yes?" Dr. Janus asks. My mind flashes back to Marta, burned up into a boxer's stance—knees and arms bent, a defensive crouch. I close my eyes and take deep breaths.

"In fire-related deaths, this heat-induced contraction results in exposure of the peripheral joint spaces like the wrists, elbows, and knees, and there is often charring of the articulating surface of the bones. Deterioration of bone here would not be unusual. But look here," she says, pointing to Joelle's elbow joint. "Here, I found that a portion of the bone was *missing,* while the depth of char is consistent with the surrounding area, as if some of the bone had been removed prior to the fire. The surrounding tissue in that area was profoundly burned, but shows evidence of deep bone-level skin splits."

"Translation, please," says Books.

"Sorry. I'm saying the subject cut through their skin, moved aside their muscle tissue or sliced through it with methodical vertical cuts, and shaved a chunk of their bone off before they died. Basically, he cut them to shreds on their elbows, wrists, and knees—he sliced skin and he removed bone. Imagine someone performing knee surgery on you without anesthetic, while you're awake, and you get some idea of what these people went through. Except it was *both* knees, *both* elbows, and *both* wrists—so multiply the experience by six."

"Jesus, Mary, Mother of God," Denny Sasser whispers.

"And he knew it would be nearly impossible to detect, because these areas of the body are some of the parts that are most exposed in a fire."

Somehow, my hands have split apart again, resuming their spasmodic quaking, and only now do I realize the lighting in the room has turned a blinding shade of white, and the buzzing in my head has reached a dizzying volume, the odor in the air turning foul and putrid—

"Are you okay?" says Dr. Janus, presumably to me.

My face is sizzling, my stomach in revolt—

"Emmy," says Books.

"I forgot," says Janus. "There's a personal connection—"

"No," I hear myself say. "Keep . . . going . . . there's more . . . isn't there?"

"There's more. In fact, this is where the two deaths diverge," says Janus. "Believe it or not, this is where it gets worse."

Chapter 49

"SO HE DIDN'T do the same things to the two victims?" Denny Sasser asks.

"Well, not entirely," says Olympia Janus. "Each of them inhaled that smoke, however he accomplished that. And the very painful slicing and bone-cutting at their limb joints was present in each victim. But yes, at this point, the examinations of the two bodies diverge. Let's start with Curtis Valentine."

She pulls out two sets of photos from her file. "I found evidence of injuries inflicted at his temporal bones—his skull, basically. You see there are two skull fractures, here and here," she says, pointing to either side of the skull just behind the temple. "Is that unusual? Not at all, for someone burned in a fire. Heat-related fractures commonly occur in the temporal bone just behind or below the temples. They are normally jagged, radiate from a center point, and may cross those suture lines. For all intents and purposes, these fractures look like normal heat-related, postmortem fractures—each of the two fractures is jagged, and each radiates from a center point.

"However," she continues, tracing the line of fracture with the eraser of her pencil, "look at the center points of each of these two fractures. They are identical in diameter. Identical. What are the odds that two heat-related fractures in the same individual would have identically sized center points? A diameter, by the way, that is consistent with your average ice pick."

"You think he punctured Curtis Valentine's skull twice with an ice pick," says Books. "In locations where a coroner would blame the fractures on the heat from the fire."

"Exactly. And in a location where you would expect to find skin-splitting, too. And while we're on the topic of skin-splitting—just like he did with the knees and elbows and wrists, here at the skull he kept the incisions on the skin parallel to the muscle tissue, so it would mimic a heat-related splitting."

The room is quiet a moment. Everyone's trying to keep up with our learned doctor, and everyone's trying to digest this information without losing their lunch.

"Curtis Valentine was scalped," I say, my voice flat.

"Exactly," she says. "Our subject punctured Mr. Valentine's skull in two places to get hold of the skin; then he tore off the skin in patches, inch by inch, like peeling an orange. The skin flaps were left attached to the skull, and as they burned, they flaked away until the damage was easily mistaken for normal fire damage."

"Okay," I say, though I'm not sure if I'm saying it to myself, to steady myself, to keep a clinical focus and not think of my sister. "And was he . . . when this happened . . . was Curtis—was he . . ."

"He was alive during all of it," says Janus. "The shredding of the skin at the elbows and knees and wrists, the cutting of the bone, the peeling back of his scalp—there's evidence in the histological analysis of the tissue that there was swelling at the sites, which only happens if you're alive."

Don't think about it. Don't think about her. Think about the case, the puzzle, the solve. This isn't personal. This isn't about Marta—

Marta. Oh, my poor, sweet Marta—

"You're describing torture," says Denny Sasser.

"*Torture* isn't a strong enough word," Janus says. "Emmy? Are you okay?"

I open my eyes into my hands. I didn't realize I'd been covering my face. I squint into the light of the room.

"Emmy?"

I spin my index finger in the air, hoping that she'll understand that I want her to continue, because I'm not sure my voice will work anymore.

"What about Joelle Swanson?" Books asks. "She wasn't scalped?"

"No, she wasn't." Lia Janus sighs. "I also ordered extensive histology on her available skin samples still capable of being tested. Her skin and muscle tissue were nearly completely destroyed by the high heat of the fire, but there are a few sections of deeper tissue on her thighs that show evidence of second-degree burns occurring prior to her death—with enough time that there was vital tissue reaction, including edema, erythema, inflammation, and hemorrhage. These preliminary burns, in my opinion, are consistent with the damage caused by scalding."

"Scalding?" Denny Sasser asks. "As in boiling liquid?"

"Correct." Dr. Janus clears her throat. "He

burned her over and over again, but only to a second-degree burn."

"Why stop at second-degree?"

She gives a rueful smile. "If it were a third-degree burn, all her nerve cells would have died, and there would be no pain. A large second-degree burn, on the other hand, is a constant source of agony. Have you ever been to a hospital burn unit? That kind of pain will test your sanity and your will to live." She shakes her head. "He knew exactly how to maximize her pain."

Books clears his throat. "So . . . he poured boiling water over her. He cut her at the limb joints. He filled her lungs with the smoke of burning rubber to asphyxiate her. And then he burned her up in the fire."

Not Marta . . . not Marta . . . these things didn't happen to her . . . .

"That covers it," Lia Janus says. "Listen, I'm not sure you understand what I'm saying about the unifying characteristics of these injuries. First of all, every single one of the injuries he inflicted—every single one—could be explained away as having been caused by the heat from an accidental fire. Could we convict him in court based on what I've told you today? No. There are too many holes. I firmly believe in what I've told you, but a skilled defense attorney could tie me in knots because I could never fully discount the possibility of accidental death.

"But more to the point," she continues, "each of these acts . . . each of these injuries was chosen with the specific intention of causing unimaginable pain *without* causing death. He sliced into their bodies with the skill of a surgeon, and he didn't hit one major artery. They didn't bleed out because he didn't *want* them to bleed out."

She looks at each of us in turn. "I don't know how you ever discovered this monster or connected these two murders. Whatever you did, I applaud your excellent work. Because these are the closest things to a perfect crime that I've ever seen. And they are also, I must say, among the most hideous I've encountered. Our subject has committed unspeakable acts of torture and managed to remain completely invisible."

Dr. Olympia Janus claps her hands down on the table and stands up.

"Catch him," she says. "Hopefully, before he does it again."

Denny says, "Today's, what, Wednesday the twelfth? He's midway through his second week on the road."

"Right," says Books. "Which means he's probably staking out his next victim as we speak."

Chapter 50

Hello? Hey, how are you? I'm good, I'm good.

Okay, I'm just doing my fake-phone-call ruse again, because I'm at a bar doing my favorite thing, people-watching. Do you like to do that? I think everyone does, don't they? Isn't it strange that almost everyone seems weird to you? But you imagine that, if the shoe were on the other foot, you would seem normal to them?

Anyway, I'm traveling again tomorrow, so I'm not really on the job tonight, but I'm going to show you an example of how I do what I do—how I draw people in, how I gain their trust, because—

[Editor's note: a woman's voice:] "Are you a writer?"

196

Invisible

I'm sorry. Hey, can you hang on a second? Someone's talking to me. Hang on a second.

I'm sorry, what did you say to me?

[Woman:] "I said, are you a writer?"

Am I a writer? Why would you ask me that?

[Woman:] "Because you seem like you're observing people and taking notes. Even though you're pretending to be on the phone."

I'm not pretending to be on the phone. I'm really on the phone.

[Woman:] "Okay, sorry I bothered you."

Hey, can I call you back? Okay . . . okay, thanks . . . bye.

[Woman:] "Sorry, that was rude of me."

You don't think I was talking on the phone?

[Woman:] "It's kind of a weird-looking phone, but these days, I can't really tell anymore. It's . . . I should mind my own business. Really."

No, you're fine, you're fine. I'm Graham, by the way.

[Woman:] "I'm Mary."

Mary, Mary, quite contrary.

[Woman:] "I can be. What is 'Graham,' an English name?"

Yes, it is. What are you drinking, Mary?

[Woman:] "Club soda. So . . . are you a writer?"

No, I'm not. You want to try another guess?

[Woman:] "Are you a cop?"

Nope. Why, do I look like a cop?

[Woman:] "Not really. But the way you observe people—I was thinking, maybe, an undercover one. Like you're following someone."

Maybe I'm following you, Mary. Have you done something wrong I should know about?

[Woman (laughing):] "That's an interesting question."

Oh, well, color me intrigued. Do tell.

[Woman:] "I was just kidding."

What have you got to lose, Mary? You don't know me. I'm just a guy at a bar. I might as well be a priest. Confess your sins.

[Woman:] "I'll take the Fifth, if you don't mind."

Oh, you're no fun. Would it help if I confessed my sins first?

[Woman:] "Sure."

I'm a serial killer. I'm recording my thoughts in my fake telephone for posterity. You know, so they can study me someday at the FBI.

[Woman:] "How many people have you killed?"

Hundreds, Mary.

[Woman:] "Mmmm . . . you don't look the part. You have a harmless quality about you."

That's why I'm so good at what I do. I suck people in. Like you, for example.

[Woman:] "So you're playing me? Trying to win my trust?"

Exactly.

[Woman:] "Did it ever occur to you that I'm a serial killer who's playing *you?*"

I guess I better be careful. Tell me, Mary, what are you doing here?

[Woman (chuckling):] "A nice girl like me, in a place like this?"

That's exactly what I mean, yes.

[Woman:] "Well . . . actually, you want to know? I was on a setup. A blind date. My friends set me up with someone and I met him here. I work here, so it seemed like a good place to come. We had a drink and he left."

And it didn't go well?

[Woman:] "Oh, it went fine. He was a nice guy."

You say that as if you were disappointed, Mary.

[Woman:] "Maybe a little. But that's supposed to be what I'm looking for, isn't it? A nice guy. That's what everybody tells me, anyway."

But you're not looking for that?

[Woman:] "Well, obviously, I want him to be nice. But for me, the main thing is they have to be . . . well, for lack of a better word, interesting. Not too vanilla. You know, maybe a little dark, a little edgy."

You're looking for a bad boy?

[Woman:] "I wouldn't quite say it like that."

But not a harmless guy like me.

[Woman:] "You can be harmless and still be interesting."

Okay, then. What's so interesting about me?

[Woman:] "Let's just . . . forget it."

I'm curious, really. Why do you find me interesting? Not

that I'm hitting on you. I'm not. Let's stipulate that there will be no flirting. But I admit, I'd like to hear this.

[Editor's note: pause of twenty-seven seconds.]

So you're going to leave me hanging? You're going to leave without—

[Woman:] "I just . . . I have an early day tomorrow. But it's been very nice talking with you, Graham. Good luck on your writing . . . or your serial killing."

Mary, Mary, you really are quite contrary.

[Editor's note: pause of eleven seconds.]

[Woman:] "Okay, fine. You really want to know what I find interesting about you?"

I am utterly captivated.

[Woman:] "You aren't going to like it."

I'll mentally steel myself.

[Woman:] "Well . . . it's just something in your eyes, I guess. Like you're wishing for something you don't have. You seem . . . well, you seem troubled. I hope I'm wrong. But I really need to run along. It was nice meeting you, Graham."

[Editor's note: pause of forty-one seconds.]

Mary, Mary. Mary, Mary.

Oh, my.

[END]

Chapter 51

THIS IS A good thing . . . this is a good thing.

Books keeps saying these words into my ear with the soothing ease he'd normally reserve for a child. I stagger out of the Cook County Medical Examiner's Office without a word, Books clutching my arm at the biceps and holding me upright. When we reach our car, I rush around to the front of the vehicle and vomit into the bushes—deep, guttural retching as I plant my hands on my knees and gasp between lurches.

Books hands me some tissues when I'm done, when it's passed, and I clean myself up before he helps me into the backseat. "I'm . . . sorry," I manage, the only words I utter on the drive back to the hotel, while Books, Denny, and Sophie assure me it's not a problem.

But it *is* a problem, I know. Everything has

changed. I've changed. Now I've seen up close what he's done. I've seen what he did to Marta.

Books follows me to my hotel room and, without a word, comes inside with me. He puts me onto the bed and sits next to me, one foot on the floor, one on the bed, his hand resting on my arm. "You want anything?" he asks. "Some water?"

I don't answer. I stare at the cheesy wallpaper and let out a low moan. "Go ahead and say it," I whisper, my voice raspy with phlegm.

"I'm not going to say it." He goes to the sink and fills a glass with water, placing it on the nightstand beside me. "At least not until tomorrow."

This is why you don't work on cases with a personal connection. He warned me. And he was right.

"You should get under the covers, Emmy. You're trembling."

"I'm not trembling because I'm cold."

"I know, I know." His hand rubs my arm, something just short of tender, just shy of intimate. How many times he caressed me that way, once upon a time, in a slower, sexier way.

"This is a good thing," he repeats once more. "Keep that in mind."

I close my eyes in acknowledgment. It's not lost on me, the significance of what happened in there with Olympia Janus. Our investigation has just been given the stamp of approval.

"What Lia said in there was right, Emmy. The work you did to uncover these crimes was nothing short of brilliant. You did it all by yourself. You fought against the tide. You fought against the entire ocean. Even *I* doubted you. But you were right all along. And now we can commit our full resources to catching this guy. We're going to catch him, Em."

I sit up on the bed, feeling woozy, unsteady. "Where's my laptop?"

Books holds out his hand. "Not tonight, Emmy. You need rest."

"No—"

"Listen to me, Emily Jean. You're only human. You've been motoring on a few hours of sleep a night for weeks—months, probably—and now you've experienced some real trauma this evening. Give yourself a break. For the sake of the investigation, give yourself tonight to sleep. I'm flying in a dozen agents tomorrow. We have the full resources of the Bureau behind us now. If you really want to catch our subject, you'll have to take care of yourself first."

As usual, Books understands me better than I understand myself. I drop my head back down on the pillow, staring at the ceiling.

Books dims the lights. "I'll sleep here in this chair," he says. "I'll be here all night with you, okay?"

"Thank you," I say.

He doesn't answer immediately. I feel myself start to drift, my eyes swimming beneath heavy lids. I know that sleep will be fitful tonight. And I know what I'm going to dream about.

"We're going to catch him, Em. Just remember that."

And it's Marta, returning to me, the images I've struggled to stifle since Lia Janus gave her detailed recitation, images I won't be able to avoid when I surrender to sleep. A knife to her kneecap, an ice pick to her scalp, boiling water from a kettle pouring over her—

"I don't want to . . . catch him," I mumble. "I want to kill him."

Chapter 52

NINETEEN PAIRS OF eyes—twelve agents' and seven research analysts'—are glued to me as I complete my presentation, my map with the blue stars and red stars, my run-through of our subject's pattern—two kills a week, every week, from Labor Day to around New Year's, a slower trend during the spring and summer months.

"Questions?" I ask. "Comments?"

I look over the room. I know only a handful of these agents, some of whom come from Hoover and some from Chicago's field office. Books doesn't even know all of them, and he was an agent for more than a decade.

Books, who is running the investigation, has organized the agents into teams, with a team leader for each one who will report to Books every night. One team is for new incidents/rapid response, for new fires that we discover, on the theory that the quicker we deploy to a scene, the more effective our investigation will be (included, within that, the rather fantastical premise that we might deploy so quickly that we could actually catch our subject before he leaves town). Another team will handle old fires, combing through the litany of murders already committed and doing in-person interviews and research to try to dig up a suspect and draw out a pattern.

And then we have two teams devoted to the most recent fires, where the bodies are still warm, so to speak, and the evidence the freshest. Team Nebraska/Colorado will handle the double murder of Luther Feagley and Tammy Duffy in Grand Island, Nebraska, last week and the murder of Charles Daley in Lakewood, Colorado, two days later.

And Team Illinois will investigate the murders of Curtis Valentine in Champaign and Joelle Swanson in Lisle. That team will include our original four-person squad—Books, Denny, Sophie, and me—as well as some others.

A hand goes up in the back of the room, a man with sand-colored hair in a charcoal suit. Even as my eyes move in his direction, I grimace in pain. Either tiny gnomes are operating jackhammers behind my eyes or I have the worst headache I can remember. I am hungover from a night of sporadic sleep, breathtaking nightmares, an ever-present nausea.

"So we presume he lives here in the Midwest, and he's traveling in the fall."

"That's right."

"What kind of a job allows you to stay home in the spring and summer, but requires travel literally every week during the fall to a different locale?"

I shrug. "I'm not convinced that he's traveling because of a job. In fact, I don't think that's the case."

"Why not?" the agent challenges me. "That's the most logical assumption. He's a trucker or a traveling salesman or something like that. He has an airtight excuse for traveling around the country. Why isn't that the most logical hypothesis? That's what I'd do. If the police questioned me, I'd want to be able to show that I had a valid reason for being in those places."

"He wouldn't do that," I say.

"Oh, really. He wouldn't do that. And why is that, exactly?" The agent folds in his lips, as if suppressing a smile, and looks around him. The typical special-agent bravado—*lookee here at this little research analyst, trying to play special agent. Go ahead, little lady, teach us all your wisdom!*

"Think about how meticulous our subject is," I answer. "Look at the medical evidence Lia Janus found. Look at the surgical detail with which he carried out his torture, so that nobody would even see it as murder. That's not a guy who wants to be tied to a paper trail, where you could trace his movements week by week just by looking at job orders or some dispatch report."

I shake my head and begin to pace as I continue. "We know from last year's data—from the patterns of the murders from Labor Day two thousand eleven until that year's end—that he traveled each week to an area, killed two people, and then returned to his hub somewhere in the Midwest before heading out again the next week. He clearly seems to have traveled by car. And that makes sense, because he wouldn't want to leave a trail by purchasing an airline ticket. He could take a train, but that's slower, less precise, and also leaves a trail. And I'd be willing to bet that he drives his own car, not a rental—again to avoid a record. I'd go so far as to surmise that he pays cash for everything when he travels—gas, food, even lodging. A man who is willing to go to so much trouble to torture people without making it look like torture—to somehow fill their lungs with smoke from burnt rubber, for example, or to inflict unspeakable pain in such a way as to mimic injuries from a fire—is not a guy who's going to be so careless as to tie himself down by a job. No," I say with a sigh, "even if we find this subject, I'd be willing to bet that we wouldn't be able to prove he was in *any* of those cities at the relevant time, or that he even left home at all."

The agent with the smirk isn't smirking any longer, but he's also not willing to give up. "You're suggesting we shouldn't even pursue that angle?"

"No. Please do pursue it. I'm just telling you what I think."

"But let's start with Emmy's premise," Books joins in. "That our subject goes to incredible lengths to avoid leaving a paper trail. No credit cards, no rental cars, etc. That doesn't mean he didn't still leave a trail, right?" Books points around the room. "For the murders last fall," he says, "for each week, each area he visited where he committed a pair of murders—check all the surrounding hotels for people who paid cash during that time period. They'd probably still have to show ID, right? Check for parking tickets issued during that window of time for out-of-state plates. And he would have had to have a large wad of cash on him, right? So before he left town each week, maybe he withdrew a large sum of money from a bank or an ATM. Let's look for that, for each week last fall—a midweek withdrawal of large amounts of cash, probably over a thousand dollars."

I feel a surge of momentum. Good. This is good. So many smart and talented people putting their heads together—surely we can think of something.

Finally. We're no longer spending our time looking backward, proving a crime was committed. Now we're looking forward, trying to solve it.

"We're hoping to have a profile worked up soon," says Books. "Until then . . . every night, team leaders, six o'clock central time, we video conference." He claps his hands. "Let's catch a bad guy."

Chapter 53

THE TAVERN IS about three-quarters full at 3:57 p.m. There is a standard full-length wrap-around bar in one corner, then an open area with some cocktail tables in the middle, with dining tables at the other end. The crowd is a youthful mix, many of them just at the legal drinking age of twenty-one, some a bit older, possibly grad students. Waitresses weave through the crowd holding platters with beers and shots. There is probably loud, lively music playing, but we don't have audio, just the grainy black-and-white video from a standard security camera mounted in the corner, which has since been downloaded to a disc now spinning inside Sophie Talamas's laptop computer.

The four of us—Books, Denny, Sophie, and I—are huddled around the computer screen. With his pen, Denny Sasser points to a man walking through the crowd toward the dining tables. From the view of the immobile camera perched high up at the back of the bar, the man is walking through the middle of the screen toward the bottom right corner. The man is short and bottom-heavy, wearing a black shirt and black jeans and a ponytail—the aging hippie.

"This is Curtis Valentine," says Denny.

My heart flutters. There is something stirring about watching this man move with such unremarkable ease, a casual gait as he holds his beer carefully and heads to a table, unaware that he has only hours to live, hours which will be excruciating.

The footage comes from Benny's Tavern in Urbana, Illinois, from August 29, the day that Curtis Valentine was murdered.

Valentine continues to walk toward the bottom right corner of the screen until he disappears out of view. He is heading for a corner table, a sensible decision for someone coming here for a meeting. Unfortunately, the security camera isn't focused on that corner; its focus is the front of the establishment, the entrance and the wraparound bar, where the cashier is located. The owners want to keep an eye on the bartenders and, more important, on the money.

"Good-bye, Mr. Valentine," says Denny, as

Valentine disappears from our view. "Go to four oh four p.m., Sophie, if you would."

Sophie dutifully fast-forwards the video to seven minutes later, or 4:04 p.m.

"Keep an eye on the entrance," says Denny, gesturing to the top left corner of the screen.

The room is quiet. Books clears his throat.

"Here," says Denny, as the door to the bar opens.

A man walks in, a profile of his right side facing the screen. He is holding a phone up to his right ear, partially obscuring his face. He is wearing a baseball cap, further shadowing his features. His eyeglasses complete the trifecta of concealment. The grainy video doesn't help, either. But we can still see a few things: a male Caucasian, perhaps bald, medium height, with what appears to be a paunch showing through a blue Windbreaker.

"This is our subject," says Denny.

Nobody speaks, but electricity fills the air. This is our man. This is the man I've hunted for months, in the flesh, so close to us that I have to restrain myself from reaching out and touching the screen.

This is the man who has killed and killed again with impunity. This is the man who has committed such heinous acts of torture that he could make a UN commission on human rights atrocities blush.

This is the man who killed my sister.

Chapter 54

"HELLO, SCUMBAG," says Books to the computer screen. That's the word Books has always used to describe the criminal he's chasing, be it a bank robber or kidnapper or serial killer, a word that is both antagonistic and, more to the point, dismissive, disrespectful—making the crucial, if subconscious, point to his team that he doesn't fear this man, and thus neither should they.

On the screen, the man—our subject, the killer, perhaps the most evil man to roam this earth—remains on the phone, his face angled slightly downward as he speaks and as he listens, occasionally putting his left hand over his left ear.

"Bad luck for us, he's talking on a phone," says Sophie.

"It's not luck," says Books. "He knows where

the security camera is. He's concealing himself as much as he can without being obvious about it."

Our subject moves through the crowd, remaining at right-profile to us for a time. We lose him periodically for a couple of beats as he wades through people, but then he turns and, for a moment, faces the camera almost completely as he heads to the rear of the tavern—toward the bottom of the screen.

"Pause," I say, as Sophie is already in the process of doing that very thing.

The screen freezes, occasionally twitching. It's the best shot we're going to have of him, but it isn't much. Facing directly toward us, but still the head bowed down slightly while he talks (or pretends to talk) on the phone, the bill of his cap concealing basically his eyes, leaving only his nose, mouth, and chin.

"Yeah, he knows where the camera is," Books says again. "Keep running it, Soph."

Soph, I note, a fleeting thought. *Not* Sophie.

When the screen comes back alive, our subject keeps his head down and moves toward Curtis Valentine's position. For the first time, we can clearly see a bag that our subject is carrying, slung over his left shoulder, no doubt containing his bag of goodies—the educated guess would include an ice pick, surgical instruments, a canister of gas and gas mask, maybe a Taser, probably a firearm.

Just as our subject reaches the right corner of the screen, he raises his head up and, as best as I can see, ends his phone call and begins to address Curtis.

But then he's gone, out of the camera's view.

"Damn," I say.

"You can keep watching if you like," says Denny, "but he doesn't reappear until they leave at five oh three p.m. And don't get your hopes up."

Sophie fast-forwards the video to that time. When Curtis Valentine leaves with our subject, Curtis is on the right. Our subject is now walking away from us, and for good measure, has turned to his right to talk to Curtis—leaving us to look at the back of his head and his baseball cap and Windbreaker. As the two men move through the bar toward the front door—the top left of the screen—our subject manages to keep his face turned away from the camera's eye, and looks quite natural while doing so.

"He's good," says Books.

"We already knew that. Sophie, can you go back to the frontal shot we had?"

The screen scrambles, everyone moving backward at rapid-fire speed. It brings back memories of old video footage from my infancy, of my father teaching Marta and me how to walk when we were a year old, a video we watched ten years later at Christmas. There was my dad, coaxing us along, then letting go of our hands to leave us on our own, twins flailing forward with heavy, awkward steps like drunken sailors, before each of us fell backward on our fannies. I remember watching all of this with Dad, Mom, and Marta, and Dad rewinding the tape over and over again at a high speed, so Marta and I were staggering forward, then falling, then standing up and walking backward toward Daddy's hands. We howled as Dad ran that VHS tape backward and forward repeatedly, kids whose buttons Daddy knew how to punch, the light dimmed in our family room, while I sipped eggnog (Marta hated eggnog, but I loved it), the warmth of the crackling fire and the comfort of those same Christmas stockings we had for our entire childhood, hanging by the chimney with care.

"There," says Books.

The screen freezes, sputtering at us. Sophie tries to zoom in, but with the low quality of the picture, too close makes it even blurrier. She works it back and forth until she's found the best shot of our subject she can.

The eyes are impossible to see in any meaningful way. But it's not a total loss. The curve of his face, the elongated, delicate nose. Even with the Windbreaker, there is some indication of his build, a slope to his shoulders, a narrow frame. It's something. Each of us is digesting it now, wondering if we'd be able to recognize this man if we ever saw him in person.

Yes, I decide for myself, but that's my stubbornness talking. Who knows if our subject is really bald? Who knows if he truly has a protruding gut? Knowing this man as we now do, it's inevitable that he's at least somewhat in disguise. Put some blond hair on him, remove the glasses, add a suit and tie, remove a fat-belly suit, and he could probably walk past all of us.

I mean, hell, let's say it—he could probably wear the exact same outfit he's wearing in this video and walk right past us. Because he looks exactly like he wants to look: an ordinary thirty-something guy. An unremarkable, unmemorable man.

A man who is normal. A man who is harmless.

Chapter 55

BOOKS PUSHES HIMSELF away from the desk where the computer is perched, a bit of frustration in his expression. Denny had warned us there wouldn't be much to this video, but still we couldn't help raising our hopes, the first chance to see our subject in person. The adrenaline now begins its slow, disappointed drain.

"We'll have the techies get on this right now, see if we can upgrade the picture quality," he says, breathing out a sigh, letting his nerves settle. "But I don't think this will be good enough for facial recognition."

He's right. I don't have great familiarity with facial-recognition technology—the IAs, or intelligence analysts, who do homeland security work have far more experience—but I've worked with it enough to recognize its limitations. A profile shot of the subject won't get us far, and even with this frontal image, we don't have his retina or complete shots of many of the other landmarks—eyes, the full nose, cheekbones. Nor is there any way of picking up his skin texture, be it a creamy-smooth complexion or something ruddier.

He just didn't give the camera a good enough peek at him.

Books rubs his face with both hands. "We got search warrants this morning for Curtis Valentine's computers," he says. "We should have them by day's end. So very soon we'll know the name of the person Curtis was scheduled to meet—the name our subject used. We're making progress, people."

I make a noise, a bit of cynicism. But Books is right—it was only two days ago that the Bureau officially recognized these fires as homicides, and yes, we're now starting to produce results.

If only we'd moved faster, I say to myself, not for the first time or even the tenth time. It's a familiar refrain running through my mind—all of this delay has led to more and more deaths.

I look back at the frozen screen, to the blurry black-and-white snapshot of our man. He's almost mocking us, coming so close within the range of the camera but not allowing a good frontal shot, knowing precisely the angle of—

Wait a minute.

"He was here before," I say. "You said it yourself, Books—he knew where the video camera was the moment he walked in."

"He wasn't in earlier this day," says Denny. "We looked at the footage all day."

"Then the day before," I say.

"Could be," says Books, slowly nodding. "Yeah, sure, could be."

I jump from my chair and move into the open space of the room. I'm a pacer when I get excited, as if my mind can't move forward unless my legs do, too.

"He came in and staked out the place. He probably sat at the wraparound bar at the front, got himself a good look around. Probably dressed completely differently."

Books looks at Denny.

"I'm on it," he says. "I don't know if they've retained video that far back. We were pretty lucky they still had the August twenty-ninth footage. But I'll check right now."

Denny opens his cell phone and walks out of the room. Books catches my eye and gives me a solemn nod.

"We're making progress," he says. "Just a matter of time before something big breaks."

"Good, because it's just a matter of time before he kills again," I say. "Like, today or tomorrow."

Chapter 56

> **"Graham Session"**
> **Recording # 13**
> **September 14, 2012**

Say it, Nancy. Say it for all of my friends to hear.

[Editor's note: sounds of a woman's voice, inaudible.]

You believed me. You actually believed that I was selling Girl Scout cookies when I came to the door. Now if that isn't proof of my proficiency, I don't know what is!

Okay, to be fair, I did a little aw-shucks routine and said that my daughter was home with the flu, and she had this deadline to make her quota, so was it okay if I just sold them for her? And I *did* have a box of Thin Mints with me.

Ah, what a day! The sun is out, the birds are chirping, the leaves are changing, the air is clean and crisp, and Nancy and I are getting to know each other quite well. How could I not be happy? Of course I'm happy.

Where does that Mary-Mary-quite-contrary get off, anyway, telling me that I look troubled? She doesn't know anything about me. *Something in your eyes,* she said. *Like you're wishing for something you don't have.* What in the world would I wish for that I don't already have? I have my health, thank goodness. I love what I do. And I'm absolutely *perfect* at it. What else is there in life?

You have any thoughts on this, Nancy? Probably hard to talk with the gas mask on. Well, don't worry, it's almost over for you. Just a little bit—

[Editor's note: a whistling sound.]

Oh, hey! Do you hear that sound, Nancy? Don't go away, I'll be right back!

She's a nice gal, this Nancy. Very pleasant and gentle. She had a baby at a young age, so her boy's in college but she's only a bit over forty. Divorced and unattached. A spinster. Do people still use that term, *spinster?*

Nancy's biggest fear in life is that her boy, Joseph, won't find someone special. She says that he has trouble with commitment. He had a rough time during high school, apparently, with drugs and a couple of arrests for shoplifting. Her ex-husband is part of the problem, not doing his duty on the child-support front and not spending much time with young Joey. But things are looking up for Joey, and he's hoping to be an addiction counselor someday.

By the way, not to harp on this, but if anybody's *troubled,* it's Mary-Mary-quite-contrary. When I met her, she'd just been on a blind date. A woman who is so lonely that she's willing to go on a date with someone she's never even met is calling *me* troubled?

I'm not troubled.

Go ahead, I can almost hear you saying it. *He's projecting his sadness. He makes himself feel better by making others hurt. Their pain is his medicine.*

Sorry, no. But thanks for playing! What do we have for the losers, Johnny? First, a copy of the *DSM-IV,* courtesy of our sponsor, the American Psychiatric Association. At the APA, remember: if you have a problem, we'll invent a word for it.

And that's not all! Next, they'll receive a copy of Dr. Sigmund Freud's *The Interpretation of Dreams,* featuring cathartic revelations on penis envy and castration anxiety and Oedipal desire. Let Dr. Freud solve your problem today! And if he can't, worry not! He'll just blame it on unresolved sexual feelings toward your mother.

Nancy, Nancy! I'm back. You remember our friend the kettle? Now, sit still, dear. I'm afraid this is going to hurt.

[END]

Chapter 57

I HEAR THE sound of typing on the other end of the phone call. Then Sergeant Roger Burtzos of the New Britain Police Department says to me, "Okay, Ms. Dockery. I've got your clearance here. So tell me again what you want?"

"The fire in your town tonight."

"Yes, what about it?"

"I want you to dispatch someone to the scene—"

"We already have officers dispatched."

"Okay, fine. Have them ask the firefighters about the number of victims in the house and their specific location within the house."

A pause. I don't know if he's writing this down or if he's expressing his annoyance with me.

"And tell them to interview neighbors to confirm with them the number of people who live at that house."

"All right, Ms. Dockery. Will do."

"I need the information as soon as you can get it."

"Understood."

It's my third call like this tonight, after hearing of residential fires on breaking-news alerts or first-responder websites. We know that our subject sets two fires a week in the area he visits during his "Fall Tour." We want to identify that first fire as quickly as possible so we're in position when the second one happens. Whether anything good will come of it is another question, but it's worth a shot.

So I'm trying to spot these fires in real time. Back when I was a one-woman operation, I was calling police departments the day after, or sometimes several days after. Now I'm doing it as soon as I learn of the fire.

It is nearing midnight, the final minutes of Friday. My attention span is waning. My eyes feel heavy. My limbs are sore. I'm about three levels past sleep-deprived, somewhere between catatonic and zombie-like.

But I have to be on my game. Because tonight has to be the night. Working backward, it has to be tonight. He never kills on Sunday, as we know. Usually his second kill in the given week is Saturday. Which means the first one is earlier in the week, usually Thursday, sometimes Wednesday (like Luther Feagley and Tammy Duffy in Nebraska), but no later than Friday. So it has to be tonight.

I push myself away from my desk on the eighth floor of the FBI field office in Chicago. I stretch my back and shake out my hands.

In the next office over, Books has just returned from Joelle Swanson's former townhouse in suburban Lisle. "Anything good?" I ask.

He shrugs. "There was no forced entry," he says. "So he somehow conned his way into her house. Just like he did with Curtis Valentine. This guy must be a charmer."

I shudder at the thought, but Books is probably right.

My cell phone rings. The caller ID is blocked, which tells me it's law enforcement. Take your pick on jurisdiction: I've called, thus far tonight, police departments in New Britain, Connecticut; Fergus Falls, Minnesota; and Cambria, California.

"Ms. Dockery, it's Sergeant Burtzos from New Britain PD."

Well, that was fast. "Yes, Sergeant?"

"Turns out my guys at the scene already knew the information. Are you ready?"

"I'm ready." I'm back in my office now, hands poised over the keyboard.

"Her name is Nancy McKinley. She lives alone. She is divorced with a son, Joseph, who goes to college in Hartford."

"Okay . . ." I hold my breath.

"She's dead," he says. "They were way too late. Her body was badly burned in the fire."

Getting closer . . .

"She was found dead in her bedroom."

Closer still. "On the bed itself?" I ask.

"On the—well, lemme ask." In the background, I hear the sergeant on the radio with the officers at the scene. I can hear the response, squawking over a radio; then Sergeant Burtzos comes back on the phone and confirms it.

"She was lying in her bed," he says.

"And the fire's origin?" I ask.

"Well, they said it's only preliminary at this point," says Sergeant Burtzos. "The fire's still raging. But they think it started right there in the bedroom."

I move the phone away from my mouth and shout, "Books!" over my shoulder.

Then I bring the phone back to my mouth. "Sergeant," I say, "I want you to listen to me very carefully."

Chapter 58

"I'M SORRY," says Sergeant Burtzos through the speakerphone. "We're short-staffed on a good day, and it's past midnight now. I couldn't possibly summon the manpower any time soon."

Books and I look at each other. This is what we figured.

"Maybe the state police?" Burtzos suggests. "They're usually the ones to do roadblocks."

Books shakes his head. "We couldn't do it fast enough, and we wouldn't know the boundaries. We don't know where he's going next. That's okay," he says. "Listen, Sergeant, can you put us through to the officers at the scene?"

"I can do that, I can do that. Give me your number."

Three minutes later, the direct line on my office phone rings. I push speaker and answer.

"This is Officer Janet Dowling," says the voice through the speakerphone.

"This is Special Agent Harrison Bookman, Officer. And I have with me Emmy Dockery, an analyst with the Bureau. Can you hear me okay?"

"I'm inside my patrol car right now, so yeah."

"Officer, is there a crowd there at the scene?"

"Not as much as there was when the fire was roaring. But yeah, there's a crowd. Maybe two dozen people?"

"Give me your cell number, if you would. I want to send you something."

Ten years ago, the idea that you could transmit an image by phone was unimaginable. Now it's annoying if it takes more than ten seconds.

"Okay, got it. Didn't come through real clear, though."

"That's because it isn't clear. This is security-camera footage. Best we can do. The subject is a male Caucasian, a bit under six feet tall, maybe bald in this picture at least, average build, probably early- to mid-thirties."

"Got it."

"Take a look through the crowd, Officer. And can someone take a picture of the crowd?"

"Yes, we can. So you think he's here, watching his artwork?"

"It's possible." Books glances at me. Neither of us really thinks the subject is there, but you never know.

"Agent, our fire captain says it doesn't look like arson. I mean, there hasn't been an investigation yet, but he's been doing this a long time and his instincts are good."

Books catches the look on my face. Several dozen fire captains and arson investigators have been wrong so far.

"We believe it's arson," I say, "and that he's very good at hiding it."

"Very good."

Books says, "Question everyone there, Officer. Treat it like a crime scene."

"Will do."

"But try to keep this below the radar," says Books. "Our subject doesn't think we're chasing him right now. No reason to let him know. Not yet."

We end the phone call. Books checks his phone, a text message. "Okay, the rapid-response team is on their way to the plane. I better get going."

I start to say something but stop. My eyes move to my duffel bag in the corner of the room. I've packed three days' worth of clothes and toiletries, should the need arise.

"Better you stay here," Books says. "You have lots to do."

If I really wanted to put my foot down and come along, Books would acquiesce. But he's right. We've already discussed this. We've just received an information dump from the Lisle and Champaign police departments, full of information on Joelle Swanson and Curtis Valentine. That's what we analysts do, right? We sift through data while the agents run out for the excitement.

An awkward moment hangs between us. Nothing makes sense, not a hug, not a handshake.

"Be careful," I say to him. "And keep in touch."

Chapter 59

BOOKS'S IMAGE APPEARS on the laptop, his words coming a beat after his lips move. "You got me okay?"

"We got you," I say, with Sophie and Denny seated next to me.

"Nothing major to report, sorry to say," says Books. "New Britain is a sleepy little town. The victim, Nancy McKinley, is an accountant who works in Hartford. She left for the day at five fifteen, stopped at a grocery store just outside New Britain, then went home. That's the last anyone heard from her."

"We didn't see anything on the video from the grocery store," says Denny. "Nothing that jumped out at us, but we're going to keep looking."

"He wouldn't have been dumb enough to put down a credit card at the store," I say. "He probably didn't enter the store at all. He just waited for her to leave."

"Her son, Joseph, said she wasn't dating anybody and didn't have any plans for this weekend," says Books. "So maybe our subject just rang her doorbell and forced his way in."

I turn to Sophie. This is her assignment, checking e-mails and any social media that the victim would have used that might tip us off.

"I'm still looking at it," she says. "But so far, nothing."

"We have the state police on standby in Rhode Island, Connecticut, Massachusetts, and New York," Books says. "Okay, so tell me what you've learned."

I take a quick look over my notes, a summary of the work of several people on our team.

"On the day he died, Curtis Valentine had an appointment on his calendar at four p.m. to meet a man named 'Joe Swanson' from Lisle, Illinois," I say.

"You're shitting me."

I'm not. Our subject used a male version of Joelle Swanson's name to set up an appointment with the next person he was going to kill, Curtis Valentine. "We've traced a cell phone call—a burner cell, of course, untraceable—from Lisle, Illinois, to Curtis

Valentine's office phone on August twenty-second. That's the same day he killed Joelle Swanson."

"So he killed Joelle in Lisle, and while there, he set up his next murder, a week later."

"Yes." I glance at my notes. "Apparently, this 'Joe Swanson' said that he was starting up a new business but wouldn't say what, and he'd been burned by his last website designer so he wanted to meet Curtis face-to-face."

"Smart," says Books. "Very smart. Curtis probably invited him to his home to show off his equipment. And what about Joelle Swanson?"

"Nothing," I say. "She had nothing on her computer, or from anything we're hearing anecdotally, to indicate she was planning on meeting anybody."

Books doesn't respond to that. It's not hard to see how this is playing out. Our subject feels comfortable confronting women at their homes, but not so much the men. From what we can tell, he somehow forced his way into the homes of Joelle Swanson and Nancy McKinley but set up an appointment with Curtis Valentine so he'd be invited in.

Is that how it happened with Marta? Did she just answer the door, thinking that our subject was a door-to-door salesman, a guy looking for directions, a meter reader with the electric company? She would have done that. Marta would have opened the door to anybody. She never saw the dark side of anything, only the light.

"Okay," says Books. On the screen, he looks down at his watch. It's just after four o'clock central standard time, an hour later where Books is in Connecticut. Today is Saturday, meaning today will be the second murder, the second fire. Oh, if we could issue a warning. But what can we tell people? A murky photograph, no name attached to it, no area of vulnerability, not even an m.o. to point to with any specificity? *Hey everyone who lives in the northeastern United States, be on the lookout for a white guy of average height—he might force his way into your house and torture you and burn your house down.*

"We've sent a bulletin to all local jurisdictions in Massachusetts, Rhode Island, Connecticut, and New York to alert us immediately to any residential fires of any magnitude," Books says. "With any luck, we'll have word of the fire tonight less than an hour after it happens."

"We'll be ready here," I say, trying to avoid raising my hopes, but knowing that we are in the game now, that tonight, possibly, could be the break we've been waiting for.

Chapter 60

I'll say this for the northeastern part of the country: you sure do change seasons well. There is nothing more majestic than the turning of the leaves up here. Granted, it's a bit on the early side, so I'll have to come back this way in October to see the full blooming of fall, but you can see the beginnings of it, like a beautiful woman's coming-of-age, so full of mystery and promise, so vibrant and invigorating. Puts a real spring in a man's step, does it not?

Well, I get like this sometimes after I'm done with a session, kind of sentimental and, I might admit, giddy, even euphoric. There is so much to love about what I do, especially the ways I do it nowadays. Do you see what I see in its beauty? In its raw honesty?

Invisible

There's an old saying that people are at their most honest at birth and at death. Do you know who said that? It was me! You probably thought I was going to say Robert Frost or Philip Roth, but seriously, it was just me. You ever read those famous sayings on the Internet or in some book of famous quotations and think, *Goodness, I wish I had just* one *of those attributed to me?* After all, Will Rogers has at least ten of them. Winston Churchill has dozens, as do many of our famous presidents. I want just one, that's all, just a single memorable utterance of truth so perceptive that it sticks with you forever.

"A remark generally hurts in proportion to its truth."

"The only thing we have to fear is fear itself."

"A lie gets halfway around the world before the truth has a chance to get its pants on."

"People are at their most honest when they are born and when they die."

Yes. Yes, indeed! I daresay my quote holds up quite nicely in that company.

But this isn't about me, dear audience. It's about you. What do *you* think of my brilliance?

Enough, then. I've had my time this evening with this fine gentleman, Dr. Padmanabhan, and my sincerest apologies if I've butchered the pronunciation of his name. Though I suppose if you asked him, he'd say it wasn't the worst thing that happened to him tonight.

And now it's time for me to take my leave. But before I do, I would only ask you, do I sound like someone who is troubled? Of course not. I'm at the top of my game and I'm still having fun. What could that Mary woman possibly have been thinking?

I'll be back to speak with you tomorrow. Traffic has probably cleared sufficiently on I-95 now, so I best be on my way.

[END]

Chapter 61

"THE NEIGHBORS SAY that Dr. Padmanabhan lived alone," says the officer.

"Thank you, Officer. Please hold." I click off the phone and punch the button on my radio for Books. "Books, do you copy?"

"Copy, Emmy."

"Scenario two," I say. "Scenario two. Call came in from Providence, Rhode Island."

"Scenario two, copy that. Make the call."

Thirty seconds later, Books and I are on a conference call with the superintendent of the Rhode Island State Police and the commander of the Connecticut State Police, both of whom have been standing by for my call.

"This is scenario two, Rhode Island and Connecticut."

"Rhode Island copies that," says Superintendent

Adam Vernon. "Our troopers are in place."

"Connecticut copies," says Commander Ingrid Schwegel. "Our troopers are in place as well."

"We feel good about I-Ninety-five?" I ask, just to ease my nerves. It's already been the topic of discussion.

"Agent," says Superintendent Vernon, mistaking my title, "if the suspect is headed back to the Midwest, his only route is through Connecticut, and the only highway that makes any kind of sense is I-Ninety-five. There are forty-one miles of border, but if he isn't expecting anyone to be waiting for him, he'd be a fool not to take I-Ninety-five."

"Very good," I say. "The fire call came in fourteen minutes ago, and I just got confirmation that it's the fire we're targeting. My map says the fire is located just north of Miriam Hospital in Providence, which means he has to travel forty miles down I-Ninety-five to reach the Connecticut–Rhode Island border."

"Even if he got a head start," says Vernon, "there's no way he's reached the border yet. But I've already given the order, Agent. As we speak, the flares are going up."

"This is Agent Bookman. I'm airborne and should be at the border in fifteen minutes. I'll be the agent in charge, but we'll have agents on the ground joining you shortly. Let's be clear on the directive: plate numbers and VINs of any vehicle with a male loosely fitting the description. Permissive searches at a minimum. Anything suspicious—anything at all—your troopers will have my direct contact."

"Connecticut copies."

"Rhode Island copies," says Vernon. "If he's on the road tonight, we'll get him."

Chapter 62

THE FEED FROM the FBI helicopter comes through with surprising clarity on my laptop. An overhead view of Interstate 95 as it moves south-southwest from Rhode Island into North Stonington, Connecticut. A split-level highway with two lanes heading southwest, plus a shoulder.

At the border, beneath signs that read CONNECTICUT WELCOMES YOU and NORTH STONINGTON, TOWN LINE, state trooper vehicles from both states have set up a vehicular blockade, perpendicular to the lanes of traffic. Flares precede the blockade for as far as the screen permits me to see—probably a half mile at least, or whatever the protocol is for roadblocks.

The road is jammed with vehicles waiting in line. At the checkpoint, officers and FBI agents shine flashlights into cars, both the front and backseats, sometimes pop the trunk and check it, sometimes direct the car to pull over to the shoulder for a more thorough search, and always record the license plate and VIN number located inside the front door. Once allowed to leave, the vehicles must do an awkward bend around squad cars, then over to the shoulder, before they proceed into Connecticut, not exactly the "welcome" they were expecting from the Constitution State.

The highway is backed up as far as I can see, even as late as it is—near midnight eastern standard time. No doubt, drivers assume that this is a Saturday-night sobriety check, and it turns out to be just that for a couple of unlucky drivers, who end up having their cars impounded and taking a ride to the lockup in North Stonington.

The helicopter moves along the highway, looking for any vehicles attempting to turn around, and I see for the first time that there is a second helicopter doing the same thing.

Books is feeding me names and license plates and VINs as we go along, and I'm running them for criminal backgrounds and for stolen vehicles. I don't think our subject would drive a stolen car. A criminal background? Hard to say. It obviously wouldn't surprise me if he had one, but for some reason, I suspect he has a clean record. He's just that meticulous.

I've been managing my expectations here, but there's no hiding the truth—we have a real chance tonight. Each car that leads our team to take a second look, to pop the trunk, even to move them over to the shoulder, raises the hair on the back of my neck.

And that gives the hair on the back of my neck a lot of exercise, because most of the cars receive extended attention from our team of state troopers and FBI agents. Most of the drivers are men, and the majority of them Caucasian, and we don't narrow it down all that much when you throw in "average height," "average build," and who-knows-what for his hair.

But in the end, each of these cars is allowed to pass.

I'm not wrong about this. He drives to a new part of the country, commits two murders, and returns home. The data doesn't lie. And he must live in the Midwest. He must. The patterns of his travel can be tied to major highways.

I'm not wrong. He's a driver, and he's driving back to the Midwest.

He could have taken a different route. Like the police superintendent said, there are forty-one miles of border. But he isn't expecting us, and why wouldn't he take Interstate 95? Of course he would.

The first ninety minutes are slow and, ultimately, uneventful. And then it speeds up, because the number of cars diminishes. The backlog disappears as the hour approaches two in the morning. There just aren't that many cars crossing into Connecticut at this time.

After a Dodge minivan passes through the blockade, there is a stretch when no cars are on the highway heading southwest. Interstate 95 is empty.

"Where the hell is he?" Books spits, exasperated. "This made all kinds of sense."

"I know," I concede. "I thought we had him. There's no chance he turned around when he saw the blockade?"

"No chance. There's a trooper up ahead at the first flare, idling on the shoulder. If any vehicle tried to turn around and cross the median, he would have seen it. We've had that covered. Damn!"

"Maybe he's getting some rest first," I say. "Getting an early start tomorrow."

Books doesn't answer immediately. Frustrated or concentrating. Probably the latter. Books doesn't let his emotions overtake him much. He was always the rational to my emotional.

"I suppose it's possible he *was* in one of those cars," I say. "Remember who we're dealing with."

"Maybe. Maybe. Not many midwestern license plates, though."

True. But that won't stop me from starting a database and throwing all these names and plate numbers in it.

"We're going to keep this checkpoint up until dawn at least," he says. "We can't do this forever. But let's give it until sunlight and revisit it then. Sound good?"

"I'm not going anywhere," I say, keeping up a brave front. But somewhere inside me, I can't help feeling that we've missed him. We set up a spiderweb, but he somehow sidestepped it. Somewhere along the way, I fell too in love with my own analysis, sure that he would behave according to the model I created from the data.

And because I missed, next week, he'll do this all over again, in another part of the country, to two more helpless victims.

Chapter 63

I SIT, POISED over my computer, running the checks, my brainpower dissipating, my eyes heavy, my back and neck in full-scale revolt. I refuse to look at the clock on the wall, knowing that the little hand is about to hit the eight and the big hand the twelve. Knowing that the roadblock's now been up for more than ten hours.

"One more hour," I say to Books through my headset.

"That's what you said an hour ago," he replies into my ear.

"One more hour."

We had originally planned on ending the roadblock at eight o'clock in the morning eastern time, or seven Chicago time. I pushed it an hour to nine o'clock EST, which is coming up now.

"There isn't even that much traffic, I argue.

A small line of cars have backed up in Rhode Island on their way into Connecticut, but nothing approaching major gridlock. "It's Sunday morning. It's not like we're causing commuters a big pain."

"We can't keep this up forever, Emmy."

"Sure we can. We're the FBI."

A pause. Maybe I'm winning another hour. *He has to come through this roadblock sooner or later,* I tell myself. *He has to.* Even though another part of me is admitting that somehow I've miscalculated.

"No, I'm calling it," says Books, as if he's recording a time of death.

"No! Please—just one more—"

"Negative. I'll call you soon."

"Books!" I yell, but there's no feedback. Books has disconnected the line. He knows what it's like arguing with me. He's correctly decided that it's better to just cut me off.

"Shit." I rip off my headset and throw it down on my desk. I get to my feet and a hot, slicing pain shoots up my back. My vision is blurred from staring at a computer screen all night. My brain, let's face it, is fried.

I make it into the hallway and head down toward the "war room," a converted conference room, minus the long table, where eight research analysts are working on our case. They came in this morning at seven and have been doing full workups on the people we stopped at the roadblock, a total of more than five hundred white adult men.

I am woozy, my reactions fuzzy. I hear animated discussion, then laughter—*laughter*—and I quicken my pace toward the war room.

Inside, one of the two male RAs is standing, doing something comical, an imitation of a goofy dance move or something. When he sees me, when the room becomes aware of me, everyone stops smiling and silence lingers awkwardly in the air. I look at each of them, these seven new RAs plus Sophie Talamas, as I enter the room. I feel like some humorless parent interrupting a slumber party, a teacher walking in on a rambunctious classroom, and I hate it, but it doesn't stop me from going off.

"The man we're after," I say slowly, my voice trembling, "scalps victims while they're still alive. You get that, right? He burns the flesh off their bodies—while they're still alive. Stop me when I've said something *funny!*"

All eyes have dropped to the floor. Sophie says, "Just blowing off some steam, Emmy. Everyone's working hard."

"Everyone's not working hard *enough*," I reply. "He's in here," I say, pointing to one of the laptop computers. "Somewhere in all this data, in some cross-reference we haven't done yet, in some database, on some blog or social media or website, is our subject. It's up to us to find him, people. You all in this room. He's not going to leave a fingerprint for one of our superstar special agents to find. He's not going to drop his wallet at the crime scene or trip and break his leg on the way out of a house he torches. He's not going to be spotted by some nosy neighbor. It's not going to be the field agents who find him. It's going to be us, the people in this room, the RAs. So screw your heads on and give me your A game, people, because this asshole just slipped away from us for another week!"

I storm out of the room and head for the elevator, needing a shower and something to eat before I continue. It isn't until I'm out in the fresh air that I realize my car keys are back up in my office.

Chapter 64

WHEN I RETURN to my office, Sophie Talamas is in there, holding my keys. "I think you forgot these," she says.

I snatch them from her.

"You had no right to say that to us, Emmy. These people are killing themselves for you. They're the most underpaid people in the entire Bureau, yet they're working fifteen-hour days, they're here at seven in the morning on a Sunday—"

"Hey, you know what, Sophie?" I throw up my hands. "You want a nine-to-five job, go work at Seven-Eleven or something. We're trying to catch a monster. It sometimes requires a little extra effort."

"I think we're clear on that."

"Are you? That's great." I head for the door.

"We're not finished," Sophie says.

I stop and turn. "What did you say?"

Sophie, with her silky hair pulled up fashionably casual, her skinny jeans and pretty knit blouse, her perfectly etched features, is fuming. When someone this attractive gets mad, her face doesn't turn ugly, exactly—it's more like her features become highlighted, her eyes a little shinier and her cheeks glowing more prominently. "We have a problem, don't we, Emmy? You and I."

I take a breath and hold out my hand. "Just do your job, Sophie, and—"

"I'm *doing* my job. I'm working as hard as anyone. But what's our problem? You've given me nothing but dirty looks since the day I arrived."

"I need you focused," I say. "I need you to focus on this case and nothing else."

"I'm not sleeping with him, Emmy."

I draw back, knocked on my heels by the comment. Sophie folds her arms and doesn't speak, letting those words linger between us. There is so much to say and think about what she's just said, none of it good. The fact that she acknowledges the issue at all means I've done something—body language, facial expression, something—to make it an issue, at least in her eyes. The fact that she is comfortable enough with Books that she feels entitled to make such an announcement. The fact that she thinks I need to hear this from her, that we're even *talking* about this when there's a vicious sociopath at large—

"I'm not," she says again. "Books has been very good to me, very supportive. We're friends, for sure. But that's all it is."

And then, I can't deny the small pang of relief that I feel, that I instantly sequester, because that's what I'm best at, right? Steeling myself, shutting down. My feelings for Books (to the extent they exist, some residual feeling, some primitive sexual attraction, nothing more) don't matter, because I can put them aside to focus on this investigation. My sense of loss for Marta doesn't matter, because I can put that aside, too. I click on any such feelings and drag them into my mental trash bin where they belong.

I'm a girl standing in a tornado, pretending like it isn't even windy, like I can compartmentalize every emotion, switch off my heart and divert every ounce of my energy into my brain, that I can be the girl who's all about the data, all about the clues, all about the puzzle, and forget about anything that makes me human.

I'll have time to be human later. *Later* is one of my favorite words.

"Do your job," I whisper to Sophie. "That's all I care about."

Chapter 65

I SPEND MOST of the afternoon in the war room, watching over the other RAs, checking their work, flagging anything that looks promising, though little of it does. There is some residual tension from my blowup earlier in the day, but it gradually subsides as we focus on the work at hand. At six o'clock, somebody mentions dinner, and we put in for some pizzas. I wander down to Books's office where our fearless leader has been taking calls from the various agents in the field since he returned from the northeast a couple of hours ago.

"Shit," he says, as I walk in, shaking his head. There is background noise, video from some source, maybe his smartphone.

Books looks like hell, having spent all night in a helicopter over the Rhode Island–Connecticut border. His eyes are red and unfocused, his hair matted. His face is drawn and unshaven.

"What's up?" I ask.

"Oh, nothing." He waves a hand. "My Chiefs got spanked for the second week in a row. C. J. Spiller, the Bills' running back, for Christ's sake, ran through our line like we're a bunch of high-schoolers." He lets out a sigh. "And Romeo's a *defensive* coach."

I drop into a chair opposite him. "Books, you do understand that I have no idea who C. J. Spillman or Romeo are."

"Spiller," he corrects me. "C. J. Spiller is the—"

"And you also realize that I don't care."

Books shakes his smartphone. "We're oh and two now, and it feels like we're light-years from the division title we won—"

"Books, what is it with men and football? I mean, it's like an addiction with you."

"Me and millions of others."

"I know," I agree. "My dad was like that, too. He'd sit in front of the television all day on Sunday and watch games. We had to work church around it, because we all knew what his real religion was."

And then something happens. The clouds separate. My heart begins to race.

"Football is the ultimate . . ." Books is waxing philosophical but I'm no longer listening. I pop to my feet, which in my current state is not a good idea, and nearly fall over as I rush out of Books's office and into my own.

I jump on my computer and bang out a solid hour of research, my body overheated, my pulse reeling, my hands trembling so hard that I can barely type. When I'm done, I have a U.S. map with a lot of markers.

Books is on the phone with an agent when I walk back in. He shakes his head quizzically and finishes his conversation before he looks carefully over the paper I've given him.

"Those are the kill sites," I say with a child's overblown pride. "The different cities during his autumn travels. Labor Day to year's end, last year."

"Okay, those are the orange stars, two kills a week, each week a different part of the country. But what are the black stars between the two orange ones in each location?"

"The black stars," I say, "are professional football stadiums."

Books looks at the map another moment; then his head pops up and he looks at me like I've just discovered another planet.

"He never kills on Sunday," I say.

"Oh, Jesus." Books brings a hand to his mouth. "Labor Day to New Year's. That's . . . the NFL season."

"He's not traveling on business," I say. "He's going to pro football games."

Chapter 66

"LAST YEAR'S AUTUMN kill spree," I begin. "September eighth, two thousand eleven—the first known kill, in Atlantic Beach, Florida. September ninth, the second kill in Lakeside, Florida. And what's right between them? EverBank Field, the home of the Jacksonville Jaguars, where the Jags hosted the Tennessee Titans that Sunday, September eleventh."

I look over at Books, the one who told me to refer to Jacksonville's football team as the "Jags," to give me street cred with the rest of the predominantly male team. We're video-conferencing with the entire task force.

"Who won the game?" someone asks. There's always a comedian in every bunch.

"The Jags, sixteen to fourteen," I answer, another nod from Books. "The following week, two more kill sites: September sixteen in Rock Hill, South Carolina, and September seventeen in Monroe, North Carolina. And the next day, he took in the Carolina–Green Bay game at Bank of America Stadium in Charlotte."

"A different stadium every week," says Books. "And no patterns to the teams, either. It's not like he followed the Colts or the Bears or anyone around the country. There's no pattern we've discerned from the locations he selected. Good teams, bad teams, evenly matched games versus lopsided ones—there's no pattern to them."

"Except that he stayed away from the Midwest," I add. "Because the Midwest is his stomping ground for the off-season."

"He never went to the same stadium twice?" someone asks.

"Not last year, no. This year, the season's just begun. In the first week of the NFL season, he killed that couple in Nebraska and then a man outside Denver, which means he would have gone to the Broncos–Steelers game in Denver that Sunday. And just this week—the second week of the season—he killed in New Britain, Connecticut, and in Providence, Rhode Island. We figured he would then speed home to the Midwest, and his only means of exit was Interstate Ninety-five, heading south-southwest through Connecticut, so we roadblocked it." I use my pointer along I-95, heading in the opposite direction. "But he didn't go home on Saturday night. He took I-Ninety-five *north* into Massachusetts. He went to the New England Patriots game today in Foxboro."

I don't make eye contact with Books. When he and I were working this all out, and we realized that we had totally pegged our subject last night, but that we blocked I-95 in the *wrong direction,* I couldn't speak for a good ten minutes.

We had him. We were so close. We had him down to the freakin' highway on which he was traveling. And still, he evaded us. And now two more people will die agonizing deaths this coming week.

Books, probably sensing my despair, jumps in. "But the point is, he didn't visit Denver's or New England's stadium last year. Which means, he seems to be on a path to keep going to a new stadium—one he's never visited—every week until he's visited them all."

"So let's assume that," I say. "Let's assume his next trip will be to a stadium he didn't visit last year. Let's further assume it won't be a midwestern stadium, because it's his backyard. So that removes the Chicago Bears, the Indianapolis Colts, the Saint

Louis Rams, and the Kansas City Chiefs. Bottom line, there are four stadiums we don't think he'll visit, plus the two that he already has."

"Okay, what does that leave?" someone asks, a woman.

"There are thirty-two NFL teams and thirty-one stadiums, because the Jets and Giants share one," I say. "So, thirty-one is the number. He visited seventeen stadiums last year and two more this year. That's nineteen. Then disregard the four midwestern teams and that's twenty-three that are off his list. That leaves eight more stadiums, folks. Eight more stadiums."

"And of those eight remaining teams, only five have home games this week," Books chimes in. "The Oakland Raiders, Dallas Cowboys, Cleveland Browns, Washington Redskins, and Seattle Seahawks."

"The Seahawks are a Monday night game, so we think we can rule out Seattle. He's going to one of the other four areas this coming week," I say.

"So what do we do?" asks one of the agents on the video feed. "Send out a general alert to be on the lookout for an average-looking white male with no distinguishing characteristics, who might have made an appointment with you, or who might show up at your door unannounced?"

He's right. That's the problem. We don't have a good image of the man, and we don't know his m.o. very well, either. He scheduled an appointment with Curtis Valentine in Champaign, Illinois, but we don't know how he got to the others. What can we tell people? What kind of an alert can we send?

"We'll put all local law enforcement on alert for any residential fire, with a quick turnaround to us, just like we did in the northeast this week," Books says. "And once we know his first kill of next week, we'll know where he is, and which football game he's attending."

We have to wait for him to kill again, in other words. It's as depressing as it sounds. But it's our only lead thus far.

"And once we know that," says one of the agents, "we'll be able to narrow him down to one of eighty thousand people watching a ball game."

"True," Books concedes. "We have to think about how to handle that crowd. But we're fairly confident that whichever location he chooses, he will be inside a football stadium for three hours this coming Sunday. Now we'll have to decide what to do with that window of time."

It will be tricky, but we'll have to come up with

something. For that short period of time, we'll have our subject in a steel box. We have to make sure he doesn't get out.

Chapter 67

I started by watching her tonight. I watched her tonight in the most revealing of ways—that is, when she didn't know I was watching her. I slipped into the bar, you see; surely you appreciate by now my abilities to move about undetected. When I met her at this bar last week, Mary had mentioned that she worked here, and it was my good fortune that she happens to be a bartender, so she was relatively stationary while I lurked in the corner, watching her from a distance.

I watched her when business was light, the dinner hour, as I ate the basic pub food and then opened a laptop computer as an excuse to linger. I watched her when business picked up for the *Monday Night Football* game. I watched her when people were rude to her and when people flirted with her. I watched her when she had moments to herself and when she interacted with the manager and other staff.

And then I slipped into the bathroom so I could remove my baseball cap and glasses and pull down the collar on my jacket. When I reappeared in the bar, crowded enough to provide me cover, I made my way to the bar as if I had just arrived. I will admit to a stirring of butterflies in my stomach. Yes, my friends, I was nervous.

I took a stool at the bar and waited my turn like any other patron. I decided I would act surprised to see her, as if I was just coming to this bar like I did last week and didn't expect to see her here. Would I pretend not to remember her name? Would I struggle a moment, snap my fingers, and say, "Mary . . . right?"

When she approached me, with a soft smile playing on her face, all of my deliberative functions ceased to operate. Her dark hair was pulled back into a loose ponytail, but a few curls had sprung loose. Her eyes squinted, showing crow's-feet at the corners. The lighting was poor, casting her eyes a shade darker than I recalled last time I saw her up close.

"Well, Graham," she said, "I was beginning to think you were going to ignore me all night."

She did it again! She put me on my heels before I even said hello. Last time, she caught me recording my thoughts while pretending it was a phone, the first person who's ever figured out my ruse. This time, she knew I was lurking in the back of the bar, not necessarily in disguise but certainly obscuring my features.

And she remembered my name!

So then it was incumbent on me to come up with something witty, yes? Something clever, perhaps self-deprecating—that would typically be my trademark. A quick comeback of biting sarcasm, delivered with a deadpan expression. Something to keep up my end of the conversation.

But before I realized it, my mouth was moving and words were coming out. I said, "I was nervous about seeing you."

Friends, I must tell you, time stopped for me just then. I wanted to reach into the air and snatch those words back. My entire soul was laid bare at that moment. *What have I done?* I thought, in those few beats of time, those few torturous breaths of oxygen. *How can I take it back? Will she think I'm pathetic?*

And this is what happened next: she broke eye contact with me, the corners of her mouth lifting slightly higher. She worked a rag across the bartop. And she said to me, "Well, Graham, that's about the sweetest thing you could say to a girl."

Do you remember what that feels like? That moment when there is a . . . a connection between you and someone else? That flutter in your chest when you realize you've crossed that small bridge, that there is at least some mutuality of feeling?

Maybe Mary and I—and I can't believe I'm saying this, but

Invisible

maybe Mary and I—

    No. No, no, no. Slow down, Graham. Tread cautiously.

    Move slowly.

    We wouldn't want anyone to get hurt.

[END]

Chapter 68

MY EYES LOOK up from the computer screen. My head lolls back so that I am staring at a blank ceiling. My vision is fuzzy from sleep deprivation and staring into a computer for hours.

Books knocks on my office door. "There's still some Chinese food in the conference room," he says.

"Sounds good," I say without conviction.

"Hey." He comes over to me and puts a hand on my shoulder. "If you're not going to sleep, you at least have to eat. You're skin and bones as it is."

Always have been. Five-foot-nine and a hundred twenty pounds since I was a teenager. Long and lanky—*athletic* would be the kind way of saying it—not demure and shapely like my sister or, for that matter, my mother.

"Okay, we have them," says Sophie Talamas,

bouncing into the room. "The teams themselves, the legal ticket brokers—we have them all now. Everyone who's bought a ticket to an NFL game this week in Oakland, Dallas, Washington, or Cleveland."

I spin my chair around and nod to her. "Okay, you know what to do," I say. The research analysts are going to perform their magic, looking through all of these names and running them through our databases.

"Don't look so excited," Sophie says.

I make a face. I'm not excited.

"Emmy doesn't think our subject's on any of those lists," says Books.

"He wouldn't buy a ticket that way, where he gets in someone's database," I say. "He'd pay in cash. My guess is he's going to scalp a ticket at the game."

I cringe at the word *scalp,* given the method of torture our subject prefers. I got the word from Books, the sports enthusiast. When he first mentioned *scalping* a ticket, I pictured someone with a serrated knife.

Sophie rubs her eyes. She's put in serious hours as well. We all have. "You think tonight'll be his first kill of the week?"

I shrug. It's Wednesday night. The earlier in the

week that our subject shows himself to us—pins himself down to some location in the country—the sooner we'll know which football stadium he'll visit, and the more effectively we can prepare. So as completely bizarre as it may sound for me to say that I'm hoping he kills someone tonight, it's the unfortunate truth.

"Go home," Books says to me—*home* being a hotel room. "You can work on the laptop from bed. We've got all sorts of people looking for this guy now, Emmy. You're not a one-person show anymore."

I drill a finger onto the desk. "I'm staying right here," I say. "And if we pinpoint him to a location tonight, I'm going there with you."

Chapter 69

I want you to listen to this. This is from tonight, from Mary and me. I met her after she got off work.

Me: Can I ask you something, Mary? Why did you agree to see me tonight?

Mary: You mean, why did I agree to go out with you after I caught you spying on me in the back of the bar on Monday?

Me: I might have chosen a more charitable account of events. But—yes. Why? I might have thought you'd find me odd.

Mary: *[Laughing]* I do find you odd, Graham.

Me: Ah. Glad we have that settled.

Mary: I told you before, I like a little quirkiness in men. It was—I don't know, it was kind of endearing. Flattering, too.

I'm not used to somebody getting nervous over me.

Me: I find that hard to believe.

Mary: You think there's a big market demand out there for a thirty-seven-year-old bartender who's a recovering alcoholic?

[Editor's note: pause of eleven seconds.]

Mary: Oops, I spooked you. That's a heck of a way to introduce that piece of information. But yes, I'm an alcoholic. I've been sober for over ten years, if that's any consolation.

Me: No, I . . . I think that's rather extraordinary.

Mary: Oh, I don't know about that. I'm just facing down my demons like everyone else.

Me: But you're building a new life. You're taking college courses during the day and working at night. That's very impressive, I think.

Mary: That's nice of you to say.

Me: Mary, why would you work at a bar if you're a recovering alcoholic?

Mary: I know, I know—it doesn't make a lot of sense, right? Mostly because I needed a job that was nights only so I could go to school during the day, and a friend of mine owns the bar. Maybe I like the challenge, too.

Me: The challenge?

Mary: Yeah. Knowing I can stare it in the face and beat it every day. It's like, every day I look at those bottles of booze and say, "I don't need you anymore. I beat you." It's empowering.

Invisible

Me: Facing down your demons.

Mary: Yeah, exactly. Don't you have demons, Graham?

I thought that whole exchange was . . . remarkable. The way she so easily opened herself up to me? The way she looked me in the eye and said, *This is who I am.* People don't do that. They don't show their true selves. They hide behind layers and layers of self-deception and outward deception. They wear masks. They put up fronts. They lie. They hide.

What was I supposed to say back to her? I really wanted to reciprocate. I really did. I mean, she lays out the sordid details of her life right there, as easily as she takes a breath, and what do I do in return? Do I say, *I have some demons of my own, Mary?* No. I change the subject, that's what I do.

And it's not like she didn't notice. She drops these revelations, and suddenly I want to talk about this-darn-weather-we're-having. It was obvious. I think she knows. I mean, she doesn't *know* know—she couldn't possibly—but she senses something about me. I know she does.

Oh, and this smile she has, I wish you could see it, the way her nose wrinkles up and her eyes squint, it is one of the most sincere and true smiles I've ever seen. She is so quick to let happiness in and so firm in keeping out the venom, the poisonous thoughts.

And her smell. There is this trace of strawberry. I think it's her shampoo. When I smell it I think of the word *fresh,* and really, there isn't a better word to describe Mary.

Oh, and then the end of the night, after I walked her to

her door. I can't remember ever being so nervous. My hands stuffed in my pockets, my eyes down, shifting weight from one foot to the other. I'm telling you, I must have looked like an awkward schoolboy on his first date.

And I kissed her! I'm not sure how I moved from point A to point B, but somewhere in there I mustered up my courage and I leaned in and she met me halfway. It was so soft and slow and sweet, our lips pressed gently together, her hand caressing my cheek. I felt a charge of electricity throughout my body. I felt weightless.

I feel weightless now!

[END]

Chapter 70

"SHIT."

I push myself away from my desk, rolling in my chair halfway across my office. I get to my feet and get a nice dose of vertigo, the walls turning sideways, the floor angling up toward me. I grip my chair to reclaim my equilibrium.

"Shit," I repeat, because it seems to capture the moment.

I'm falling apart. I know that. I'm pulling virtual all-nighters and not eating. I'm not going to be able to sustain this much longer.

And what do I have to show for it? First, Wednesday night, and now Thursday night, tethered to my computer and phone, waiting all night for the call from one of the locales where we expect our subject to go—Oakland, Dallas, Washington, Cleveland—awaiting any notice of a residential fire that we can link to him.

And so far, nothing. Sure, a few calls came in, a house fire in Sausalito, a diner in Cleveland that went up in flames—probably a "Greek lightning" fire, an arson by a restaurant owner going out of business, looking to collect insurance money—but nothing that comes close to our guy.

It's five in the morning now, Friday morning. I haven't had more than a catnap since Tuesday night. I need to get a few hours of sleep so I can stay up again tonight—Friday night—when he's sure to attack. Simple math: if he's going to kill two people this week before Sunday, he'll have to do the first one Friday night.

Great. I know for certain that tonight will be the night, and I'll be falling asleep at my desk.

Deflated and groggy, my neck and back reaching the status of rigor mortis, my fingers tired from the rapid-fire typing all night, my vision as clear as fog, I leave the FBI building and take the rental car back to my hotel. I get out of my car and slam the door shut. The crisp air of a fall morning provides a moment of relief (outdoors—yes, I remember there is such a thing as outdoors, fresh air).

A tinge of pain hits me behind my eyes, dark circles clouding the fringes of my vision, as if I'm looking through a tunnel. I have to go to bed, I realize. Maybe just a few hours—

"That's her!" I hear a woman yell. My reaction time is slowed but I'm jumpy all the same, and my immediate response—*danger*—takes longer than normal to dissipate before I realize that the man and woman rushing toward me are not coming to do me harm. Not physical harm, anyway.

One of them is carrying a recorder in her hand. The other, a handheld camera.

"Agent Dockery," says the reporter, a pretty young African-American woman. "Diane Bell, from the *Tribune*."

This is a new one for me, the first time a reporter has ever confronted me like this. The words shoot into my brain—*no comment* and *I'm not an agent*—but instead I just say, "Yes?"

"Agent Dockery, I understand that you're chasing a serial killer around the country, a man who has killed possibly dozens of people and burned up the evidence to hide his crimes."

"I . . . I . . . ." I shake my head, show the cameraman the palm of my hand, and start walking toward my hotel. "I can't comment on an ongoing investigation." I say it robotically, something I've heard others say, politicians under fire and stone-faced prosecutors. *No comment. We can't comment on an ongoing investigation.*

"So there *is* an investigation," she says. "Great. Thank you."

I shake my head violently, which doesn't help my shaky equilibrium. I keep walking, picking up the pace, turning my shoulder to shield myself from her as I near the entrance to the hotel. If I'm not careful, I'm going to fall over on camera.

"Curtis Valentine," she says. "Joelle Swanson?"

I reach the door of the hotel and push it open.

"Your sister, Marta?"

I snap my head around to her but don't say anything. She raises her hand in a calming gesture and approaches me. "I know it all, anyway, Agent," she says. "Your sister was one of the victims and you've been on a crusade. You found this killer when nobody else believed you."

My mind is racing. I'm out of my league. I don't even know the protocol. Special agents are trained to deal with the press. Research analysts? Nobody ever wants to talk to us.

"Who . . . told you that?" I manage.

She drops her head a notch, a *tsk-tsk* look. Right—reporters don't reveal their sources. It's all a one-way street with them.

"Take my card," she says, and for some reason

I do. "This is an amazing story, Emmy. Don't you want to tell your side?"

"No," I say, and I push my way into the hotel.

Chapter 71

BOOKS RUNS HIS hand over his face. His eyes are red and unfocused, his face drawn. He's had more sleep than me, but that's not saying much. College students cramming for final exams have gotten more sleep than me.

"We never comment on the existence or non-existence of an investigation," Books says to me gently, like a parent to a child.

I dig a knuckle into my eye. "I didn't say anything."

"You confirmed that there was an investigation."

"She knew names. Including Marta's. She already knew there was a damn investigation."

Books's eyes meet mine, but he doesn't push it. He's made his point. No matter how much that reporter already knew, she didn't have FBI confirmation of an investigation until I gave it to her.

I throw up my hands in surrender. "I screwed up."

Books doesn't quarrel with that assessment.

"How did they get the story?" I ask, but it's a rhetorical question. The reporter will never tell, and it doesn't matter, anyway.

"My guess, one of the local cops working the Joelle Swanson or Curtis Valentine cases." Books shakes his head. "These guys are always looking for favors. 'I give you this tip, remember to make me look good next time there's a story involving one of my cases,' that kind of thing. Or maybe it was one of the victims' families. Frankly, I'm surprised it took this long to leak out."

"Well, the timing sucks." I throw a pen across the room. "Here, he thinks he's gotten away with everything. He's going about his business, wherever he is this week, killing these people with the clever cover-up, thinking he has everyone fooled, and he's going to walk into a football stadium this Sunday and we're going to nail him. And now? Now he's going to know we're coming!"

Books's cell phone rings. He looks at me with an apologetic smirk. "The Dick," he says. He punches the button for speakerphone and answers.

"This is Books," he says. "I have Emmy with me."

"Ah, yes—well done, Emmy! On the eve of the greatest lead we have in this case, you tell the *Chicago Tribune* all about our investigation."

Books rolls his eyes, mostly for my benefit. The Dick is probably enjoying having the upper hand again, being able to call me out on a screwup, however much he exaggerates it.

"I just got off the phone with the editors," Dickinson tells us. "They weren't very forthcoming with what they knew. They have some victims' names, they know that Emmy has a personal involvement in this investigation—"

Books and I exchange looks. A nice jab from Dickinson. I'm sure the Dick would like nothing more than to fire me for this. If I didn't have that episode in his office hanging over his head, he'd surely do just that.

"—and it sounds like they might have an autopsy report. They know there are multiple locations throughout the country where our subject has killed, but they don't seem to have it all in a tidy package. And they didn't say anything about our most recent information, like the video footage of the subject from the bar, or any connection to professional football games."

I shake my head. "It doesn't matter. They know that Curtis Valentine and Joelle Swanson—and my sister—are being classified as murders, not accidental fires. That's the whole ball of wax for him. He doesn't want us looking for a murderer, period, much less him. Once he sees this article, he'll know we're onto his methods. So much for sneaking up on him."

The Dick says, "Then you'll thank me for getting the editors at the *Tribune* to hold off on the story until Monday."

"Oh, that's great," says Books. "That's great!" He puts out his hand and calms the air between us. "So there's hope for us yet."

"What did you have to give them?" I ask.

"First access, if and when the case breaks."

Books gives a who-cares shrug.

"So you have this weekend, this one chance to isolate the subject in whatever football stadium he visits," says Dickinson. "Do us all a favor and try not to fuck up anything else between now and then."

Chapter 72

Mary, Mary, quite contrary,
How does my love for you grow?
With sweet little smiles and feminine wiles,
And your ponytail tied in a bow.

I THINK WE can all agree that needs a little work. Mother Goose, I am not.

But in a good mood, I am. Oh, listen to me, I'm starting to sound like Yoda from *Star Wars*. As opposed to Yoda the Supreme Court justice, or Yoda the union carpenter. There's only one Yoda! I don't need to qualify it. "Silly I am!"

Oh, God, I do feel silly. I'm giddy, changing my clothes twice before tonight's date, fixing my hair, brushing my teeth twice. I even did some push-ups so that if she touches my arm or puts her hands on me, she'll feel some hard muscle. Is that normal, to primp like that? What do I care? If this is abnormal, then I'll take abnormal!

Okay, take a deep breath. I don't want to spook her. I don't want to push her away by seeming too eager. You can be too eager, can't you? I mean, maybe she just enjoys my company but isn't ready for some big commitment.

God, look at all my instruments. The forceps are a mess. The chisel will need to be replaced soon. I think I'm going to switch from the ten-millimeter to the eight when I get a new one. Harder to sharpen and probably harder to clean, but greater precision, too. It's all about precision. And the bone curettes have seen better days, too. What's happening to me? Once upon a time, I'd clean the instruments meticulously the moment I returned home. This is what you're doing to me, Mary. You're distracting me.

But I don't mind being distracted!

Am I ready for a commitment? Oh, see, I'm doing it again—I'm making this too big, too fast. She's a nice girl, Graham, a very sweet woman. Maybe there's something there long-term, but you don't have to make that decision right now, or tonight. Take it slow. Isn't that what people say—*take it slow?*

Okay. Yes. That's just it. If I seem too eager, she'll pull back. Just be yourself, be relaxed, and let it happen.

Oh, here's the bad news about Mary: she works Mondays

through Wednesdays, which leaves her best nights to socialize Thursday through Sunday. What rotten luck! Those are the nights that I take my little road trips. The nights I'm away are the nights she's free! Is that a sign that we're not meant to be?

Okay, see, this is what I can't do. I can't put too much pressure on this. Let's just have a nice Saturday night date and . . . take it slow.

God, I'm speaking in clichés. But they're clichés because they're true, I guess. Just take it slow, relax, let the relationship breathe, like a young Cabernet Sauvignon.

But don't overthink it the other way, either—don't spend so much time trying to look disinterested that you give off the wrong vibe. Don't try too hard. Be yourself.

Be myself? How can I *be myself?*

I'm making myself crazy. Just go and have fun and don't have any expectations. Good. Yes. That's the ticket. Just go have fun and don't think beyond tonight.

And don't forget to change the blade on the amputating knife.

Just in case.

[END]

Chapter 73

MY EYES SO heavy I can hardly raise them, I watch the clock in my office hit four o'clock. Four in the morning. Saturday night has come and gone without incident.

I pick up the stapler on my desk and throw it at the clock, missing badly, putting a dent in the wall, chips of paint scattering on the carpet. Four consecutive nights of all-nighters—Wednesday night through Saturday night—with nothing to show for it but bags under my eyes and failing vision.

Books, hearing the commotion, enters my office with trepidation, wary of being the target of a flying office supply.

"What, he—he took the week off?" I shout. "He just decided, 'Oh, no, not this week'? He doesn't do that. He's never done that. He's like a robot. The one week we're ready for him, the one last chance we have before the newspapers run their story and tip him off, and he takes a fucking *vacation?*"

Books leans against the door. "I know. I don't get it. But we deal with it. We have no choice—"

"Oh, would you stop being so damn *calm?*" I hiss. "We could have ambushed him this week, Books. We *had* him. Now, he's going to know we're coming."

"Maybe not, Em. We don't even know what the *Tribune* article's going to say. Let's just do our best to control what we can control."

I shake my head, my vision blurring in the process. When my eyes come back into focus, I am looking at the article from Marta's hometown paper, the *Peoria Times,* the one written last month about how I was demanding that the Peoria Police Department treat Marta's death as a murder, not an accidental fire. *We understand Ms. Dockery is distraught,* the police chief was quoted as saying. *But we can't allocate our resources based on the whims of a grieving sister. The police detectives, fire chief, and forensic pathologist all agree that Marta Dockery died of smoke inhalation from an accidental fire.*

Books follows my line of vision and sees the article, stuck to the cushion board on the wall by my computer with a blue tack. "Look how far you've come. What's the date of that article—August seventh of this year? That article made you look like a quack, like an irrational sister who believed in Santa Claus. And now look at you, Emmy. Six weeks later, you've not only convinced the Bureau that you were right but also put into motion an intensive manhunt—and we're getting close. Look how close we are, Emmy. Before he threw us this curveball, we were ready to throw a net over a football stadium and catch this asshole today. We'll have another chance. I promise you we will. We're inside his head now. We have his pattern down, no matter that he took this week off. Hey, look at me."

Suddenly he's right next to me, hovering over me, without my noticing. Maybe that's because his invasion of my personal space never used to *be* an invasion—it was his space, too. That was a simpler time. It was easier with him than it was without. It felt more natural. It felt right. Like we were just jagged puzzle pieces that made no sense alone, but together we fit perfectly. That's what life's supposed to be about for normal people, right? You find that other piece that matches yours, that completes yours, and you make the jags and the crevices fit, even if they don't go in perfectly smoothly, even if they require a few adjustments. You don't demand perfection. You make it work and appreciate the parts that fit instead of obsessing over the small angles that don't.

I look up into his eyes. I've seen the longing in his eyes before—I've returned that longing—but I know that I'm too broken right now for any meaningful response. Books knows it, too. As I've said before, he knows me better than I know myself.

"We're going to catch him," he says. "And we're going to do it soon."

Chapter 74

I don't know what to do. I'm in deep. Deeper than I ever would have imagined. I didn't know what to say when she said it to me. I just sat there and then—

Oh, I'm not making any sense. We went for a walk after dinner and then we went back to her house and she has this old wood-burning fireplace, and even though it wasn't that cold, she thought it would be romantic to fire it up, so we did.

Then we started kissing, and we touched each other. It was so tender and warm and gentle. I'm not talking about sex. I'm talking about something much deeper. I'm talking about intimacy. Just caressing and stroking, looking into each other's eyes, feeling each other's breath on our faces. We shared a moment like I've never shared anything with anybody ever. I could have stayed there forever.

Then I said to her, "Mary, you're very special to me." It really just came out. I didn't plan it. That's unusual for me, right there—since when did I shoot from the hip? I plan everything I do—everything, you know that, you know that about me—but not with her. I wanted to say it. It felt good to say it.

And then she said, "Do you mean that?" And I told her, of course I meant it. Of course I did. But then she got quiet. I felt her withdraw a bit. And that's not like her. She's the open book, remember. But here she was, drawing into herself, holding back. It was the first time I saw vulnerability in her eyes. I'd moved her to a place where she didn't feel comfortable. I didn't know what to do. I thought I'd somehow made some huge mistake. I wondered if I should apologize. But that didn't make sense. Apologize for telling someone they're special? And then all kinds of thoughts were swirling through my head, *This goes to show your inexperience, Graham,* or *This just proves that you're not cut out for a relationship like this,* but then instead of remaining frozen or falling back into my normal calculated self, I trusted my emotions, and I just spoke from my heart and I said, I think what I said was, "Did I say something to upset you?"

And then tears welled up in her eyes, and at first I thought she was going to try to play off the whole thing in a casual way, but then this is what she said—it was a whisper, really, our faces only inches apart. "If you mean that, then I'll give myself to you. I will. I'm ready to do that. But only if you'll give yourself to me. If you can't do that, it's okay. But I'm ready to do that if you are."

I'll give myself to you. That's what she said!

I didn't—I didn't know what to say. I kissed her then, and maybe she took that as an answer, or maybe she's giving me time to decide. But I don't need time to decide. Mary, I *do* want to give myself to you. More than you could ever know, I want to give myself to you. I want to put myself in your hands, to open up every locked door inside me and reveal myself. I want you to be the one person in this world who knows everything about me. Don't you see? This is what I've always wanted. This is all I've ever wanted.

But how? How can I do that? How can I expect you to accept me?

I think—I think she could be the one, though. She knows what it's like to overcome a past, to move forward as a new person and not look back. Granted, my history is a bit more complicated than a bout with alcoholism, but in the end, isn't the point the same? Looking ahead. Putting your past where it belongs, in the past. Becoming someone better.

That's what I want, Mary. I want to move forward with you. I can do that. I mean, I *think* I can do that. I want to try. Isn't that what matters—that I want to try?

But I have to be able to trust you, Mary. Can I trust you, Mary?

[END]

Chapter 75

I TAKE A long breath before I turn to the front page of Monday's print edition of the *Chicago Tribune*.

Feds Probe Series of Fires As Work of Serial Killer
Cross-Country Spree of "Criminal Genius" Includes Fires in Champaign, Lisle

Chicago—Federal agents in Chicago and elsewhere are probing a series of residential fires, previously believed to be accidental, as the work of a "criminal genius" who has repeatedly fooled investigators and forensic experts across the country over the last year, sources close to the investigation say. The fires, which are now being reclassified as homicides, include the recent deaths of Curtis Valentine, 39, of Champaign, and Joelle

Swanson, 23, of suburban Lisle. Authorities would not comment on the number of deaths involved but estimated they number "several dozen, if not a hundred" deaths across the country. "He makes the fires look accidental," said one source, "and the deaths look natural." New forensic procedures and updated police work, according to sources, have uncovered brutal torture-murders that were largely concealed by the intense burning of the fire. "Most of the evidence went up in flames," said one investigator.

I get a mention in the sixth paragraph, referring to me as an "FBI staff analyst" whose sister, Marta, perished in a house fire outside Phoenix, Arizona, last January and who had been lobbying for a federal probe of several seemingly similar fires. "Emmy's persistence was the catalyst," said one source. And the lone photo accompanying the article, where the article continues on page five, is of me hustling away from the reporter in front of my hotel.

But here's the most interesting paragraph of all:

Sources familiar with the investigation say that forensic evidence and fieldwork have allowed investigators to pinpoint the general location of the perpetrator, though that information was not disclosed to the *Tribune*. "We know generally where he lives," said the source. "It's only a matter of time."

Where do they get this stuff? We know generally where he lives? Yes, if by *generally* you mean somewhere in the Midwest.

"Well, on the bright side, you're famous," says Denny Sasser, putting his hand gently on my shoulder. "This could have been a lot worse," he adds with less levity.

It's true. There is no mention in the article about the patterns of his cross-country travel, or about NFL football games, or any indication that we have moved beyond a very preliminary investigation.

"Nothing about football stadiums," Books says, rushing into my office.

"No mention of football games," says Sophie, entering the room as well. "So that's good, right?"

"It's good, everyone," I say, patting the air with my hands. "Yes, it's good."

We are all silent as we reread the article. For me, it's the fourth time.

"The leak was local," says Denny. "Whoever

spilled it doesn't know much about what we're doing."

Probably true . . . still reading . . . talking about the initial conclusions of the medical examiners here . . . the work of the FBI forensic pathologist that contradicted the locals . . . other kill-site locations, not known to the reporters, but reportedly reaching all corners of the United States . . . some general information and statistics about house fires in the United States and the known incidents of arson . . . ending with some more drama: "This is one of the most ingenious murderers we've ever seen," according to some source.

Mentally exhausted, coming down from our initial trepidation, the four of us are quiet for a moment. Books, as usual, breaks the silence by clearing his throat.

"So?" he says with a shrug. "What does our subject do now?"

Chapter 76

No, no, no. This can't be happening. Not now. Not *now!*

I don't understand. How did this happen? How could they have possibly figured this out? I did everything right! They even said so: "A criminal genius," they said, "who has repeatedly fooled investigators and forensic experts." Of course I did. My execution was flawless. And yet this criminal genius apparently wasn't so genius after all, was he?

That stupid girl. Oh, that stupid, stupid little girl named Emmy Dockery. The "catalyst" behind this investigation, that article said.

I shouldn't be surprised. Marta told me you were relentless, Emmy, brilliant and dedicated. And I was cocky. *Who cares if her sister works for the FBI?* I told myself. *Nobody could possibly figure this out.*

What am I supposed to do now? Just pick up my marbles and go home? Just call it a good run and move on? That's what they want, you know. They leaked this story just for me to see it. Don't you see that? There's hardly any detail in there. They don't know what I'm doing or how or why. If they did, they wouldn't have leaked the story to the press. No, they've somehow managed to figure out what I've done, but they have no idea who I am or where I am. I'm as invisible to them as I've always been. So they're trying to scare me off. Yes, of course—they're trying to spook me into believing that they're close. But I know they're not close. No—that's right, they aren't close, they couldn't be close, they're not close. They're not close.

No, no, no. No, no, no!

How did they figure this out? I just don't see how. I was so careful. I was so disciplined.

You think you can make me stop? Is that it? You think planting a vague, stupid newspaper article is going to deter me? You think I don't know that you guys deliberately plant stories to spook suspects? You could put a hundred agents on this case and you'd never find me. You could put me on a bus filled with FBI agents and they'd never find me. You guys are way out of your league—you do realize that, don't you?

Well, what's that saying? "You can't have a rainbow without a storm, you can't have a diamond without friction"?

You're just going to make me better. Yes, that's right, that's the old Graham talking. Maybe I needed a new challenge. Maybe this can be chapter two of our story. In the first chapter, I move about the country with virtual impunity while the FBI sleeps in blissful ignorance at the Hoover Building. In this new chapter, the FBI wakes up but still can't find its own shadow. Yes, I'm going to turn it up, that's what I'm going to do. I'm going to turn it up and do it right under their nose and show them how impotent they are.

But how—*how* did they figure this out? I can't believe this. I can't believe this. I really can't. Somebody please explain this to me.

No matter. No, it doesn't matter. I'm actually glad this happened because it was getting too easy. And now I really have a taste for it again. This week's going to be a lot of fun. I'm going to make this week extra special.

You think you can scare me? Watch what happens this week, campers, and then you can decide how scared I am.

[END]

Chapter 77

BOOKS CLOSES HIS eyes and winces as the Dick completes his tirade through the speakerphone.

"...so instead of spending our resources chasing down a predator, we're spending it addressing media inquiries."

Well, technically, *Dickinson* is working with the media inquiries, not any of us in Chicago, and it's not like he was doing any work on the case, anyway, unless you count stealing all the credit as work.

"What happens now?" he asks.

I look over at Books, slumped in his chair, who nods to me to answer. Just moving my focus from one side of the room to the other causes a lightning strike behind my eyes.

"This week is week four of the NFL season," I say. "Of the eight stadiums our subject has yet to visit that are outside the Midwest, only three of them have home games this week: Detroit, Philadelphia, and Dallas. Dallas is playing on *Monday Night Football,* so he won't go to Dallas. He doesn't do Monday nights."

"He doesn't, eh? You know him that well? Then maybe you can explain why he decided to take last week off."

I respond to the substantive point, not the jab. "He's never gone to a Monday night game. That's not his pattern. So it's either going to be Detroit or Philadelphia."

"Which one?" Dickinson asks.

"Philadelphia," I say.

Books looks at me with a quizzical expression.

"Our subject likes to spread himself out geographically," I explain. "He never wants to go back to the same general area within a close window of time. That's why, when he's gone to the different stadiums in Florida, for example—Miami, Jacksonville, Tampa Bay—he spreads out his visits so they're not too close together. When he's gone to the New York area for Buffalo, the New York Jets, the New York Giants, same thing—he's always careful not to do it too close together in time. He's trying to avoid anyone detecting a pattern."

"You still haven't explained why you're sure he'll

go to Philadelphia this weekend," says Dickinson.

"Because there are two stadiums in Pennsylvania —for the Steelers and Eagles," I answer. "And he hasn't gone to either one yet. He only has eight weeks left to complete his tour of these stadiums, and he's got two trips to Pennsylvania to fit in. If I wanted to spread out my visits, I'd hit Philadelphia this week and do Pittsburgh at the end of my tour."

A pause.

"Makes sense to me," says Books.

"Given your track record, Emmy, I'm not so sure," Dickinson scoffs.

Books starts to object on my behalf, but I wave him off. Let Dickinson get his licks in. I don't need his approval. I don't need anyone's approval.

Marta used to say that about me, that I was militantly independent, that I made a point of alienating those close to me. *Strong, independent Emmy,* she used to say, with her usual combination of scolding and love. *Always trying to prove you can go it alone.*

"The question," says Books, "is whether our subject has read that *Tribune* article and, if so, what effect it has on him."

"Do you have an answer for that, too, Miss Dockery?"

I don't. Not grounded in data, at least, which is

typically how I form my opinions. But I do have a hunch.

"It's going to motivate him," I say. "He needs to prove to himself that he won't let the FBI scare him off."

Books inhales deeply, his eyes moving with worry to the ceiling.

"It's going to get worse," I say.

Chapter 78

Okay, well, I just want everyone to understand—it didn't have to be this way. And who knows? Maybe it wouldn't have been. We'll never know now, will we? No. No, we won't.

But meeting Mary . . . meeting her has . . .

[Editor's note: pause of eleven seconds.]

. . . meeting her has changed me. Or it could have changed me. If you'd just given me a chance to find out.

But no. No, you pick now to discover what I've been doing. Not a year ago or even six months ago. No, you wait until I've met this perfect woman and then you suddenly grow a brain and figure out what I've been doing and blab about it to the newspaper and turn my whole life upside down.

So now I'm . . . well, I'll say it like this. I'd like to express my displeasure to you. I'd like to show you what happens when you mess with my life.

No more Mister Nice Guy.

[END]

Chapter 79

"THAT DOESN'T SOUND right," I say into my phone as I pace in my office. My eyes drift to the wall clock, which says it's nearly midnight, Thursday night.

Officer Glen Hall responds breathlessly: "I'm just reporting what I was supposed to report, ma'am. I was told if there was a residential fire, I had to immediately call it in. And then our dispatch forwarded my call to you—"

"No, I understand. You did the right thing."

Officer Hall did what he was told. We'd put out a blanket advisory to the two possible areas where our subject might strike this week—Detroit and Philadelphia—to alert us of any residential fires immediately. He responded to a residential fire and he immediately called it in.

I was certain that our subject's next stop would be Philadelphia. But Officer Glen Hall works for the police department in Allen Park, Michigan—a suburb of Detroit.

I pinch the bridge of my nose. "How many victims did you say?"

"Ma'am, there are . . . there are . . ."

His voice breaks off. I don't know if it's a bad connection or, more likely, emotion.

"There are six bodies," he says.

"Okay, Officer, and they were found in a single bedroom?"

"That's . . . cor—correct."

"I'm sorry to ask, Officer, but can you describe the position of the bodies?"

"I . . . it . . . it looks . . ." I hear him take a breath, gather himself. "They're lined up like a morgue in there."

It's him. It has to be.

"I got your text." Books comes rushing into my office. "It's him? With six dead?"

I nod my head, my eyes down.

"Six people? He's never done that, Emmy."

"It's him," I say. When I hear nothing, I look up and meet his eyes. "It's him."

Books opens his cell phone. "This is Bookman," he says. "Mobilize the rapid-response team. We're going to Detroit."

Chapter 80

NINETY MINUTES AFTER getting the call from Allen Park, Michigan, I'm in a small ten-seat plane with Books and six members of our rapid-response team. Books is on the phone talking with the special agent in charge in the Detroit field office, barking out directions. I'm looking out the window, my mind spiraling in countless directions, when the man sitting across from me, to whom I've just been introduced but whose name already escapes me, interrupts my thoughts.

"So there's no pattern to his victims?"

"No pattern," I say. "Men and women. White, black, Hispanic, Asian. No children, but otherwise all ages from twenty to seventy-seven. All socio-economic backgrounds. Accountant and lawyer and doctor and shoe salesman and janitor and grocery clerk. The only thing these victims have in common is they live alone."

"They don't have anything else in common?"

I shake my head. "Nothing we can figure. And we've tried everything. We've cross-referenced them down to the towns they grew up in, the schools they attended, clubs they've joined, religious affiliations, social media they use, everything. No," I say, blowing out a sigh. "They're all normal, regular people with no unifying characteristic."

Books hangs up his phone and looks at me. "The victims tonight were all women," he says. "Six women. Four have been identified and they're working on the other two. Looks like there are severed limbs and stab wounds and possibly GSWs, but that won't be clear until the autopsy."

"That's different from his m.o., right?" says one of the agents on the plane.

"It's different," I say. "Six victims at a time is different. The methods of killing are different. The fact that they're able to discern as much as they have from the crime scene, that the fire hasn't totally obscured matters—also different. It's all different."

"He's losing his discipline," says Books. "He's coming unglued."

"He doesn't *need* the same discipline," I say.

"Because now he knows that *we* know what he's doing. He doesn't need these obscure methods of killing that look like natural causes because he knows we won't buy it. Frankly, I'm not sure why he even bothered setting a fire at all."

"He wants to be sure we know it's him." Books thinks about that and nods. "He's sending us a message. He's saying, 'I'm not afraid of the FBI. In fact, you ain't seen nothin' yet.'"

I shudder at the thought, as if it hasn't been my fear since the moment the media got hold of the story and published it.

"He'll make a mistake now," says another agent. "If he starts lashing out, he'll do something wrong."

Maybe. This is their area of expertise, not mine. I'm not sure I buy it. And I'm not sure, at the moment, that I care. Right now, I only want one thing.

I want our subject to attend the Vikings–Lions football game this Sunday.

Chapter 81

BOOKS PACES AT the front of the luxury suite at the north side of Ford Field, where we've established Command Central. He is on fire, focused, completely in his element up there, debriefing our crew of state, local, and federal law enforcement employees, all 150 or so of them in plainclothes, undercover, looking like men and women who are taking in a football game. This is the Books I first met, the steely Joe Friday agent whom you couldn't envision having a life outside the office, who appeared to care about nothing in this world except catching the bad guy, getting the job done.

"Okay, everyone, quiet down," he says, and within seconds the posh luxury suite is totally silent. "This may be our best chance to catch the worst serial killer I've ever seen, so it's important we remember the fundamentals." He takes a nervous breath. "There are going to be sixty thousand people here today, and one of them is going to be our subject. If you look like an FBI agent, he will notice you. If you look like a plainclothes police officer, he will notice you. If you look like you're searching for someone, he will notice you. He is smart, perceptive, and supremely careful. You *must not be noticed.*"

Books's voice lowers with intensity, and the room hushes with him.

"Because of this, we are going to do things a little differently. We want him to come into the stadium. And once he's in here, we don't want him to leave. If we have to stop every white male in his thirties or forties—maybe with a protruding gut, maybe not; maybe bald, maybe not—but if we have to stop every one of those men on the way *out* of the stadium, then we will. But you must first let him *in*. Your job here today is to identify potential suspects once they enter the stadium and phone them in to us here at Command Central. *Do not apprehend anyone* until you hear from us.

"You will not wear earpieces, and you will not use radios. You will call the numbers issued to you on your cell phone, and you will look like you're asking your wife or husband why it's taking so long to get back from the bathroom. You will do your best to look like you're actually here to watch the Lions kick the shit out of the Vikings."

"Amen to that," whispers a young local officer wearing a bright-blue Lions jersey. Urban decay may be devouring the city from the inside out, and we may be hunting the most brilliant serial killer in history, but football is football, I guess.

"The group up here in Command Central will be watching everything that walks, crawls, or flies within a half mile of this stadium on our monitors. Lucky for us, when Ford Field hosted the Super Bowl in 2006, they installed an extensive wireless surveillance web to monitor crowd activity, entrances, exits, and the surrounding area. And God bless Detroit, it still works. You phone us with a location and a description, and we'll zoom in on him. Then we'll make a decision about what to do next. We *do not* want to scare this guy off before we're ready to snatch him."

Books hands the briefing over to the local sergeant in charge of issuing assignments and joins Sophie, Denny, and me along the side wall. Caterers arrive and begin setting up chafing trays on the counters along the wall next to us. I raise an eyebrow, and Books gives a humorless smirk. "Well, we *do* have to look like any other luxury suite. We're on the north side, and all the suites on the south side will be able to see us if they try. We're just keeping up appearances."

"How nice that your appearances seem to include Italian beef," I whisper.

I hear our names called out. "Agent Bookman, Command Central. Sophie Talamas, Command Central. Denny Sasser, you're leading a team scalping tickets over at the Eastern Market. Emmy Dockery, Gate A . . ."

"*Gate A?*" I say to Books. "You put me at *Gate A?* You know as well as I do that he won't use Gate A."

With Comerica Park right across Brush Street to the west and the 36th District Court across Beacon Street to the southeast, there are enough cameras there to show us what the local ant population had for lunch. He'll choose one of the entrances on the north side: Gate B, C, D, E, or F. Those gates have better access to the parking lots and fewer tall buildings nearby where people could be watching.

Books blinks his eyes patiently. "Really?" he whispers. "Well, then, he won't be likely to recognize you from your photo in the *Tribune,* then, while you're watching Gate A, will he?"

He has a point. I hate it when he has a point.

When the assignments have been doled out, Books reasserts himself and looks over the crowd.

Grown men and women are hopping in place, stretching out, shaking out their limbs to release nervous energy. It is as if we are about to play a football game ourselves.

"Most people don't go to football games alone," he says. "So he should stand out in that regard. But he's smart. So he'll probably try to walk in with a family, or some group of people, as if he fits in with them. He'll probably strike up some conversation with them, so he looks like he belongs with them. But at some point, he'll break free from them. I can't write this out for you in a script, so all I can say to you is, keep an eye out for what I'm talking about—without *looking* like you're keeping an eye out. Easy, right?"

Some muted laughter. This is classic Books, empathizing with their difficult task, trying to bring the team together.

And then reminding them of the importance, one last time.

"This man has scalped, scalded, and meticulously dissected seventy or more individuals in the last year. He has committed acts of torture that would make a Nazi war criminal blush. He butchered six women on Thursday night in Allen Park. On Friday, he executed a mother and three children before setting them on fire. He's the most prolific serial killer I've ever seen, and he's spiraling now. He's actually getting worse."

Books looks around the room. "This man is a monster. And today, we're going to bring him in, dead or alive."

Chapter 82

"EMMY, YOU'RE GOING to wear a hole in the ground if you keep pacing like that," Books says when I answer my phone, "and you couldn't look any less like you're actually going to a football game. Just stand still and look bored, like you're waiting for your boyfriend to show up with your tickets."

"It's hard for me to pretend," I counter. "I never had a boyfriend who took me to a football game."

"That's cold. You never showed the slightest interest in football."

True enough. "Any luck with the scalpers?" I ask for the hundredth time. We've assumed that our subject is a cash-only guy who wouldn't want to throw down a credit card for his ticket to the game, preferring to buy it outside the stadium before the game.

"We have some leads," he responds with annoying vagueness. "Just worry about your assignment."

"Thanks for the great advice." He's right, of course. I'm nervous and it probably shows. So is Books. Everyone's nervous, and coping the way cops and agents typically cope, with sarcasm and one-liners.

The gates opened two hours before kickoff, and I've seen probably fifteen thousand paunchy white males wearing different shades of blue on their shirts, pants, faces, and other body parts. I haven't seen any loners, though; every man seems to be walking into the stadium with at least one other person.

I end the call. I check my watch and shake my head as if I'm annoyed, playing the part of the girlfriend waiting for her boyfriend. Why am I stuck down here while Sophie's upstairs at Command Central? I know the answer, of course; it turns out that Sophie has specialized experience in operating complex networks of surveillance technology, which is why she is up in the luxury suite and I'm enduring a modified pat-down by a woefully under-trained security guard on my way into the stadium. No courtesy wave-through for law enforcement here. We must keep up appearances.

Though I can identify about twenty places on my body I could have hidden contraband unnoticed by stadium security.

I weave in through the security checkpoint, deliberately not noticing the five other agents doing the same thing. Many of the undercover agents are in pairs, to keep up appearances, but we also need to spread out as much as possible.

I'll admit, I never thought I'd say the interior of a football stadium was "pretty." But this one is, at least where I'm entering. All glass and steel and brick, the atrium open, breezy, and flooded with natural light, more like a shopping mall than a stadium. It was built up around an old department store, and the architecture was preserved, including the old cobblestone street. I had gathered that the locals were all pretty proud of it, and I don't blame them. Plenty of balconies here, though, where our subject could be watching us file in.

And not all of us good guys are entirely . . . inconspicuous. I glare at a middle-aged man with close-cut hair standing in the entrance of the More Than a Roar team gear store, spending a lot more time looking over the crowd than admiring the toddler-size jersey he is clutching. He might as well be wearing a sign that says, I'M JUST PRETENDING TO SHOP; I'M REALLY A COP.

I make my way through the Adams Street concourse around to my seat—I'm stationed at the head of section 112. The playing field was built well below street level, something about not wanting to build the stadium too high and obscure the skyline. As I enter past the long wrought-iron gates separating the concourse from the field, I can see that the whole first seating section is downstairs, rather than up.

It is overwhelming. The noise, the sheer mass of humanity—everything. *We're never going to find him here. There are too many, and we are too few.*

Get a grip, Emmy.

I scout the section while walking slowly to my seat. I call Books.

"Hi, honey!" I say brightly. "The stadium sure is full today! Boy, I wish you could be down here. But I'm so glad you're getting to see it on TV!"

"Nice, Emmy," I hear Sophie say on the other end. "What do you have?"

"Section one eleven, row nine, seat three or four. Section one thirteen, row twenty-six in the middle, and row thirty, seat five or maybe six. And section one twelve, row eighteen or nineteen, couldn't be sure, in the middle. All either bald or with their heads and faces obscured. I'll have a dozen more by the half, I'm sure."

I sit down to at least pretend like I'm watching the game, and the Vikings return the kickoff for a touchdown. Helluva start, Detroit.

Chapter 83

WHEN THE FOURTH quarter begins, Detroit is losing 20 to 6. I could not possibly care less about the outcome of this event, where grown men dress up in colorful gladiator costumes and try to carry a leather ball across a demarcated line—but I do care about how close the score is. If it's what Books calls a "blowout," then the fans might start to leave, and we'll have to be ready for the exit of our subject a little earlier than planned.

Does 20 to 6 constitute a blowout? I don't really know, but I do know, from my chatty friends in section 112, that this remains a "two-score game," and I had to nod as if I knew what that meant. I've done a lot of that while in my seat. I had to feign anger at a returned punt at the start of the second half, curse along with my seatmates at the incompetence of Detroit's special teams coordinator, nod agreeably when the Lions defense "finally woke up." And I had to invent pretense after pretense to call my mother/sister/brother/ husband/boyfriend/aunt every time I saw a possibly bald man that might have a slightly slender nose and sloping shoulders.

Books and his team must have looked closely at nearly every male in the stadium by now. One of the locals actually called in Denny Sasser as a suspect when he arrived at the stadium.

"I miss being a research analyst," I say to my "brother" over the phone as I make my way, yet again, to the Adams Street concourse. "I'm not cut out for surveillance."

"Copy that," says Sophie. "Why don't you go check out the portable kiosks in the concourse? There are a few blind spots when they put up the umbrellas."

"Okay." The adrenaline courses through me as we near the end of the game. I just *know* he's here. I can *feel it*.

I find myself strolling through the concourse, people-watching, the way Marta and I used to do in the summers at the mall. The stadium is starting to empty a little, but Lions fans aren't quitters. They'll stay until the last gasp—more wisdom I picked up from section 112. The game is still perfectly audible, because the stadium is open to the concourse on two corners. I can see our law enforcement teams setting up checkpoints at the exits. We are preparing to screen the fans as they leave the stadium, our method of last resort. My gut writhes. There's not a chance he would let himself be caught in a crude net like that. He's too precise. Too proud. Too smart.

I'm leaning against the wall of the escalators leading to the second floor, watching people walk past. My fingers and palms are beating a nervous rhythm on the metal surface in time with the music echoing from the stadium. If there's one thing I can say about the game, it's that Detroit sure plays good music. The home of Motown is proud of its heritage. They have worked in homegrown heroes Kid Rock and Eminem, and as I move back down the atrium toward my seat, Aretha Franklin starts asking for her R-E-S-P-E-C-T.

As I walk, I begin to sense an inexplicable oddness, or an absence, to my right. Maybe this is what the field agents mean by "gut feeling." It makes me profoundly uneasy. The stadium is to my left, and the stair-step ceiling unique to the underside of a stadium makes the right side much taller. There is nothing unusual I can see immediately among the restaurants and stores.

But I sense a void of movement in a place where everything and everyone else is moving.

I stop and scan the small crowd. There's nobody that looks anything like our subject, but that feeling just isn't going away. It's growing. I'm starting to hear the echo of Aretha from the stadium as though it is much farther away, like I am suddenly enclosed in walls muting the surrounding noise.

My heart is beating like crazy, my palms wet and sticky. I can't explain it . . . I just somehow know—

I spin around.

And twenty yards away, standing motionless, a man is staring right at me.

Chapter 84

FULL HEAD OF hair. Full beard. Lions cap on his head. Horn-rimmed glasses. Jacket collar pulled up high. A disguise. And even though I can't specifically make out his eyes, I know they are fixed on mine.

I blink twice, startled and still disbelieving. The man is squared off and facing me. People pass between us, fans heading to or from bathrooms or concessions, but every time he comes back into my view, he is still motionless, still staring directly at me.

It's him.

A woman accidentally bumps his shoulder. His body gives with the jolt, but he never stops looking at me.

It's him.

He cocks his head slightly, like he's angling for a better look at me.

In those few moments that pass, I am frozen, breathless, paralyzed. But I want him to see me. *Here I am,* I want to say to him. *I found you.*

In those timeless beats of my heart, I hear Aretha Franklin crooning, the crowd noise cresting and falling, while we stare at each other.

Two seconds? Ten? I don't know how long it takes before I remember why I've held the cell phone in my hand all along, so I wouldn't have to fumble in my pocket for it if the moment presented itself.

The moment has presented itself. My heart pounding in my throat, I look down at my phone as my thumb poises over the speed-dial button, instant access to Command Central.

Instead, I look back at our subject, whose facial expression has changed from a poker face to some kind of sympathetic smirk.

And now, in his hand, is a small black device of his own, probably his cell phone. But why would he need a cell phone right—

And then an explosion, a pop so deafening that I barely notice something ricocheting off my face, cutting me, a blast so jarring that I know I've cried out but I can't hear my own voice, and suddenly the floor has risen up to smack me in the cheek.

In my temporary stupor, nothing makes sense,

not the sticky floor or the sight of my own blood, not the strobe-light effect of the sirens flashing, and even though I cannot hear a thing I sense it, I *feel* it while I lie on the floor, the sudden change in the vibration of the stadium, which is now a constant thumping, a stampede—

I lift my head in the direction of the subject, the man I've hunted for more than a year, but instead I see a silent horror movie, no sound but the agonizing images of a mad rush of bodies, panicking, fighting through the narrow aisle and, once freed from the logjam, bursting toward the exit. I move like a terrified dog on my hands and knees toward a pillar on the interior wall of the stadium and embrace it like a loved one as the throng rushes past, stepping on my legs and ankles, tripping over me, until I pull in my legs against the swimming tide and ball into the fetal position.

I hold on for dear life to the pillar as people push and trip and climb over one another in a desperate attempt to escape. I lift my head upward to compete for oxygen with the stampede, gasping for air and struggling, with my failing limbs, to keep hold of my anchor. If I let go of this, I know I'll be crushed.

My head ringing viciously, my oxygen short, I struggle to fight the rising nausea and my rising dread. How many will die here today? I don't know. I can't think about that now. Because I'll be among the dead if I lose my grip on this pillar.

He did it again, I think. Our subject, once again, has escaped. He has buried himself within the crush of sixty thousand people racing for the exits, soon flooding the streets outside Ford Field, after this unidentified explosion that has blown out my eardrum. He outsmarted us once more. He was ready for us. Of course he was. He's been ready for us all along. Every time we think we're close, we realize that he's anticipated our move and countered it.

He's never going to stop. And we're never going to catch him.

Chapter 85

"SIT STILL," SAYS the paramedic.

"I'm fine. It was just a scratch."

"You have a concussion, and you need stitches on your cheek."

The sun has fallen and darkness begins to color the sky. It's been four hours since the explosions. The paramedics long ago took the most seriously injured to trauma units. There are very few civilians still around in the parking lot outside Ford Field, which is now filled with vehicles from Homeland Security, the FBI, and state troopers, as well as media trucks and news copters flying overhead. An explosion in the middle of an NFL football game isn't going to go unnoticed for long.

Apparently there were eight explosions in all, each occurring within seconds of the other, at various points on the south end of the stadium.

They weren't bombs per se, I'm told, but rather very powerful fireworks, placed strategically in overflowing garbage cans at locations where the acoustics would maximize the sound of their blasts within both the concourse and the stadium, including Gate A, where I was stationed.

The fans at Ford Field didn't wait for an explanation when they heard the blasts; they didn't explore the distinction between a massive pyrotechnic and a terrorist's bomb. When the explosions went off, one after another, it was a frenzied race to the exits that nobody—not even the FBI—could stop. And even if our agents had been able to hold up the throng, protocol wouldn't allow it. Evacuation procedures required that all doors be flung wide open to allow people to, well, evacuate. We literally had to let everyone leave. For all anyone knew in those critical first minutes, it *was* a terrorist attack.

Books and the team did everything they could to contain the pandemonium, but it was too much. People were jumping into their cars and speeding away before we even knew which way was up.

Books walks over to me and puts a hand on my shoulder. "You're lucky your eardrum wasn't blown out," he says, which was what I thought had happened, initially. "You were right next to one of the garbage cans where the M-Eighties detonated."

I gingerly touch the gauze on my cheek. "The M-what?"

"They were M-Eighties," he says. "They were originally military explosives. They were outlawed for consumer purchase in the sixties, but people still buy them illegally. Hell, I think I used to set them off when I was a kid. Loud as hell. Like forty or fifty times as strong as the fireworks you can purchase legally."

I jump off the back of the ambulance and take a moment to steady myself. "How did he get explosives into the stadium?" I ask.

"Oh, it's easy, Em." Books makes a one-inch space between his thumb and index finger. "They're each about this big, and they don't contain metal."

"And the detonator?"

"He must have used a remote detonator. Could buy it at any fireworks store."

Great. Just great.

"He was expecting us," I say.

Books purses his lips. "The media reports didn't say anything about us linking him to football games. But he's smart. We know that. So this was just a precaution on his part, I'd guess. When he saw you, he knew he needed a route to escape. And he used it."

I sigh. As always, we were playing checkers, but our subject was playing chess.

"Nobody dead?" I ask, I pray.

"Not so far, no. Some people were seriously wounded in the rush for the exits. I've never seen so many people so scared." His eyes drift away; then he shakes himself free of the memory. "The blasts themselves didn't hurt anybody other than people standing near the garbage cans, like you. It was the panic afterward. They tell me there are hundreds of people with broken bones, crushed ribs, all kinds of bruises and abrasions, but so far nobody has died."

Thank God for that. The first good news of the day.

Books holds up a police artist's sketch of the subject, taken from my description. Thick dark hair, full beard, thick glasses, Lions cap, army jacket pulled up high.

"An obvious disguise," I say. "But that basically looks like him."

"Okay. Then let's see if we can find him on the video monitors entering the stadium today," he says. "And then we can see where he sat, and we can work backward."

"Okay, let's do it," I say. "I should be there. I'm the one who saw him."

Books takes my arm. "You need to go to the hospital, Em."

I wiggle free of him. "I'm fine."

"No, Emily Jean. You're going to the hospital. You need stitches at a minimum. That's an order."

I stare at him, and he blinks first. Neither of us is going to pretend that he can order me to do anything.

"Harrison Bookman, you get me in front of a video monitor right now," I say. "Or *you're* going to be the one who needs stitches."

Chapter 86

TWO HOURS LATER, the smell of the catered food still lingering in the luxury suite doubling as Command Central, Books, Sophie, Denny, and I are bleary-eyed and exhausted.

"So now we know, at least, that he didn't arrive in the disguise he was wearing when you saw him," Books says, stating the obvious. We've combed through video of every gate entrance to the stadium and never spotted him. Our subject was wearing a different getup when he waltzed past security to start the game.

Books rubs his forehead furiously, like he's trying to remove an ink stain. "That was our best chance of knowing where he sat," he says. "But not the only way. He'll show up on various cameras, and maybe we'll get lucky with crowd footage."

I nod my head as if I find hope in that statement,

but I don't. Our subject has thought of everything. He's a mile ahead of our thinking every time.

"Who even knows if he'll go to another NFL game," I say. "We can hope he does so out of pure stubbornness, but I wouldn't bet a nickel on it. This was it." My head drops back on the chair. "This was our chance."

"Okay, well, let's not go dark," says Sophie. "Let's look at next week's games and make a plan. Week five of the season, right? And, Emmy, you still think he's likely to hit one of the Pennsylvania stadiums soon—Pittsburgh or Philadelphia. So let's see . . ." She pulls out an NFL schedule. "Oh, look! They're playing each other next Sunday. The Eagles at the Steelers, Sunday, October seventh, at one p.m. That's good, right?"

I close my eyes. Despite Sophie's laudable attempt to inject some sunlight into the room, I see only darkness.

"He knows we know about the NFL connection now," I say. "You think he's going to walk into another spiderweb?"

"I'm sorry, I must not be up to speed on this thing about Pennsylvania," says Denny. We've all been sequestered in our narrow tunnels in this investigation. Denny's been spending more time doing fieldwork.

"Emmy was looking at the pattern of his stadium visits," Books explains. "Whenever the subject goes to an area where NFL stadiums are clustered together, he separates the visits by many weeks so he's not hitting the same general area too regularly. So, like in Florida, he spreads out his Jacksonville, Miami, and Tampa Bay visits."

"And he hasn't gone to Pennsylvania yet," Denny gathers. "Okay. And there's just a few weeks left in his stadium tour, so if he's going to hit Pennsylvania twice, he better start now. I see."

I'm glad he sees. My life is so much better now.

(I have a concussion, so I can be rude as long as I keep it to myself.)

"Might an old, retired agent like me raise a suggestion?" Denny says.

"Shoot," says Books.

"Might we consider the possibility that he *isn't* going to visit Pennsylvania?"

"Why wouldn't he?" I ask.

"Well . . . isn't the answer obvious?"

"Not to me, it isn't," I say, growing impatient. The concussion again.

"Maybe he *lives* in Pennsylvania," says Denny. "And he doesn't want us looking there."

I sit forward in my chair.

"We think he lives in the Midwest," says Books. "Remember?"

"I remember that you said that, yes. That doesn't mean I agree."

I point to Denny and wag my finger. "The pattern of his kills during the off-season in the NFL are all centered around the midwestern states," I say. "So the pattern shows that, during the part of the year that he's not touring NFL stadiums, he kills close to home."

"I understand that's the theory," says Denny.

"But your point, Denny," I say, standing up now, "is why couldn't our subject be screwing with us on *that* part of the case, just like he's screwing with us on every *other* part?"

"In a nutshell, yes," says Denny.

Books looks at me, color returning to his cheeks. "He created a pattern to make it look like he was a midwestern guy, in case we started figuring out what he's doing: Is he really *that* forward thinking?"

I actually laugh out loud at that question. "He's a galaxy forward compared to us, Books."

Books gets out of his chair, nodding. "He lives in Pennsylvania?"

"If someone has a better lead right now, let's hear it," says Denny.

I look at Books. "I sure don't. It's worth a shot, at least. Check the plates in the parking lot?"

Books raises his radio to his mouth. "This is Bookman to rapid-response team leader Dade."

A moment later, the radio squawks back. "This is Dade."

"Dade, you're going over the video footage of the parking lots outside Ford Field during the game, right?"

"Affirmative, Agent. Running plates as we speak."

"Any license plates from the great state of Pennsylvania?"

"Let me check on that."

The radio goes silent.

"The Commonwealth of Pennsylvania," I say, allowing some giddiness with my hope.

"What's that?"

"It's the *Commonwealth* of Pennsylvania."

The radio squawks back on. "Agent, there are three license plates from Pennsylvania."

"Run those right now, Dade."

"Copy that."

Books nods to me again. "So Pennsylvania's not a state?"

"I think it still counts as a state."

"I hope so. That would really fuck with our flag."

Sophie and I have our laptops open, ready to run searches the minute we get the names.

"What *is* a commonwealth, anyway?" Books asks me.

"Bookman, how the hell am I supposed to know?"

"You're the one who brought it up."

It's another five minutes of this supremely engaging banter, each of us trying to cope with our jagged nerves, before the radio comes back on.

"Okay, Agent, are you ready?"

"Ready."

"First vehicle is registered to David Epps in Beaver Falls." Dade reads out the address.

Sophie says, "I'll take that one," and starts typing.

"Second vehicle to a Marlon Cumer—Cumerford, I guess." He spells the name for us and reads an address in Erie, Pennsylvania.

"I have that one," I say.

"And the third one," says the agent, "is listed to someone named Graham. Winston Graham."

Chapter 87

IT'S JUST A hunch, just one of hundreds of theories and leads we've explored, but something about Denny's guess—that our subject lives in Pennsylvania—somehow rings true to me. And the fact that only three vehicles traveled to this game from Pennsylvania makes it easy enough to investigate, true or not.

But we don't get off to a good start. It takes Sophie and me less than twenty minutes to rule out the first two names on the list we were given. David Epps from Beaver Falls, Pennsylvania, is an elementary school teacher, married with three children, and he has a brother who lives in Detroit, thus explaining why he'd attend the Lions game. Marlon Cumerford from Erie, Pennsylvania, is a sixty-two-year-old retiree from a position with the city transportation department, and a cross-reference with the Lions ticketing office shows that he is a season ticket holder who travels to every Lions home game.

Winston Graham is number three. Sophie and I tag team him, desperate for a score, our last chance. "Single, never married," I say, as I fly through the relevant databases. "No criminal record. No fingerprints on file."

"Parents—Richard and Diana—deceased, the last one dying nine years ago," says Sophie. "No other family. An only child. Raised in Ridgway, Pennsylvania. He has a postal route for an address, so it's rural."

Books and I look at each other. "If I had to write a bio of our subject," I say, "he would be a loner who lives in a remote location, and he would have time on his hands."

Books thinks about it and nods. He picks up his cell phone and says, "Get me in touch with the agent on duty in the Pittsburgh field office." After a long pause, Books is apparently connected, and he introduces himself to that agent. "I need a warrant," he says. "There's an on-duty AUSA I can talk to? Great. Patch me through."

Another pause, while Books waits for the federal prosecutor working the late shift in Pittsburgh, whose job it will be to talk to the federal magistrate hearing emergency warrant applications this time of night.

"The name is Winston Graham," Books says hurriedly into the phone, spelling the last name and providing the Social Security number, driver's license number, and home address. "Phone records, bank accounts, credit cards, and a warrant to search the premises. I'm working on an affidavit right now. What? Why—why not?" Books begins to pace. "Yes, it is. Yes, it *is*. Hey, listen . . . listen to me. I don't give a royal rat's ass if the magistrate's asleep. The guy we're hunting is the guy who set off the explosives at Ford Field today. Yeah, *that* guy. And he's not only *that* guy, he's also the arsonist serial killer who's been roaming the country. This . . . okay, but listen to me, we don't have time for baby steps. Because we don't! Just do . . . get me whatever you can, as fast as you can. Think you can handle that?"

Books hangs up. "Lawyers," he says. "They don't think we have enough for a warrant."

"They may be right," says Denny. "We think our subject might live in Pennsylvania and Graham lives in Pennsylvania, like thirteen million other people. We think our subject was at the game today and so was Graham, along with sixty thousand others. And he lives alone. It probably *isn't* enough for a judge."

"Maybe this is." Sophie spins her laptop around so it's facing us. It's Winston Graham's records from the Pennsylvania Department of Transportation. "He renewed his driver's license eight months ago and took a new photo," she says. "Does this man look familiar?"

The picture isn't the greatest quality, which makes it all the more reminiscent of the grainy image we have of our subject from Benny's Tavern in Urbana, Illinois, when he was meeting Curtis Valentine. But unlike that image, which showed little of the curve of his face and only a long, slender nose while he kept eyes downward and his face away from the camera, the photograph he took for his renewed driver's license is full-frontal. He is squinting for the photograph, his eyes beady and lidded, looking like someone who wears eyeglasses and was told to remove them (and is none too happy about it). Unlike in the video from the bar, where he might have been completely bald, here Winston Graham has some semblance of wispy brown hair above each ear but is otherwise bald. His jowls mask his chin, a function of age and weight. He looks a bit older than his forty years, but to me, there's no question.

"It's him," I say, feeling a surge of adrenaline,

a sense of momentum that hours ago would have been unfathomable.

"Shit, that's him," says Books. "That's our subject."

"When do we leave?" I ask.

"Everyone, go back to the hotel and get your stuff," says Books. "We leave as soon as possible."

Chapter 88

I'M IN THE final stages of packing up, toiletries dumped into a bag, listening to CNN on my television with its breaking-news coverage of the explosions at the game today and the hunt for the "Ford Field Bomber." The repetition is endless. They can't come off the story, but they have nothing fresh to report other than the occasional new anecdotal testimony from a fan at the game who discusses the loud blasts and the mad rush for the exits. *It was like the Fourth of July,* says one man. *I thought I was dead,* says another. *It sounded like it was coming from all directions at once,* another claims.

We see diagrams of Ford Field and arrows and red glowing dots showing the points of explosion on the south end. He chose the ideal spot for the acoustics in the concourse, says a city official, to maximize the sounds of the blasts and the resulting panic.

Authorities have ruled out Islamic terrorism, we are told. The suspect is a white male in his thirties or forties, they say. An intense manhunt is under way, viewers are assured, involving local, state, and federal authorities.

Three people have now been pronounced dead, all injuries sustained in the mad melee that ensued as fans swarmed for the exits.

I jump at the knock on my hotel room door. Under the circumstances, a cat's meow could make me jump.

It's Books. I let him in and go back to my belongings.

"I thought we were meeting in the lobby," I say.

"Yeah, we were. I just . . . I just thought I'd come up."

"Okay. Change of plans?"

"No. No change. But the pilot won't be at the plane for another hour, so we have a few minutes."

"Oh, okay." I wonder what he wants with these few minutes.

When I look back at him, Books is turned away from me completely, addressing a smudge on the cheap chest of drawers in the room. He raises a hand tentatively, then makes it a fist.

"When I heard that first . . . ," he begins, then clears his throat aggressively.

I pause. He doesn't go on. So I do it for him.

"When you heard that first blast, coming from the south end zone," I say quietly, stepping closer to him but giving him his space.

"I . . . thought you were dead."

"But I'm not, Books. I'm fine. We get past it and move on, right? Isn't that what you always say?"

He nods his head. Books and his emotions have always gotten along like oil and water.

"Okay," I say, "so let's just focus—"

"I kept calling your cell phone, and you didn't . . . you didn't answer."

I don't say anything. The room suddenly feels very warm.

"You know, when this case started, I didn't really think your theory was going anywhere," he says. "You had some interesting data, but in all honesty, I was very dubious." He turns his head to the side, so I can see his profile, his tired eyes and mussed hair falling forward. "I just wanted to work on the case because *you* were working on it. That sounds silly, now, after you ended up single-handedly uncovering this monster."

"Well, I'm glad you did," I say. "Look at us now. I think this Winston Graham could be our—"

"Emmy, I need to say this. Just let me say it." Books takes a breath. "I still—"

His cell phone rings. His half-completed sentence looms between us. *I still . . .* He sweeps his phone off his belt, annoyed. "This is Bookman," he says. And then he rifles to attention. "What? Who? MS—"

He turns to me. "Turn on MSNBC."

I grab the remote and flip around, unsure of where to find that cable news channel, but it's only a few clicks away, it turns out.

The breaking-news line at the bottom of the screen says it all.

BREAKING: MANHUNT MOVES TO PENNSYLVANIA

" . . . *believe the Ford Field Bomber is located. To repeat, a source close to MSNBC has confirmed that federal investigators are focusing on a location in rural Pennsylvania where they believe the Ford Field Bomber is located.*"

"Oh, shit," Books mumbles. "How did this happen?" Books shouts into his cell phone. "How the *hell* did this happen?"

I raise a hand to my face. It could have been anybody, I realize. We've been in touch with authorities from local cops, Elk County sheriffs,

Pennsylvania state police, and the Pittsburgh FBI. It only takes one to spring a leak.

"I want that perimeter around his house sealed tight," he says into his phone. "Because if he's watching the news, now he knows how close we are. And you damn well better believe he's watching the news."

Chapter **89**

They're coming to take me away! They're coming to take me away!

Oh, this is great, this is just great, great, great. You're out there somewhere, aren't you, ladies and gentlemen of the FBI? What did it? I really want to know. I really do. What did it? *How* did you pin me down to that football game?

Oh, shit, fuck, *fuck!* How the . . . what the . . . ahhh! Ahhhhh!

You think you're going to take me alive? Is that what you think, you miserable stupid fuck shit fuck fuck fuck! You're going to lock me up and study me like a caged rat and strap me down and analyze my brain waves so you can stop the next one like me? Oh, that's rich, that's the plum jewel of the whole thing right there, thinking that you can ever stop someone like me. You can't! Don't you see that? Don't you understand? You can't prevent the next one like me because the next me is you! I'm inside all of you! The only difference is I don't hide behind some mask, driving my SUV and sipping Starbucks at my kid's soccer game. You're just like me and you don't even know it!

You hear me? Do you fucking hear me?

Why should I let you take me alive? Huh? Why should I? Why should you know anything about me? You don't deserve it. I was trying to help you, I was . . . fuck! Fuck! I was trying to get you to understand, but why the hell should I care if any of you understand me? Why should I care about anything anymore? You've done nothing to deserve it. You and the miserable little sheep that follow you haven't done a single thing in life to deserve what I can teach you, what I tried to teach you.

So just go on with your little sheep miserable lives, doing what everyone says and telling yourself that your life is normal and good and happy and never mind who's pulling all the levers and never mind what's really going on in the world or who the real people are hiding behind those smiley faces and blow-dried hair and—whatever, whatever, you know what? I'm done with this. I'm—but you won't get me alive. You could have learned so much from me but now it's too late. Why should I give a shit about you when you don't give a shit about me? About me! Why don't *I* matter?

You think you'll stop people like me? You can never do that. Do you hear me, FBI boys and girls? You won't ever, *ever* stop people like me!

[Editor's note: pause of fourteen seconds.]

Oh, I can't . . . I don't believe this. I can't believe this! But too bad for you, I won't go quietly, I can't, don't you see I just . . . I just can't . . .

[Editor's note: pause of eighteen seconds.]

It shouldn't be like this. It shouldn't be like this. This isn't right. This isn't fair. I'm not what you think I am. But you'll never understand. You'll never even try to understand. I'm finished trying to help you understand. I'm done.

I'm so tired. I'm so, so tired. I really don't want to do what I have to do now. I really, really, really don't want to do it, I swear to you I don't, please believe me, I don't.

But I have no choice. She knows too much.

[END]

Chapter 90

FOUR O'CLOCK IN the morning. A deep, still darkness, not even the first hint of light creeping over the horizon. A peaceful autumn morning in rural Pennsylvania, about to be not so peaceful.

The farmhouse belonging to Winston Graham is located in unincorporated Elk County. Surrounded on three sides by acres of scrub brush, former farmland long neglected, with a small forest of trees behind it, the farmhouse is a sprawling brick ranch. The floor plans we've obtained from the county recorder show three bedrooms in the back of the ranch, a kitchen, a living room, and a front parlor. There is a basement as well, spanning the entire floor plan.

From the main streets, a long dirt road winds its way for more than a quarter mile to the farmhouse, where Winston Graham's Buick Skylark rests next to the attached garage.

Members of the Hostage Rescue Team have crawled into position, surrounding the farmhouse and lying in the weeds, literally, waiting for the signal in their ear from Books. They are dressed in black, head to toe, with gas masks and helmets, submachine guns and holstered firearms, stun bombs on their belts.

From our perch a quarter mile away on a small hill, I raise the infrared binoculars to my eyes again. There is no movement at the farmhouse. No light inside or outside the house. For all we can tell, the ranch has been abandoned.

"Thank you, Your Honor," says Books into his cell phone.

He lets out a breath of relief. "We got our warrant."

Books has been on the phone for half an hour with a federal magistrate judge in Pittsburgh, explaining the basis for his probable cause to search the residence of Winston Graham. The last thing we needed, after all this work, was to have some judge rule the search invalid and leave us with nothing.

Books raises his radio to his mouth. "Team Leader, this is Bookman. Do you copy?"

"Copy, Bookman." The reply through Books's radio breaks the stillness of the night air.

"Team Leader, we are now in status yellow."

"Copy that."

"Are you in position, Team Leader?"

The team leader on the HRT does a quick check with his people around the perimeter before coming back to us. "We are in position, locked and loaded."

Books looks around at the other agents and me. We are in a small convoy of vehicles out of sight of the farmhouse: the Elk County sheriff's office, Pennsylvania state troopers, the local fire department, the bomb squad, and federal officials from the FBI as well as the Bureau of Alcohol, Tobacco, Firearms and Explosives.

"Team Leader," says Books, "we are sending in Kevin. Do you copy?"

"Copy that."

Books nods to the ATF agent standing next to him, a man named Moore. But right now I'm more interested in the contraption Moore is holding, which includes a video monitor and a toggle stick. He looks like a teenager playing with his Xbox.

But "Kevin" is no video game I've ever seen. "Kevin" is an explosives detection device, operating like a little remote-control truck with tractor wheels and a 360-degree pivot capacity. And we can see what Kevin sees from this remote device.

A member of the Hostage Rescue Team approaches an open window. That's odd. Winston Graham is inviting us in. The HRT member lowers Kevin into the living room and scrambles for cover a few yards away. The screen in Moore's hands comes alive. We are now looking inside Winston Graham's house, seeing what Kevin is seeing on a small screen.

The living room is filled with antique furniture and a rather small open kitchen. Dated, but lived-in, no doubt. A bottle of beer rests on the breakfast counter. Newspapers are strewn about the floor, everywhere, almost covering up the hardwood floor.

Newspapers.

Fires need three things to burn: oxygen, fuel, and heat.

The open window is oxygen. The newspapers are fuel.

The light on Moore's remote device begins to blink red, a mini siren. Kevin is telling us something.

He's telling us that he detects a heat source.

"It's gonna blow," I say.

"Team Leader, retreat," Books calls into his radio. "Retreat, Team—"

And then the explosion, a muted blast that interrupts the dark night with a flash of bright orange cascading across the living room, engulfing the room with the snap of a finger, like one fiery dragon's breath.

"Fire team, go! Go!" Books shouts to his right. The fire truck blasts into action, followed by SWAT officers in fire coats and the bomb squad, tires squealing on the paved road.

"He doesn't want to be taken alive," says Denny Sasser.

I throw on my thick coat and helmet and carry my gas mask in my hand.

"All agents," Books cries out, as he starts running toward the inferno, "you keep that perimeter secured! Every inch of that perimeter secured! This could be a diversion!"

I run along with Books, each of us ignoring the available car and just racing with all our speed toward the house, the beacon of blazing orange and thick smoke blowing through the roof now.

"The basement," I call out between breaths. "He's in . . . the basement!"

Chapter 91

"STAY BACK!" BOOKS calls out to me, a hand extended, as he stands a few yards from the house. "You aren't authorized to enter, Emmy. That's an order!"

Tactical agents, covered in firefighting gear, move in along with the firefighters, acting as armed escorts, their submachine guns drawn and blast shields raised, ready for anything or anyone. Moments later, high-powered hoses do their work on the flames, blowing out the windows in the process, inky black smoke snorting out of every orifice of the ranch. I keep my distance behind a bulletproof shield, awaiting another blast or gunfire or something else, something unexpected, for Mr. Winston Graham has become the expert of the unexpected.

Before long, any semblance of fiery orange

radiating from the house has disappeared, leaving a drenched, drooping structure still coughing polluted smoke. The fire was precisely planned and well executed, but the fire department was, after all, only a quarter mile away when it started.

"Clear!" a voice yells into my earpiece. "Main floor is clear!"

Clear of human beings, they mean, dead or alive. And clear of threats.

The basement. The fire didn't reach the basement, I'd bet.

"Stay . . . *here*," Books says to me through his gas mask, turning to me.

I take a step back in compliance.

He disappears into the black smoke engulfing the house, no longer burning but radiating a heat so fierce I can feel it through my shield and helmet.

Remember your place, I tell myself. *Not your place to run in there. You could do more harm than good. You could fall through the floor and they'd end up spending valuable time saving you. Not your place.*

I put on the fire boots that go with the rest of my costume, the helmet and shield and gas mask with oxygen tank, the heavy coat and pants. Why did they give me these things if they didn't expect me to go in? I wait five minutes and then I head inside.

It's almost impossible to see through the smoke, but I know the layout of the house, just as all the agents do, from the floor plans. I suck in clean oxygen off my gas mask while the dirty smog surrounds me. I focus on the floor, partially scalded from the fire, charred bits of newspaper scattered everywhere and floating through the air like remnants of a ticker-tape parade. This floor is unsafe to traverse, but I'm not the first or the tenth person to cross it and I'm not good at patience. I know that if I keep walking straight down the main hallway, past the kitchen and past the bedrooms, the door to the basement will be there.

I find the door, open, the staircase heading down to the basement free of smoke. I take the steps downward. *There are at least ten agents down there*, I tell myself. *No matter how good he is, he can't overtake ten of them.*

Right?

I hit the bottom of the stairs and turn. The main part of the basement is unfinished and dingy, concrete walls and floors, a hot-water heater, water softener, washer and dryer in one corner, and a weight-lifting bench with barbell and free weights in the other corner.

But then there is a long corridor with doors on each side. Agents pull each one open and rush in, weapons first. Shouts of "FBI!" and "ATF!" and "federal agents!" echo back to me. I remove my gas mask and follow down the corridor as agents clear one room after another.

"All clear!" shouts one of the agents to Books, who nods and looks around in vain. When he sees me, he lacks the energy to complain. He just shrugs. The entire house, first floor and basement, have been cleared.

Where are you, Winston Graham?

I walk back into the main area of the basement, the appliances and the workout area. And then I notice the cabinet in the corner, a gray metal structure almost as tall as me, with twin doors and a padlock that is unlocked and hanging over one of the handles.

For a man as precise as Winston Graham, that's practically an invitation.

"Here," I say. "Look in here!"

"Get back, dammit," Books says, taking my arm and yanking me backward. He gestures with a hurried finger to the cabinet. Agents approach the cabinet on each side. One slips off the padlock. Then, in sync, each agent grabs a handle and yanks open the doors.

The interior of the cabinet looks like any other. Three shelves, two of them completely empty.

There is, in fact, only one thing resting on the center shelf.

A stack of paper.

With a purple bow tied around it.

"What the hell is this?" Books asks, approaching the cabinet and looking at the first page of the stack of paper. "What the hell are 'Graham Sessions'?"

Chapter 92

DAWN HAS BROKEN, the sky above us coloring into day, but still it is relatively dark. We are back down the road now, at the back of a SWAT team truck, using the floor of the cabin area as a desk and spreading out the stack of documents, the random musings of a serial killer, which he has dubbed "Graham Sessions." They are numbered—twenty-two in all—and dated. They appear to be recorded orally. He probably used one of those high-tech recorders that automatically transcribe his words into a document.

Each Graham Session is spread out over the truck's floor. We read them quickly at first. There will be plenty of time for analysis of his word choices and colloquialisms, days that will be spent deconstructing every sentence.

But right now, we're looking for any leads on

where this monster is hiding. So I pass quickly over the disgusting self-glorification contained in these pages, the revolting passages where we read along as he tortures victims, looking for anything, anything that might give us a clue—

"Mary," I say aloud. Someone named Mary is mentioned in recording number twelve, a conversation with her that he recorded in a bar. And then she keeps coming back in subsequent chapters. She becomes the focus, in fact, with each new passage that I read. He has feelings for her. He is opening up to her. He's becoming tormented over her. He is falling in love with her.

Mary is a bartender, a part-time student, a recovering alcoholic. But what is her last name? Where does she live? Are we going to have to search all of Pennsylvania for a woman named Mary?

Then we see him melting down, as he realizes we're closing in on him. The self-gratification still pops up in spurts, but he's getting nervous. He's losing confidence, while trying to convince himself—and us—that he isn't.

What will he do about Mary?

"We have to find her," I mumble.

Books raises a radio to his mouth. "How are we with the cadaver dogs?"

"They're here," a voice pops back. "We're

starting with his property and then we'll move to the wooded area behind the ranch. We have agents combing the woods right now."

"Let's keep reading," Books says to me. "There's got to be some clue about her in there."

But I'm almost done, and there isn't much yet. In recording number twenty-one, dated yesterday, Sunday, after he eluded us at Ford Field, Graham is coming unglued. Good. Fine. But it's his last words on that day that chill me to the bone.

She knows too much.

"He's going to kill her," I say.

And then I get to the final recording, dated today, October first.

Chapter 93

I didn't . . . I didn't want this for you, Mary. I didn't want this for us. You have to believe me. Please, tell me that much—tell me that you believe what I'm saying. I've been lying to you. I've been lying to myself, convincing myself that I could be different with you, that everything could be different. But please believe me now. Please believe that if I'd met you earlier, things would have been different, I would have changed, I know I would have, I would have changed for you, Mary.

But now it's too late, and I can't let you . . . no, Mary, I can't, I'm sorry, I'm sorrier than I've ever been in my life. I've never been sorry before, actually, never, but I am now, because you've opened up things inside me and I wanted to let them out and explore them together with you. I know we could have done that and everything would have been okay. Please understand, Mary—please!—that I have no choice, I have no choice but to do this, because no matter how much you might love me back they'll turn you and make you tell them things about me and I can't let them do that to you. If I could leave you here I would but I can't, I don't have a choice. You see that, don't you? I don't have a choice. It's outside my control.

They're coming for me now, Mary, and they're going to tell you all kinds of things about me and I can't let you hear them because they'll make them sound so much worse than the truth—that's what they do and I can't let them. I'd rather you remember me as the person who loves you, because I do love you, Mary, I swear to you that I do love you and I'm capable of love because of you.

You won't love me if you hear what they say. You won't love me if you know the truth. You never would have, I guess. No, I guess not. Nobody would love me! How could they? How could anyone . . . now hush, Mary. Hush now.

You're my special Mary, my dear, dear Mary Laney and I'll always love you and always remember you, and that will have to be enough. Please understand, my sweet Mary. Please understand that I'm doing this out of love and I wish it could be different, I wish it could be different, oh, why can't it be different? Why can't they just leave me alone and give us a chance to be different and be better?

There's nothing left for us now and I can't let them hurt you or turn you against me. I won't let them destroy what we had. I won't.

Now sleep, my dear, sweet princess. Sleep and carry me with you in your heart, and I'll always carry you in mine.

I promise you that one day soon we'll meet again.

[END]

Chapter 94

"MARY LANEY, L-A-N-E-Y," Books calls into his radio.

I'm sitting on the floor of the SWAT team truck with my laptop open, scrolling the motor vehicle registrations in Pennsylvania, the property tax records.

"There are four Mary Laneys in the greater Pittsburgh area," I say.

"Assuming it's Pittsburgh."

"It has to be close," I say. "Whatever he did to her, he came back here and included the transcript in his stack of papers before he vanished."

"Maybe he killed her right here in his house," says Books.

"Don't say that. Don't say he killed her."

"It sure sounded like that, Em."

"Wait," I say, looking up from the computer

screen. "Her age. She said her age in there, right? I think it was thirty-seven?"

"That . . . sounds . . . right." Books flips through the passages concerning Winston Graham's beloved Mary. "Yes, thirty-seven. So she was born in nineteen seventy-five, or a late birthday in nineteen seventy-four."

I cut over to the Pennsylvania Department of Health for vital records. "If she was born in Pennsylvania, she'll be . . . right . . . here! Here we go: Allentown, Pennsylvania, Mary—oh, shoot. *Shoot*. This isn't Mary Laney. This is Marty Laney."

"Are you sure?"

"Of course I'm sure," I say, edgy and agitated. "I can tell the difference between 'Marty' and 'Mary,' for God's sake."

"Maybe it's her brother."

"Maybe. But let's keep looking."

Back to the property tax records, finding Social Security numbers and cross-referencing them with criminal records databases. She was once an alcoholic, so maybe she got in trouble with the law.

Nothing. The four Mary Laneys in the greater Pittsburgh area were all law-abiding citizens.

"Okay, let's do taxes," I say. "Department of Revenue . . . Department of Revenue . . ."

Tax records are chock full of information. All I

need is date of birth, for starters. She may not have been born in Pennsylvania, but she pays her taxes here.

Four Mary Laneys, with four dates of birth, pop onto my screen.

"DOB, six, twenty-two, ninety-four," I say. "DOB, five, thirteen, eighty-two . . . DOB five, twenty-seven, sixty-nine . . . DOB—"

I bounce off the floor of the truck. "Date of birth, seven, eleven, seventy-five!"

Books nods. "Is that our Mary?"

"Hang on, hang on, hang on. Let me check the W-2 for her employer."

Please be a bar or restaurant, some place that would hire a bartender.

"Yes!" I call out. "Her employer is listed as Ernie's Sports Bar."

"That's our thirty-seven-year-old bartender!" Books grabs his radio. "This is Bookman. I need the helicopters. Mobilize HRT. We have a location."

"I'm coming with you," I tell him, pushing him out of the way and jumping out of the truck before he can answer. "She's still alive," I say. "She has to be."

Chapter 95

STATE ROUTE 85 in Kittanning, Pennsylvania, has been shut down for a half mile in each direction of the home belonging to Mary Laney. There is a vacant lot across the street from the house, giving the helicopters a safe and convenient landing pad. State troopers have already surrounded the house. Fire trucks idle less than a hundred yards away.

The Hostage Rescue Team members spill out of one of the other helicopters and briefly huddle. This is, on its face, a rescue mission, but we can't take any chances with Winston Graham. He has managed to avoid us on more than one occasion when we had him pinned down. He has out-maneuvered us constantly. Yes, his last Graham Session made it sound like he was leaving her—*I promise you that one day soon we'll meet again*, were his last words to her—but I wouldn't put it past him to be inside that house waiting for us.

Books jogs over to the HRT members and confers with them while I stand across Route 85 from the house. It is a simple two-story home, some kind of shingle siding painted sky blue with white trim and a pitched roof. It is perched on a small hill with a stone path leading to the front porch.

While Pennsylvania state troopers look on with their rifles poised, two members of the HRT cross the street with a ladder and post it at the side of the house. When the time comes, they will climb it to reach the landing hanging over the front porch, allowing them to enter the second-story windows at the same time they storm the first floor.

But nobody is climbing yet. I look at my watch. It's past seven in the morning now.

"Send in Kevin," says Books.

"This is taking too long," I say. "She could be dying in there."

Books nods but says nothing.

"Books, she could be—"

"I don't have time for this, Emmy."

"*Mary* doesn't have time."

"Listen to me: who knows *what* he has planned for us in there? His own house burst into flames when we got close to it. I'm not sending agents into a suicide mission. We check for bombs first, then if it's clear—"

"And what if that's the window of time that she dies, Books? We could save a life and we're sitting out here following protocol—"

"It's not just protocol. It's the right thing to do. You want a bunch of agents to die because I didn't take simple precautions? Their lives are my responsibility."

"She's our best chance to catch Graham."

Books spins toward me. "Emmy, if you don't shut up, I'm going to put you in handcuffs. I'm not sending in men with absolutely no idea what's inside waiting for us. Not after all the surprises he's had for us so far. Would *you* want to be the first person to go through that door?"

He turns and walks away from me, speaking into the radio.

She's in there dying, calling out for help, praying for a miracle, that someone will find her and rescue her. You prayed for that, too, didn't you, Marta? You prayed that someone would save you, but nobody came. I didn't come. I wasn't there for you.

I race across Route 85 toward the house.

"Emmy, what are you doing? Stop! Emmy, stop!"

I run up the path of stones leading to the house.

"All agents, stand your ground!" says Books through my earpiece. "Emmy, this is a direct order: do not enter that house!"

I whip out the earpiece and run up the three steps to the front porch, to the front door, a simple wooden door with an old-fashioned knocker.

I'm coming, honey. I'm coming to help you.

I brace myself for impact as I turn the knob.

Chapter 96

I ENTER THE house, steeling myself for a moment, but nothing comes. No explosion. No pop or blast.

My eyes immediately move to the floor, a hardwood foyer and a hallway. And blood smears leading down the hallway, disappearing around the corner.

"Mary Laney!" I call out, as I follow the path of blood, keeping to one side of the hallway to avoid stepping in the blood and contaminating the scene. "FBI!"

I reach the end of the hallway, by a small half-bathroom. The blood trail leads into a family room with old shag carpeting and dated furniture. The trail ends at a door.

The basement.

I open the door. "Mary Laney!" I call into the dark basement.

I reach along the wall and find a light switch. I flick it on but nothing happens. Nothing but consuming darkness beneath me. I pull out my iPhone and use my flashlight app and aim downward, a thin beam of light showing me the way. There are a dozen wooden stairs and a staircase railing. At the bottom, there is nothing but a landing that I can see.

"Mary Laney!" I call out.

I take the stairs down as quickly as I can, knowing that they could be booby-trapped or set up to undermine my footing or trip me, but having no other choice.

I'm coming, Marta, I'm here and I'm going to help you, just give me that chance, just hang on, please don't die, please come back to me.

I sweep my small scope of light back and forth, listening for any sounds. "Mary," I say again, my voice trembling now as I reach the last step, then the basement floor.

Then I hear a cough, a single, soft echo somewhere to my right.

I spin and shine the light haphazardly, my pulse racing. Nothing, I don't see anything but a closet and a—

I jump as the beam of light lowers toward the floor—a figure, an immobile figure, something, some*one* lying prone on the floor.

A woman, I think, from the long hair spilling out onto the basement floor. But where are the eyes and nose and—

"Oh, God," I mumble, moving closer, training the small beam of yellow light on her. Her face is bloodied and purple, her eyes swollen shut, her nose askew, her mouth a pulpy mash.

I bend down beside her. Her body is rising and falling, wet, raspy breaths. I touch her shoulder and she recoils. I run the flashlight over her body, her bloody white shirt and blue jeans. The blood looks like spatter to my untrained eye; it doesn't look like she was stabbed or shot—beaten terribly about the face but not the body.

"Mary? I'm with the FBI. You're safe now, sweetie."

Above me, the sounds of thunderous footfalls as the cavalry arrives, the FBI sending its team in.

Mary's head moves ever so slightly, some sign of acknowledgment.

"Do you know where he is, Mary?" I ask. "That's okay," I say when she doesn't respond. I rub her arm gently. "We're going to get you help."

Footsteps pounding down the basement stairs now, larger beams of light from the Maglites the agents use.

"We need a medic!" I call back. I begin to rise,

to show myself to the agents, when Mary's hand reaches out and takes mine. I put both of my hands in hers and lower my head close to her face.

"Don't . . . leave me," she whispers.

"I won't, honey, I promise," I say, my voice choking, my eyes filling with tears. "I'm right here. I won't ever let anybody hurt you again."

Mary begins to tremble furiously, a high-pitched whine escaping her throat. I put one arm over her back and my hand under her cheek, cradling her while HRT agents storm the basement with beams of light and an army's worth of firepower.

"It's going to be okay," I say with a conviction I do not feel. "He can't hurt you anymore."

Chapter 97

I OPEN MY eyes with a start, the noisy explosion vaporizing the moment I'm awake. The dreams have been like that lately, less about the consuming flames and more about the powerful explosion that creates them.

I squint in the powerful lighting. I don't know why hospitals do that with the overhead lights. When Mary Laney opens her eyes, she'll barely be able to see.

And she *will* open her eyes, or so the doctors say. The bandages covering her bruised face and the IV drip snaked into her arm show a damaged woman, but the doctors say there's *normal brain activity*, which is reassuring, I guess, though any time someone has to look at your brain waves, it can't be a good thing.

Mary has a concussion and shattered nose.

Her teeth are fine and she doesn't appear to have suffered any other facial fractures, just deep purple bruising that leaves her with slits for eyes, a swollen mouth and cheeks.

I watch the rise and fall of her chest, listen for the soft sounds of her breathing. When she awakens, we will pump her for information. We tried already, after we found her, but all she could speak was incoherent babble. She was in shock, the doctors said, traumatized. They treated her bruises and did a few tests and then ordered at least two hours' sleep before we could talk to her again.

Meanwhile, agents are scouring Graham's house. They found tires in the back of the house that he'd been burning, and gas canisters and gas masks—that's how he forced smoke into the victims' lungs to mimic the fire's smoke. They found all sorts of surgical instruments for the torture he inflicted and medical treatises about surgery. A search of his Internet activity shows that he frequented torture-porn sites and sought additional medical information. It also revealed that he'd visited the Facebook pages of many of his victims, never "friending" them but just checking out their information so he knew where they lived, where they worked, all sorts of factual data that would help pin them down before he went after them.

And it's clear that he learned how to set his fires from the Internet, a site that explained precisely how to rig a time-delayed explosion: he used tape to dangle a balloon down from the ceiling until it was suspended over a lit candle. The balloon was full of gasoline. Beneath the candle, he placed a pile of paper. After Graham had left, the candle's flame melted the balloon, causing the gas to splash over the flame and spread to the papers. *Ka-boom.* By the time firefighters arrived, the string would be long incinerated, and traces of the candle would remain, leading to the conclusion that the fire was caused by a candle that fell over onto newspaper or magazines.

His driver's license photo has now been shown everywhere, on every cable news station and on every online news source in the nation. Everyone in the country is seeing that photo of an overweight, nearly bald, beady-eyed man named Winston Graham.

He'll look different, of course. He'll have hair and probably a mustache, change the eyebrows, wear glasses, whatever—he won't make himself obvious to anyone.

But where did he go? Where *can* he go?

We have no idea. All we know is that he withdrew more than two hundred thousand dollars from his bank account, so he's got the cash to do a lot of things.

The door opens, and Books walks in. He nods at me with an icy glare and looks at Mary.

"It's not two hours yet," I say.

"I thought maybe she woke up on her own."

"I told you I'd call you as soon as she did."

"You told me a lot of things," he says, an introductory sentence to a speech that, something tells me, he's rehearsed. "You told me if I took this case, you'd follow my directions, and you didn't."

"I don't want to talk about that," I say.

"Emmy, I gave you a direct order and you disobeyed it. You could have gotten yourself killed. You could have gotten Mary killed. You could have set off an explosion that got *all* of us—"

"But I didn't, okay, Harrison? I didn't. So shut up already."

Books, still standing, lets the silence work for him. We both know what's coming next.

"I don't care," I say. "Kick me off the case. Fire me. Whatever. I'm not going to stop looking for him."

"Oh, I *am* taking you off this case," Books says. "I can't fire you. But I assume Dickinson will take care of that. He's already asked for a full report about your actions. There were only about two hundred sworn law enforcement officers as witnesses. And I'm not going to stand in his way. You deserve to be fired."

I put my forehead against the rail of Mary's bed, the same position I'd been in when I dozed off a moment ago.

"So," Books says.

"So what?"

"So you're off this case."

"I heard you the first time."

"So you have to leave."

I look up at him. "I'm not leaving. I promised her I wouldn't leave her."

Books gives me that look he always gives me when I'm being stubborn. "You held her hand all the way into the ambulance and to the hospital. You held her hand when the doctors were treating her, which I still can't believe they let you do. But then, trying to talk you out of something is like trying to reason with a brick wall."

"When she wakes up, she's going to see me standing here, Books. I'm not leaving. Get used to it."

"Get used to it. Get used to it! Same old Emmy, doing whatever you want, whenever you want, however you want." Books's eyebrows start their familiar twitch. His neck glows crimson. He'd like to drag me out of the room by my hair.

And he might do just that. But he doesn't.

Because at that moment, a sharp intake of air comes from Mary Laney.

Chapter 98

MARY LANEY LEANS forward in bed as she expels a violent cough, thick with phlegm and dried blood. I use the automated buttons to angle her bed upward so she's at about sixty degrees, and then I hit the button for the nurse.

"We're here, Mary," I say, taking her hand and caressing it. "You're in a hospital and you're safe."

Once her coughing attack abates, Mary holds completely still. Her eyes, mere slits through purple-black bruising, stare forward.

She is remembering everything now.

And then she lets out a low moan. Her shoulders begin to tremble, and tears find their way down her swollen cheeks.

"He can't hurt you anymore," I say.

"Is he—is he—did—you . . ." She spits out

words through halting breaths, through her gentle sobs.

"We haven't caught him yet," says Books. "But we will. We need your help to do that, Mary."

Still weeping, Mary inspects herself, looking at her arms and legs, patting her hands down her torso as if searching herself for a weapon. Then she gently brings her fingers to her face, her horribly bruised and puffy face.

"I'm Special Agent Bookman and this is Emmy Dockery, a research analyst with the FBI. I'm sorry, but we really need to talk to you right now."

After a while, Mary nods, and her body stops heaving with sobs. I hand her a tissue and she blots her face gently. Then she looks at me.

"You . . . found me," she says. "It was you. You . . . didn't leave me."

I take her hand and give her a soft smile. "You're going to be okay."

"What did he . . . what did Winston do? Did he k-kill . . . ?"

I look at Books, who nods. "He's wanted for murder. A string of murders."

She takes that news badly. Judging from the last Graham Session we read, where Graham talked to her while he bloodied her face, she must have had some hint that he'd done evil things.

"Okay, everyone back off," says a doctor, pushing his way into the room.

"Real quick, Mary," says Books. "This is important. Did he give any clue as to where he was going? Or what he was doing next? Anything at all?"

Books holds off the doctor with a stiff-arm.

Mary clears her throat. "He said . . . he said . . ."

"I have to insist on treating my patient," says the doctor.

"This is important," says Books. "Go ahead, Mary. What did he say?"

Mary swallows with some effort. Her eyes close.

"He said you'll never catch him," she says. "He said he's invisible."

to me." He wags his finger in my face. "Well, guess what? You've used me for the last time."

"So a killer stays on the run that much longer because you can't get over the fact that I wouldn't marry you."

Books draws back, his lips parting. "Wow. You are something."

Yeah, that was over the line. "I'm—I'm sorry, Books. I didn't mean that."

Books works his jaw, avoiding eye contact. "If you don't leave this hospital in the next five minutes, I'll have you arrested."

"Agent!" One of the federal marshals jogs down the hallway toward us. "Ms. Laney said she's ready to talk some more."

"Great," Books says, grateful to exit this conversation.

"She, uh"—the marshal raises a shoulder in apology—"she said she wants Ms. Dockery there."

Books drops his head and shakes it. Then he casts a look of steel in my direction. "Ms. Dockery has been relieved of her duties on this case."

"Yes, sir, but . . ." The federal marshal clears his throat. "She said she'll only talk to Ms. Dockery."

With an audible groan, Books runs his fingers through his hair.

I can't help smiling just a bit.

"Well, this is awkward," I say.

Books storms past me, toward Mary's room.

"Well, let's go already!" he calls back to me.

Chapter 100

"HE SEEMED SO . . . normal," says Mary Laney, her voice still raspy. She has fresh gauze covering her nose. The bruising surrounding her eyes now has a shade of blue to go with the purple and black. I can't look at her without wanting to cry.

They found a Louisville Slugger aluminum baseball bat with Mary's blood on it in her basement. That's what Graham used to strike her face repeatedly, causing it to swell up like a hideous balloon.

An interesting choice Graham made there, the baseball bat. Is there a significance? I wouldn't have expected him to torture Mary like he did his other victims. He wouldn't burn her or scalp her or chisel away at the nerve centers at her knees and elbows and wrists. But why use a baseball bat? Why not just use a gun and do it quickly with one pull of the trigger?

"I mean, he was kind of odd and insecure," Mary continues, "but he seemed totally harmless. Maybe . . . not comfortable with himself. But he lightened up the more we got to know each other. He was gentle and sweet."

She looks at us with those words—at least I think she does, based on the turning of her head. Her eyes are so buried behind the swelling that it's hard to see them move.

"I know that sounds crazy now," she says.

"Not at all, Mary," I say. "Winston Graham fooled a lot of people. He was masterful. He got women he'd never met, who lived alone, to let him into their homes. That takes a special kind of con artist."

Mary scoops some ice chips into her mouth from a Styrofoam cup and sucks on them. "The first time I met him? He told me he was a serial killer."

"Really," I say. She doesn't know that we read about their first exchange in one of the Graham Session transcripts. She doesn't know those transcripts even exist. Books said he wants to wait before telling her.

"That was at the bar I work at," she says. "He—" Mary raises a hand to her ear, as if talking on the phone. "He looked like he was recording his words on this contraption. He held it to his ear like a cell phone. I made a comment to him about it, and he seemed really interested in me after that. He told me he had killed a bunch of people. I just assumed he was kidding."

"Like anybody would have," I say.

Mary takes us through her several dates with Graham—dates that we already know about, but we play dumb. She doesn't hit every detail that was recounted in the Graham Sessions but generally covers the same ground. The night he skulked into the bar to observe her while in disguise ("I guess that should have been the first tip-off," she concedes before adding, "but it was flattering. Men don't usually pay much attention to me"). Next they met for drinks after she got off work one night. Then their Saturday night date, the week that Graham took off from his murder spree. And then lying by the fireplace, kissing and nestling together, where they first broached the topic of having a serious relationship.

The conversation lasts for nearly three hours. Books, who is the best interviewer I've ever seen— patient, detailed—covers everything that they said and did, every emotion that Mary felt, while Mary holds my hand.

"This is incredibly embarrassing," Mary says when it's over. "You must think I'm an idiot."

"I think you're special," I say. "And so did he. I think you got to him, Mary. I mean, he didn't kill you, did he? He killed everyone else. And not just killed, Mary. He tortured them. Brutalized them. But not you. He had every reason to kill you, but he couldn't bring himself to do it. There was something different about you."

"I just got lucky," she said.

"It wasn't luck," Books says. "He was hitting you with an aluminum baseball bat. It would have been easy to kill you if he'd wanted to. Believe it or not, Mary, as bad as your facial injuries are, he didn't hit you nearly as hard as he could have. Even one solid swing of that bat could have given you brain damage. I think he was hesitating."

"You're kidding," she says.

"No. You see something similar with suicides. People who slit their wrists. At first, they hesitate, they can't do it, so you'll see minor, superficial cuts, before they drum up the nerve to actually open a vein. They're called hesitation cuts. This is something like that."

"A hesitation *swing*," I say.

"More or less, yes," says Books. "He told himself he had to kill you, but every time he swung, he pulled back. Because deep down, he *couldn't* kill you. He cared about you too much."

She gives a bitter laugh. "I have to say, a lot of things went through my mind while he was hitting me with that bat. But 'he must really care about me' wasn't one of those things."

But Books is right. That's why Graham used a baseball bat and not a gun or a knife. He was still deciding, up to the end, whether he could actually kill her.

"So . . . what happens now?" she asks.

Books nods. "You'll spend a day or two in the hospital. We'll keep watch over you. When they discharge you, we should place you in protective custody. Move you somewhere."

Mary places a hand on her chest. "You think he'll come *back*?"

"We have to consider the possibility. But don't worry. He won't know where you are. We're just being extra cautious. And we'll have someone guarding you."

"Who? You mean, like, FBI agents?"

"Or federal marshals. Professionals."

Mary's head drops, deflated. "I don't want to hide. I can't hide."

"Just until we catch him," I say.

"You could be in danger," says Books. "He may

change his mind and decide he doesn't want you alive. Or he may just want you, period, and try to take you with him."

Mary shakes her head and takes a deep breath. Then she looks right at me.

"I'll do it if you go with me," she says.

Chapter 101

SOMETHING IS WRONG. Something is wrong here.

I'm in the hospital cafeteria, reading through my copy of the Graham Sessions once more, trying to scratch an indefinable itch. Denny and Sophie, who have joined us in Pennsylvania, are sitting with me, looking through their own copies. It's not much, but right now it's all we have in terms of clues.

"Why did he start doing these Graham Sessions just last month?" I ask. "Just last August. He started his murder spree in September of two thousand eleven, but he didn't start recording these transcripts until eleven months later?"

Denny throws a toothpick into his mouth and chews on it. "Who knows? He decided that his brilliance should be memorialized."

I shake my head. "He's too methodical. He

403

would have planned these Graham Sessions right along with his killing spree. I don't think he does much of anything on a whim. We know that from his actions and from what he brags about in this diary of his—discipline, preparation, execution."

Sophie says, "So the question is, what triggered this decision? What happened in August of this year, two thousand twelve, that was different from when he began the killing spree in September two thousand eleven?"

"We don't know of anything traumatic in his personal life," says Denny. "Graham's parents died a decade ago. He didn't have any siblings. No wife or children. No girlfriend that we know of— at least until Mary, of course. No loved ones, no relationships. Not even a pet."

I think back to last August. Nothing particular stands out about his methods of killing during that time period. For my part, I was just conducting my research and sending e-mails to Dickinson and arguing with the Peoria Police Department in Arizona—

"Wait," I say, jumping in my chair, spilling coffee from Denny's Styrofoam cup. "Wait a second. August—that was when my dispute with the police in Arizona went public. That's when the Peoria newspaper ran that article about how I was claiming Marta's death was a homicide. And they made a point of mentioning that I worked for the FBI."

"He might have read that," says Denny.

"Of course he read it," I say. "He kept tabs on everything. Absolutely. So he reads that and he's thinking that the FBI is going to start breathing down his neck."

In truth, my own agency had cast me out at that point, had rejected my theories until Books came in and helped persuade the director. But Graham wouldn't have known that. For all he knew, the FBI was about to start a nationwide investigation.

"It was the first time that Graham felt threatened," I say.

"And he responded by writing a diary?" asks Sophie. "Why? Just in case he got caught, he wanted to explain to the world what he did?"

I make a face. That doesn't sound right. Nowadays, a serial killer like him would be glorified in the media. Even if we caught him, he'd have every newsmagazine and cable channel in the country wanting to give him a sounding board, wanting to run a special with an ominous title like *The Mind of a Predator.*

"You know what I think?" I tap the pages of the transcripts in front of me. "I think this is misdirection. I think there's a lie in these pages somewhere. Something to throw us off, just in case we got too close. Why not? If the FBI were on your tail, why not leave behind a note that feeds them the wrong information?"

"So the question is, where is the lie in those transcripts?" Denny asks.

"That's a very interesting question." Books walks up to our table. "Something you can ponder from your secluded location with Mary Laney."

The temperature seems to drop in the cafeteria. Sophie and Denny excuse themselves. Books doesn't take a seat, so I decide to get up and stand across the table from him.

"You leave tomorrow," says Books. "Denny's going with you, by the way."

"Okay, great. I'll keep doing my research and I'll send you e-mails or give you a call—"

"E-mails will be fine," he says. He won't even look at me. He rubs the top of the chair with both hands, then pats it presumptively. "Anyway, good luck and be—"

"Oh, Books, come on. I know I broke protocol out there but it's not like I shot somebody, or even personally insulted you. I was trying to help somebody. You're acting like I spit in your face."

Still not making eye contact with me, Books

shakes his head in bemusement. "I'm just done with you, Emmy. In every way. Go ahead and send an e-mail if you think of anything—I'm not going to stop you from doing your research—but I don't consider you part of this investigation anymore, and I don't consider you part of anything else having to do with me. Honestly, I don't ever want to speak to you or see you again."

I draw back. I didn't realize how badly I had embarrassed him. And how raw that nerve was already.

"Is that clear enough, Emmy? Do we understand each other?"

I wave my hand. "Fine, okay, sure."

Books nods and walks away.

"Books," I say. "For what it's worth, I really am sorry."

He stops but doesn't turn back. "It's not worth anything," he says. "Not anymore."

Chapter 102

WHEN I SEE Mary Laney the next evening, for the first time she is wearing her own clothes, not a hospital gown. And she seems the better for it, however beaten and bruised her face may be, now complete with a gigantic splint covering her nose.

"All set?" I ask. "They're picking us up in a few minutes."

"I'd feel better if I didn't look like the Elephant Man."

At least she has a sense of humor about this.

I leave the room. Down at the end of the hallway, Denny Sasser is talking to another man.

"Oh, Emmy," he says, pointing to the other guy. "Want you to meet Jim Demetrio. Jim, this is Emmy Dockery."

Jim Demetrio is just a bit taller than me, which makes him about five ten, a middle-aged man with a stocky frame. He's wearing a polo shirt and a baseball cap.

"So *this* is the infamous Emmy Dockery," he says. "The one who cracked the case."

I shake his hand. "I wouldn't go that far."

"The one who discovered there was a case in the first place, then. Sure, sure." He smiles at me. "You've made quite a name for yourself."

"Jim's retired FBI," says Denny. "He worked in the Pittsburgh field office until about a year and a half ago. One of the best profilers of serial killers I know. But he decided to turn to the private sector to make a killing doing security consulting."

Nice for him. I'm still wondering why I'm shaking his hand.

"He's been volunteering for the canvass."

"Oh, great, thanks very much," I say. There are several square miles of thick woods in Elk County near Winston Graham's ranch, and we are tracking every inch of it, looking for burial sites, hidden weapons caches, anything. We'll take volunteers if we can get them.

"My pleasure," says Demetrio. "Nice to get my hands dirty again."

"Jim's letting us use his place in Oregon," says Denny.

Ah, okay. They're sending Mary Laney to a

cabin on the coast of Oregon, a town called Cannon Beach. Apparently, it's Demetrio's place.

"It's perfect," says Demetrio. "I wired it for security myself. Perched on top of a hill, impossible to access except by a paved driveway with a gate. Your witness will be completely secure." He draws a horizontal line through the air. "Completely."

"Well, thank you very much," I say.

"Can I ask?" he says, leaning into me. "How'd you do it? What made you put this together?"

I shrug. I don't really have time for this. But I guess this guy's loaning us his cabin, and he's volunteering to boot. A little professional goodwill may be in order.

"The data," I answer. "The patterns of the crimes. Individually, they were brilliantly disguised. But collectively, they showed a pattern."

"Brilliant," he repeats. "You think he's brilliant?"

"I think he's a monster. But a very smart one."

Demetrio's eyes narrow. "Probably best you not think of him as a monster. He's a human being with his own reasons, however misguided you may think those reasons—"

"He's a monster," I say again.

Demetrio blanches at my rebuke. "If you say so."

I look over at Denny. "She's ready to go."

"Oh, then I should leave," Demetrio says, retreating to the elevator and punching the button. "Good seeing you, old friend. Listen, I have some business up that way in a couple of days. Maybe I'll stop by?"

"Sure," says Denny. "Thanks again, Jimmy."

Demetrio looks at me for a long moment. "What will this *monster* do next, Emmy? What's your prediction?"

I wipe my right hand on my jeans as the elevator door chimes.

"My prediction is we're going to put him in the ground," I say.

A smirk crosses Demetrio's face. "Never underestimate him," he says, before he disappears into the elevator.

Chapter 103

WHEN WE LAND at Portland's airport, we are welcomed by an FBI escort and a steady downfall of rain. Mary, Denny, and I deplane and hurry into one of the cars, and the driver—an FBI agent from the Pittsburgh field office named Getty—speeds us away.

Mary looks out the rain-slicked window. "Are we positive nobody knows where we are?" she asks me.

I look over at her. "We're being very careful about that. Only the four agents guarding us, you and I, and Agent Bookman know our whereabouts."

"That's it? Nobody else?"

"Nobody else. Try to relax. You're not good at sitting still, are you?"

"Oh, God no," she says. "My dad used to say I never stopped moving, never stopped having some task. I was like a busy bee, he said. He'd make a *bzz-bzz-bzz* sound when he'd walk past me."

Our vehicle pulls up to a ticket booth on our way out of the airport. Mary turns away from the window and ducks her head down. She tries to be casual about it, but there's no mistaking her fear.

It's an odd contrast to see her cower like this, because she is physically impressive, a bit taller than me and muscle-toned, like a competitive biker or runner. (Exercise, she told me, helped her beat alcoholism, became a replacement buzz.) Her hair is light brown and straight, cut simply and falling just below her ears. I have no sense of how attractive she is given her current state, the tremendous bruising and discoloration, the large splint over her nose. The bandages holding the splint in place look like a landing strip across the center of her face.

The rain pelts the car as we maneuver onto the open road. I'm hoping she'll settle in, maybe even get some sleep.

"Nobody else knows where we are?" she asks again. "Just the four guards and Agent Bookman and you and I?"

"That's it, Mary. I promise."

"He wouldn't come after me, anyway. Right?" She looks over at me.

"I can't imagine he would," I say. "We're just being very cautious."

An SUV passes us on the left and Mary ducks down again, shielding her face. This time, she catches me noticing her. "Sorry," she says.

"You're making yourself crazy." I put my hand on her arm. "Nobody knows you're here. I promise."

We drive into Cannon Beach, Oregon, under cover of nightfall, as planned, moving along a narrow street not fifty yards from the Pacific Ocean. I roll down the window and take in the salty, misty air. This is no vacation, but for just a moment it feels like one. We pass some resorts, then assorted shops and restaurants and tourist souvenir stores, all of them closed up and dark at three in the morning.

Mary grows edgier as we near our destination. She slides down in the car so that nobody can see her from outside—not that there's anybody outside this time of night. But it's easy for me to be rational. I'm not the one with a target on my back.

Then we turn right down a road, away from the ocean and the well-lit storefronts, and drive down a narrow, winding lane until we reach a car awaiting us, with two men leaning against the vehicle. They right themselves to attention when they see us.

These men, I presume, are the U.S. marshals from Portland.

Mary puts out her hand and I take it, interlocking my fingers with hers. "We're going to be safe here," I say.

Suddenly, a gate that I didn't even notice swings inward. The marshals get into their car, and we follow them up a steep, twisty paved drive until we reach the cabin.

Both cars pull up on the gravel parking area to the west and shine their lights on the house, various insects dancing in and out of the light beams. The cabin is all cherrywood, a wide ranch. There is a small yard surrounding it, but then, on all sides, there is darkness, a void, empty space—a drop-off, I know, though I can't see it this time of night. We are perched high on a hill. It's just like Jim Demetrio said: to reach this cabin, you'd either have to drive up the driveway into the waiting arms of federal agents or scale the side of a mountain.

The U.S. marshals leave their car and search the cabin before we enter. In our front seat, Denny and the guy driving the car, Special Agent Norm Getty, wait patiently.

"The house has updated security," says Getty. "There's a front door and a back door, each with a deadbolt. Each door chimes when it's opened, and if the alarm is set and goes off, the noise can be heard across the Pacific." He points at the house. "There are security cameras and motion sensors surrounding the house, another camera down by the front gate, and we can see all of it from here." He looks back at us and shows us an iPad, a video monitor with a screen split four ways to show the different cameras.

"It's completely secure," he tells us.

"Let's get out," I say to Mary. "It's okay."

I slide out on Mary's side, still holding her hand, taking in the mild, damp air, the smell of the ocean carried on a light breeze. We are, indeed, high up on a hill, but it feels more like an island than a mountain. The property on which we are standing is maybe a quarter acre, maybe less, most of it occupied by the cabin or the gravel parking lot. The grass surrounding the cabin is minimal, and then the drop on each side, all fenced in. I approach the fence to the east and look down into nothingness.

"There's nothing down there, on any side, except thick branches and wild foliage," says Agent Getty. "He'd have to scale a mountain and overcome insurmountable natural obstacles. And even if he got that far, he'd have to get over this five-foot fence, which has barbed wire. It's impossible, ladies. Impossible. The only way to this cabin is up that driveway, through us, through cameras and motion sensors that will alert us to his presence long before he reaches you."

Mary nods her head. "It *does* seem safe," she concedes.

I squeeze her hand. "Absolutely," I say, hoping to convince both of us.

Chapter 104

THE CABIN IS roomy and updated inside. There is a large living room with hardwood floors, a half bath off that room, a decent-size kitchen with a laminated countertop, and two bedrooms in the back with a Jack-and-Jill bathroom between them.

The room I'm in has two twin beds, for Jim Demetrio's two daughters, I assume. I don't know anything about his life, but the framed photos on the bureau show Jim at a younger age, with his wife and two preteen girls, waving to the camera on a boat somewhere and, in another shot, the four of them dressed formally at some event. I'm sleeping in a room that belongs to someone else, which always makes me uneasy, unwelcome.

We all meet back in the living room, which is decorated like a hunting lodge, a deer's head mounted on the wall, a bearskin rug covering the center of the room, antlers on the countertop from which coffee cups hang by their handles.

"This should work," says Denny. The other federal officers—Getty and the two U.S. marshals—work out their plan for the night and going forward. Two agents will be stationed in their vehicle in the gravel parking lot, one of them sleeping and one of them awake. The other vehicle will be located at the base of the driveway, again with the partners trading off sleep. Each team will have an iPad that will have all of the security cameras and motion sensors accessible.

Denny hands both Mary and me a small device that looks like your basic key fob for a car remote, only it contains a single red button. "Push the button for an emergency," he says. "We'll all get it immediately."

An emergency. The gesture is intended to reassure us, but the implication does just the opposite. We'll only need the emergency button if Winston Graham has somehow, some way, against all odds, managed to call on us.

A hush falls over the room.

And then a chime goes off, a loud rattle, a shifting of mechanical gears. Denny spins around. Agent Getty draws his weapon. My heart leaping, I rush for Mary and embrace her.

Meanwhile, perched on the wall, a door opens on a small clock. A bird pops out and says, "Cuckoo!" before disappearing again inside.

It is 4:00 a.m.

"Jesus," says Getty, holstering his weapon. Everyone takes a breath. The bird is no threat. Presumably, it has an alibi for the murders.

But it's a reminder of how jangled our nerves are, that no matter how much we reassure ourselves of our safety, nobody is completely convinced.

Chapter 105

I WAKE FROM the dream, from the nightmare plunge toward the window to escape the flames rippling across my bed. I wipe the thick lather of sweat from my forehead and sit up in bed. Coffee. I smell good coffee.

I walk out of my room and pass Mary's door. The door is closed most of the way but not shut completely. I see a glimpse of her sitting up, so I knock on her door, pushing the door open in the process.

On the nightstand beside her bed, a number of pill bottles are lined up, medication prescribed by her doctor. Understanding that she might be forced into seclusion for a considerable amount of time, the doctors gave her extra medication to last her a few months. She has pills for pain, pills for anxiety, and pills for sleep.

She is seated on the bed against her propped-up pillows, on top of her covers, with her legs out in front of her and something resting between them. Something she is bent over, staring at—at least until she sees me.

She straightens up when she sees me. Her face is at least as swollen as yesterday, perhaps more so, and still discolored.

"I didn't mean to bar—" My eyes move to the object, and then I see what it is, long and cylindrical. It isn't any of the pills prescribed to her. It's alcohol. Specifically, a bottle of Grey Goose vodka.

"I didn't drink it," she says quickly.

"But you're thinking about it."

She doesn't answer for a long time, looking away from me. After a time, I think she's going to just wait for me to leave.

"I just—don't know if I can do this," she says. "I don't even want to open my eyes and face the day. I've overcome so much and I've been so proud of myself for doing it. But this. *This?*" She shakes her head absently. "I really cared about him," she says. "I know that sounds ridiculous but—"

"It's not ridiculous, Mary—"

"So now I lose the first guy I thought was decent and honorable, and on top of that, I have to live in fear of being maimed and tortured, *and* with the knowledge that I'm so stupid that I actually let this guy into my life and didn't see him for what—"

"Mary, don't—"

"And you know what?" She shows me the bottle. "I drink this bottle and I don't have to think about any of that. Not *any* of it."

I come over and sit across from her on the bed.

"I'm such a freak!" she cries. "How do you fall in love with a serial killer?" She covers her face with her hands.

I put my hand on her arm and let her get it out. After a short time, she takes a deep breath and lets out a moan.

"Y'know, my whole life, *I've* kind of felt like a freak," I say. "My sister, Marta? She was my twin. But she was so much prettier than I was. She looked like my mother. Prettier, more fun, popular. I was the tall, gangly bookworm who memorized square roots and took up causes like the environment and animal cruelty while she was on the cheerleading squad and making the Homecoming Court. I always thought of myself as a mistake. Like a piece of bad fruit you toss out."

Mary peeks at me, then drops her hands. "You don't seem like a freak to me. And I don't think Agent Bookman thinks you're a freak, either."

"Well." I throw up my hands. "I'm fine. I

learned to deal with it. But I was always so damn jealous of Marta. And she was so nice to me. That's the real insane part. She loved me like crazy. She'd do anything for me. All I did back was resent her. And now I'd do anything . . ." I shake my head and take a breath. "My point is, *freak* is in the eye of the beholder, Mary. You're no freak. You've overcome incredible obstacles. You'll overcome this one, too."

She looks at me, a hint of gratitude on her face. Behind that athletic body she has honed over years of exercise is a lonely woman who overcame adversity with her head held high but hasn't been able to find love. She thought she'd found it with Winston Graham, only to learn the absolute worst about him. Can she recover from that, like she overcame alcoholism?

"Come with me." I put out my hand. "Let's get some coffee and go out on the porch. It looks like a beautiful day. That bottle will still be there, if you want it, afterward."

She takes my hand and we get off the bed. As she gets up, a white teddy bear falls off the bed.

"Who's your friend?" I ask.

"Oh, that was already here," she says. "But I had a white teddy bear growing up. Took it with me everywhere for years. You know what I called it? White Bear."

"Very creative," I say.

She laughs, which is nice, a start. "Then I left it at the grocery store one day in a shopping cart. Never saw it again. I was inconsolable for days. For years afterward, every time I'd go to a supermarket, I'd look for White Bear. I'd make my dad ask the store manager if anybody had found it. I made up a whole story in my mind, that some nice little girl found it and gave it a good home."

"That's a real tale of tragedy." I lock arms with her. "Well, I'm no White Bear, but I'll be a friend forever."

"Do you mean that?" she says, caution in her voice.

"I promise," I say. "One freak to another."

Chapter 106

I FRY SOME eggs in a pan and pop in some toast while Mary sits outside on the porch, drinking coffee with Denny Sasser. I can't hear what they're saying but I can see them, and Mary looks more upbeat, more animated. I think I even see her laugh.

Denny's good for that, the comforting grandfather figure. He's also a shrewd investigator with decades of experience whom all of us, at various times, have grossly underestimated. If it weren't for Denny, we wouldn't have looked at Pennsylvania as a possible location for our subject. Denny thumbed his nose at my precious data, applied some common sense, and led us to a huge break in the case.

I grab a cup and join them out on the porch. "Breakfast is ready when you want it," I say.

"Excellent!" Denny says. He's a little too high

on life a little too early in the morning for me.

Mary's hair is still mussed from sleep. She's wearing a running outfit, matching top and shorts, though she isn't going running any time soon. But all in all, she looks a heck of a lot better than she did a half hour ago. That's the life of an addict, I suppose, always on the roller coaster, always living one step from the brink.

I sit down in a cushy chair next to them, the breeze on my face, while they continue their conversation.

"So, homeschooled," says Denny. He turns to me. "Mary was homeschooled."

"It's true," she says. "My dad was really strict about that sort of thing."

"Was he in education?"

"Oh, gosh, no," she says, waving a hand. "He worked the overnight shift for a meat-processing plant. Not a lot of heavy thinking going on there." She nods. "But he was very interested in my having a good education, and he didn't like our school system in Allentown. So he got a bunch of books and schooled me himself during the day."

Allentown makes me think of the Billy Joel song of the same name, about a Pennsylvania town struggling with a devastated economy, the loss of blue-collar factory jobs and, along with them, hope.

"Your mother wasn't around?" Denny asks.

"No, she died in childbirth."

"God, Mary, I'm sorry," I say.

"Yeah." She shrugs. "It's kind of weird to suffer a loss like that and not even realize it. I mean, I literally never met her. It was always just me and Dad. We did okay. No pity parties for me."

A tough life, by any measure. A single parent, not planning to raise the child alone, suddenly being forced to. And then homeschooling as well. Nothing traditional about her upbringing. Then, of course, the alcoholism, which sidetracked any career she had planned, hopefully not forever. And now she has to live in fear, and with the realization that she fell in love with a serial killer.

"Are you still in touch with your father?" Denny asks.

"No, no. He passed away in two thousand eleven. Heart attack. Died immediately." She sucks in her lips. "Oh, I'm sure a shrink would say that I was looking for a strong male figure to fill the void. Right? Leave it to me to find a serial killer instead. I sure know how to pick 'em, don't I? A *reallll* good judge of character, I am."

She puts down her mug of coffee and looks out

over the mountains toward the Pacific. A change of subject is in order, before she starts down that road again.

"Mary, I need your help on something."

Mary's eyes move back to me. "Sure. Anything."

I tell her for the first time about the Graham Sessions, how Winston Graham recounted his thoughts and many of his killings over the last two months. She reacts with horror, especially when she hears that she was prominently featured in the diary.

"You want me to . . . read them?"

"I do," I say. "Because I think there's a lie in there. Some misdirection. And you might be the only person to spot it."

Mary nods. "I'll do it," she says. "Of course I'll do it."

My cell phone buzzes. A text message from Sophie Talamas: urgent private.

"Denny and I need to make a phone call," I say to Mary. "I'll be back in a minute and we'll start working on those transcripts."

"You guys stay here. I'll go. I need to wash up and change my bandage." She pushes herself out of the chair and touches my arm. "Sorry about earlier," she says. "I'm fine. Really. You have enough to think about without worrying about me."

She's probably right. She's a strong woman, I'll give her that. When she's gone, I punch up the speakerphone on my smartphone and dial Sophie back.

"Hey," Sophie says.

"It's me and Denny. You have big news?"

"I do," she says. "Winston Graham is dead."

I look at Denny, relief coursing through me. Did she really just say that?

"Hate to say it," I say, "but thank God."

"Don't thank God just yet," she says. "Winston Graham died over a year ago."

Chapter 107

A HALF HOUR later, Mary returns to the porch, her hair hanging wet.

"What happened?" she asks, surveying the surroundings, the looks on our faces.

I give her the *Reader's Digest* version. After the raid on Winston Graham's house in Elk County, they found his DNA from a strand of hair on a comb in his bathroom and ran it through the database. There was a positive match on a John Doe who washed ashore off the Atlantic Ocean in October 2011. Given the condition of the body when it washed ashore, the best estimate is that it was in the water for a month, at least. Which means that before our subject began his murder spree in Atlantic Beach, Florida, on September 8, 2011, he dumped Winston Graham into the ocean.

"He took over Winston Graham's life," I say.

"Graham was a recluse, and a wealthy one, so he was the perfect target. Our subject killed Graham, probably after gaining access to his bank accounts and the like, and then used Graham's house as his base of operations. If anybody ever saw his Internet searches, they'd be searches on *Graham's* computer. If anybody ever traced his car—which we did, of course—they'd trace it to Graham."

"That's why he recorded those Graham Sessions," says Denny. "Just in case we ever got close, he wanted to make sure that we believed that Graham was our man. *That* was the big lie. The lie was that the killer isn't Winston Graham."

"But I . . . I've been to his house," says Mary, not thinking clearly. "I had dinner with him. I felt . . . I felt . . ."

"Whoever he was, he was an impostor," I say. "He took over Graham's life and made you believe he was Graham. Why *wouldn't* you believe it? You had no reason not to."

Mary takes a seat and places a hand on her chest. "I think I'm going to be sick."

"Nothing's changed," says Denny. "There's still a guy out there, and we're still going to catch him. And you're still going to be safe. The only thing that's different is his name."

He's right, technically.

But however we spin it, we've been thrown for yet another loop. "Winston Graham" wasn't Winston Graham at all. We have no idea who our subject is.

Once again, he's demonstrated that he's several steps ahead of us. Up is down, left is right, black is white. We are chasing our tails all over again.

And for some reason not grounded in logic, not based on empirical data that has always been my lifeblood, I can't shake the chill in my bones, the sense that we are less safe than we think up here in this secluded cabin.

Chapter 108

EIGHT O'CLOCK AT night. The sun has gone down, leaving across the sky a dazzling array of pink and green and orange, a delicious sorbet of color.

And then the sky turns to ash, and up here in our remote hideaway, beyond the exterior lights that illuminate the property, it is suddenly consuming blackness again. With darkness comes a heightened sense of dread, for me, anyway, our first full night up here. And our first night realizing that Winston Graham isn't really Winston Graham.

I'm pacing the bedroom, finishing up a call with Sophie (Books has chosen not to participate, continuing to shut me out). "Okay," I say. "So we have Visa and AmEx charges in Pittsburgh and surrounding suburbs. We have a couple of restaurants and bars, and one of them in particular, he seemed to frequent every Sunday in the fall of two thousand ten. Drinking beers and watching football, I assume."

"And with the amount of money he spent, he must have had company," says Sophie. "A drinking buddy. Maybe this is where Graham first met our subject. Where our subject gained Graham's trust, got close to him."

"Keep on it," I say. "Call me with any news." It's coming up on eleven o'clock at night in Pennsylvania, so I doubt there will be anything new from her tonight.

"Mary, I'm going to take a quick shower," I call out.

"Okay, no problem!"

I throw off my clothes and place my emergency key fob with the red button on the vanity. I hate to spend even one minute away from Mary, though the truth is, she has four guards outside, and I wouldn't be any help fighting off our subject anyway.

The cabin has good water pressure and one of those fancy rainfall showerheads. It feels good to lose myself, to escape all of this, to let the massaging water pound my neck and shoulders, to close my eyes and turn my face upward into the torrent of water.

But then it's over, and my nerves return, the

gnawing in my stomach. I dry off quickly, throw on my kick-around clothes, and grab the key fob off the vanity. I head down the hall to the living room. From the hallway, I see the stack of paper that constitutes the Graham Sessions, but no sign of Mary. *Where could she—*

"Hey there," Mary says, startling me. She's in the kitchen, pouring boiling milk into a paper cup.

The flutter of panic subsides. I must have rushed right past her. I didn't even look in the kitchen. What did I think—she'd be kidnapped in the ten minutes I spent in the shower? I need to get a grip. I'm becoming paranoid.

I blow out a sigh.

Then, suddenly, a chime goes off, the mechanical rustling of gears, and the damn cuckoo bird blurts out at me from his wooden perch on the wall before disappearing for another hour.

It must be nine o'clock.

"Shit," I say.

Get a grip, Emmy. Mary's safe. We're in a remote spot, unknown to just about anybody, and surrounded by armed, well-trained officers. Mary's safe.

"I made some hot chocolate for everyone," Mary says. "I figured it's the least I could do for them, after what they've done for me."

She places four paper cups of hot cocoa on a large plate.

"What are you doing?" I ask.

"I'm taking the cocoa out to them."

"No, you're not. You don't leave this house."

Mary frowns at me. "I can't even walk out to deliver some cocoa?"

"Nope. I'll do it." I take the plate away from her. "Be right back."

"You think he's coming for me, don't you?"

"No, I don't."

"Yes, you do. I can feel it. I can read it all over you."

"Mary, I'll be right back."

I walk gingerly with the plate into the cool evening air and deliver two cups to the U.S. marshals sitting in the car on the gravel parkway. "Two cups of hot cocoa," I say. "Courtesy of Mary."

"That's very nice," says the driver, a guy named McCloud. "Smells great."

"Thanks for all you're doing," I say.

Now only holding two cups, I leave the plate on the hood of their car and head, double-fisted, down the driveway to its base.

When I get down there, there are three people, not two, standing next to the vehicle.

Chapter 109

I SLOW MY pace instinctively, though it takes some effort walking downhill, my strides lengthening to keep balance. My eyes adjust to the darkness, and I make out the features of the third person standing next to Denny Sasser and Agent Getty.

The three of them are laughing and gesturing. When Denny sees me, he turns in my direction.

"Emmy," he says, "you remember Jim Demetrio."

Jim Demetrio. Sure. The former FBI agent who retired about a year ago and lives around Pittsburgh. The one who lent us this cabin. One of the best serial killer profilers Denny's ever met, he said.

"Nice to see you again," I say.

"Cabin treating you okay?"

"It's great," I say. "Thank you again." Suddenly aware of the two very hot cups I'm holding, I put them on the trunk of the car. "Hot cocoa for our security guards," I say.

"How's she holding up?" Demetrio asks, gesturing toward the cabin. "The witness. Is she scared? Nervous?"

"She's fine," I say, a protective tone to my short statement.

"Hmpf. Well, that's good."

"Hey," I say. "How about a photo of the three of you?" I raise my smartphone up to my eye. "For old time's sake?"

"Oh, I don't need to see myself in a photo," says Demetrio. "It'll just remind me how old and soft I'm getting."

"Old and soft and wealthy," Denny adds.

"Oh, come on, guys. Just get together for a shot."

"Nah, in fact, I have to get going," Demetrio says. "I might stop by later to say hi, guys. Be safe."

Jim Demetrio jumps into his fancy sports car and peels away.

"Thanks for the hot chocolate," says Denny. "Smells great."

But something else smells bad.

I walk back up the driveway filled with adrenaline. I dial up Sophie, even though it's past midnight her time. I doubt she's sleeping.

"Hey," she says.

"Sophie," I say, out of breath, "I need some really quick research on someone."

Chapter 110

ANOTHER HOUR PASSES. I stare out the window by the back porch into the darkness, seeing nothing but stars filling the sky. Ordinarily, a calm, peaceful setting.

"What's wrong?" Mary asks. She's in the living room on the couch with her copy of the Graham transcripts.

"Nothing's wrong." But I feel, somehow, that something is, my senses heightened, attuned to everything, every tweet of a bird, every rustle of the leaves, every whistle of the wind, every creak of the cabin.

"You didn't drink your hot chocolate," she says. "It isn't so hot anymore."

"Actually, I'm allergic to chocolate." I smile at her. "Didn't have the heart to tell you."

"Oh, *I'm* sorry," she says. "I'll make you some tea."

"Don't bother."

"It's no bother. Remember, I'm the busy bee." Mary pops off the couch and moves past me into the kitchen. She fills the kettle with water and puts it on the stove.

"Thanks," I say. "Maybe a little tea would be nice."

She squeezes my arm. "You sure you're okay? You seem more nervous than me." I don't respond, and she walks into her bedroom.

I look again out the kitchen window, the water beginning to simmer in the nearby kettle. No sense in getting Mary anxious. As if she isn't already.

She returns from the bedroom and sits on the couch, dropping down on one leg and flipping through the transcripts. "These transcripts are freaky," she says. "But I don't see anything in here that jumps out as wrong. Other than describing me as beautiful."

Off in the distance, a shot rings out. A car back-firing? Ordinarily, I wouldn't place any importance whatsoever on it.

I move cautiously toward the front door when a bell rings out, and the mechanical gears shift and slide. The cuckoo bird tells me it's 10:00 p.m., after it's given me a heart attack and caused me to jump out of my shoes.

"Dammit, that stupid clock," I say. "You think anyone would care if I ripped that thing off the wall?"

Mary gets a chuckle out of that. "I like cuckoo clocks. We had one growing up. It was actually kind of a nickname I had."

"Is that right? A nickname?" As casually as I can, so as not to alarm Mary, I look through the window over her head toward the gravel parkway, where everything looks as expected, the U.S. marshals' vehicle parked with its engine idling, headlights beaming toward the cabin.

All good.

But still, I head back to the kitchen window, playing sentry, notwithstanding the fact that there are four armed guards outside, with access to security cameras, who can do a much better job of it than I can.

"Just a silly nickname," says Mary. "Do you remember that song 'La Cucaracha'?"

"What?" I say, snapping my head around.

And over her head, out the window, suddenly everything is wrong. The dome light on the U.S. marshals' sedan is on, illuminating the interior. The driver, McCloud, is motionless, his head against the steering wheel. His partner is slumped against the passenger window, also perfectly still.

And a man is running from the gravel parkway toward the cabin.

"Run, Mary, run!" I shout, as Jim Demetrio's face plants against the small window in the front door, one large eye peering into the cabin.

Chapter 111

MARY DUCKS DOWN and rolls off the couch to the floor as Jim Demetrio pounds on the front door.

"It's him, Mary, it's him!" I hold out my hand, beckoning her to run with me, but she crawls along the floor on her elbows parallel to the couch, as if trying to avoid gunfire, moving toward the front door.

"Mary, he's *coming!*" I shout. "It's him!" I stifle my instinct to flee, because I can't leave Mary alone with him. I open kitchen drawers, looking for a knife, as I hear a key moving in the lock.

He has a key. It's his cabin.

I promise you that one day soon we'll meet again.

The door pops open. Demetrio looks at me. "Emmy, where's—"

Mary leaps off the floor into his peripheral vision. Before Demetrio can turn, Mary drives something sharp into his neck. Blood launches from his throat as Demetrio, stunned, stumbles backward and falls against the door before crumpling to the ground.

Mary shuffles backward away from him, like he's radioactive.

I move from the kitchen toward him, looking for any signs of breathing. The adrenaline dump is catching up with me now. My entire body is trembling. I manage to fish my cell out of my pocket but I can't hold it, dropping it to the floor.

Demetrio's eyes have gone lifeless. He is slumped on the floor, his head propped up awkwardly. The blood continues to spit out of his throat, as the heart completes its final contractions, not yet having received word that it's supposed to stop pumping.

Mary looks at me, her chest heaving like an animal.

"Do you know . . . his name?" she asks me.

"J-Jim," I say, finding my voice. "Jim Demetrio. The owner of the cabin. Ex-FBI, out of Pittsburgh."

She looks back at him. "Dammit," she says. "You never said anything about him."

I put my hands on my knees, struggling for air. On the floor, my cell phone beeps, a text message from Sophie.

Jim Demetrio all clear. Out of country most of September on security job. Bought a Porsche in Pittsburgh on day of Detroit bombing. Couldn't be our subject.

Jim Demetrio . . . isn't our killer? Then—what just happened?

I look up at Mary, who is watching Demetrio closely, probably making sure he's dead.

"We should go check on the agents," I say. "They might still be—"

"No." Mary shakes her head, turns and blocks the front door. Suddenly, she is in much better control of herself, more self-assured than I've ever seen her. "No, no, Emmy. We're not going to do that."

At first I'm lost, disoriented, overwhelmed, dazed and confused.

And then my blood goes cold.

Mary watches me carefully. I don't have a poker face. Never did. So she must notice my expression as it washes over me, information hurtling at me like meteors, all of it, the things I missed. The birth certificate I pulled up when we were first trying to locate Mary Laney—the same year of birth as Mary, the same hometown as Mary, but the name "Marty" instead. The bruises on her face from a baseball bat that could have—should have—caused far greater injuries. And just now, the story she began to tell about "La Cucaracha."

"You're the lie," I say. "The lie in those transcripts . . . was you."

She watches me but says nothing, her breathing evening out. There's no use pretending at this point.

"You should have drunk the cocoa," she says. "This would've been easier."

Chapter 112

RUN, EMMY. RUN. It's your only chance.

But there's nowhere for me to run. She's blocking the exit to the front door and is closer than I am to the porch door. And besides, I've waited almost a year to find my sister's killer. Now that I have, I'm not going anywhere.

"You never got to finish your story about the cuckoo clock," I say. "You were a little kid dancing to 'La Cucaracha'?"

She shrugs but doesn't speak. Her bandaged face and white shirt are covered in blood spatter. She holds her weapon—a scalpel, it looks like, probably stolen from the hospital—at her side.

"Let me finish it for you," I say. "Your dad wanted to give you that nickname. But you couldn't pronounce it. So you said you were his little *cuckoo-clock-ah*. Do I have that about right?"

I know I do. At least that's the way Gretchen Swanson described it to me when I sat at her kitchen table after noticing her porcelain figurine cockroach. Except the little girl in that version was her daughter, whom she had recently buried.

"Joelle Swanson," Mary says. "Nice girl. Very trusting."

I remove the key fob from my pocket and push the red button for emergency.

"Your friends outside aren't going to hear that," says Mary. "They're having a nice, long nap right now."

"Maybe this signal goes to people you didn't drug with your sleeping pills," I say. "Maybe it goes to Agent Bookman. Maybe to the local police." I push it a second time for good measure.

"Maybe it would," says Mary, "if that thing had any batteries in it."

I look at the key fob again, pushing the red button but noticing that the tiny red light isn't lighting up in response. It's as dead as Mary's many victims.

"When you were taking a shower," Mary explains.

I consider my dwindling options. Mary has thought of everything. Inventing those Graham Sessions, just in case we somehow caught up to her, so she could use "Graham" as a scapegoat. And that final line she wrote—*I promise you that one day soon we'll meet again*—knowing full well that she'd escape and leave us to assume that the prophecy had come true. It was even smart of her to insist I come to Oregon with her, so she could keep a close eye on the investigation.

"You can kill me, but you'll never get away with it now. Your cover is finally blown."

"Is it?" She takes another step toward me, an animal stalking its prey, her knees slightly bent, ready to respond to any move I make. She is, at most, four strides away from me. "True, I'll have to stop going to football games, which is a real shame. I do love watching it live. But otherwise, I'll just disappear. Don't you see? The killer found me and kidnapped me," she says in a faux-innocent voice. "I'm still the victim."

She's right. I see it now. She'll take the iPads away from the agents, so they'll have no record of the security cameras. She'll probably spill a little of her own blood in the cabin to make it look like she put up a fight. Why not? If she can hit herself with a baseball bat and fool us, cutting her fingertip to leave a little blood behind would be easy. And she'll just be Mary Laney, kidnapped victim of our unknown killer.

"And—then what?" I ask. "You start a new life? Adopt all the characteristics, the little stories and anecdotes that all your victims told you, that you *made* them tell you while you tortured them? That's what all this has been, right? How your dad would say *bzz-bzz-bzz* to you? The white teddy bear you lost in the supermarket? The 'Cucaracha' story from Joelle Swanson? What about Marta?" I scream, spit flying from my mouth. "What about my sister? What are you going to take from *her* life?"

Mary takes another step toward me. "I'm going to take *you*, Emmy," she says.

And then she smiles.

I make a break for it, against all odds but with nothing to lose, pivoting to my right, toward the door leading to the porch, grabbing the handle as my body slams against it—

I feel the hot sting of the scalpel sinking between my ribs, the searing pain as it enters then exits in one fluid motion. Then a hand grips the back of my hair and I'm falling backward until I hit the kitchen floor. I put my hand over the wound, the hot blood spilling out of me, the pain like a deafening echo in my head.

Mary slowly approaches me, helpless on the floor. She plays with the scalpel in her hand. A whistle sounds to her left, to my right, from the kettle on the kitchen stove.

"Oh, goodie," she says. "The water's ready."

Chapter 113

MARY WATCHES ME, the kettle of boiling water in one hand, the scalpel in the other, a tortured expression—a cross between a grimace and a grin—on her face.

I inch backward, sliding along the kitchen floor. I am trapped. I can't outfight her. I can't match her physically or tactically. I only have my head, swimming right now with images of my sister and all the brutality we've witnessed, the autopsy photos, victims scalped and burned, sliced and diced, tortured beyond human capacity. With my remaining strength, I press my hand over the wound to my rib cage as blood seeps out between my fingers.

"Marty," I say, my voice trembling. "You're . . . Marty."

"Ah, you saw the birth certificate? I was

wondering if you would. Yes, Daddy wanted a boy. He got me instead. Didn't stop him, though, did it?"

Mary tips the kettle, and a stream of searing liquid splashes my thigh. My leg recoils, and I cry out in pain as steam comes off my leg.

"Don't move," she says.

I slide backward. Mary steps down hard on my foot, snapping it sideways, breaking my ankle with a horrific crack. I reach forward, toward the pain, and more scalding water burns my arm and shoulder, my neck.

"I said don't move."

Use your head, Emmy. There has to be a way.

"So you . . . kill people . . . because Daddy made you be . . . a boy?"

Another splash, boiling water scalding my chest, blanketing my shirt. I let out a scream so loud I almost can't even hear it, can't identify it.

"That's what you think? You think this is about killing people? You, the great Emily Dockery, the brilliant FBI analyst—you haven't figured out what I want?"

And then she's on top of me, her knees pinning down my arms, hovering over me, dominating me. With one hand she grabs a fistful of my hair and pins my head to the floor. She poises the scalpel over my face, taunting me.

Use your head, Emmy. Think of something.

"You want those normal people . . . to feel . . ."

"Those safe little people with their safe, sheltered lives," she says. "They have no idea what suffering is. Not until they meet me."

The first incision comes at my scalp line, a precise break of the skin, moving left along my hairline, slicing skin and scraping bone. I scream with all the air my lungs can muster, my legs kicking up uselessly behind Mary, my vision going spotty, like the lights are being flicked on and off, until the screams I hear are unrecognizable, some high-pitched animal cry from far away, not my own—

Use your head, Emmy. It's your only chance.

The incision stops at my ear. I try to move my head, but she has me in a tight grip. And my strength is fading, my arms limp from the pressure of her body weight, my legs of no use, blood still spilling from my midsection as well.

"Not bad," says Mary, admiring her work. "Usually I have a Taser and restraints and smelling salts and a full set of surgical instruments, but you know what? This isn't half-bad. Sometimes artists do their best work under pressure. You're going to be my masterpiece, Emmy."

Make it stop . . . make it stop . . . think of something . . .

"Admittedly, I can't make them feel what I felt," she says matter-of-factly. "I can't inject them with steroids every day of their childhood or force them to pump iron or make them worry about whether their voice will seem too high every day at school. I can't make them get dressed in a bathroom stall every day of football practice so their teammates won't see their private parts. But I can do *this*, Emmy."

Mary pulls on my hair at the base of the incision, testing it, feeling it give way. The ripping pain is so unbearable I can't—I can't even—I can't—

I'm coming Marta, I'm coming to see you, I want to come see you, please please oh please let me come—

"You want to die now, don't you, Emmy? You want me to put you out of your misery. But you don't get to. You have to live with it. You have to live in pain, like a disfigured freak, until I tell you it's over. Be grateful it'll just be a few hours of your life, and not thirty-seven *years*."

Use your head. Something, anything . . .

There is one thing . . . one advantage . . .

"Don't you die on me," she says. "Not yet. I haven't finished."

Mary pins my head down again, this time with her right hand, the scalpel poised in her left, ready to begin the incision on the right side of my hairline, to complete the act, to separate my scalp from my forehead and turn me into a freak like her.

This time, I do not resist. My body goes limp. I hold my breath.

This time, I use my head.

Chapter 114

"NO, NO, *NO!*" Mary says. "Wake up! Wake up!"

Mary releases the grip on my hair and leans forward, her breath hot on my face, shouting at me. "You don't get to die yet! You don't get off that—"

With everything I have left, I jerk my head upright, my forehead connecting solidly with the splint covering Mary's broken nose.

Mary howls in pain from the head-butt, a wounded, tortured monster, her hands immediately pitching a tent over her nose. She falls backward and off me. I take a delicious, full breath of air and lift myself up, blood pouring into my eyes and out of my rib cage, the room moving sideways.

The scalpel, wet with my blood, resting on the floor. I reach for it, missing at first, seeing double, but finally getting hold of it while Mary writhes in pain on the floor, having broken her nose for the second time in a week, this time not of her own doing.

I try to get to my feet but fail, my right ankle shattered, my body so weak I can't support myself. The lights are flashing in and out again like a strobe light, Mary closer to me each time they click on, the splint on her nose now gone, her face a bloody purple mash with a gruesome snarl and a hideous squeal—

I'm coming, Marta.

The strobe lights flickering, a gong echoing between my ears, Marta and I on prom night with our dates, hers the football captain, mine a sophomore buddy from math club three inches shorter than me, the day I identified Marta at the morgue, the time we stole one of mom's cigarettes when we were ten, the night Books got down on one knee and showed me his grandmother's diamond ring—

The stabbing pain in my ribs, Mary's contorted grimace, snarling at me—

And then for a moment, everything is still, and Mary and I lock eyes, and she lets out a deep cry and rushes toward me. But I lunge toward her, too, pushing off with my good foot. The crown of my forehead crashes into Mary's face. She cries out as she falls backward, as I fall on top of her, as I slap my left hand down on her chest and hold her down with my body weight.

Mary flails with her arms, reaching for my face, going for the scalpel in my hand.

My balance begins to wobble, my strength fading. This is it. My last chance.

My right hand strikes downward, the scalpel sinking into flesh and bone, then again, then again, *thump, thump, thump,* blood spattering my face, until Mary's screams go silent.

And then everything is dark and warm.

Chapter 115

WHEN I FIRST see Marta, she looks radiant. She looks younger, more refreshed, happier. She looks like the best version of Marta.

At first, neither of us speaks. We move fluidly, weightless, into each other's arms, and we cry. And then we laugh, because now we have each other again. And this time, as I promised her, it is different.

I tell her everything. I tell her how stupid and insecure I was, how much I admired her all those years, how I wished I could make myself be more like her, and to my surprise, to my infinite shock, she tells me the same thing. Oh, we laugh, how funny life can be. We each admired and envied the other without realizing it.

We laugh about those holidays with our flatulent Uncle Phil, the time when Marta first got her period and she cried, but I cried, too, out of jealousy that she beat me to it. We remember the time when she was eight and stepped on a nail in the woods behind our house, and Andy Irvin and Doug Mason fought over who would carry her back home, until I finally picked her up myself and carried her over my shoulder.

It feels as if our conversation never stops, has no beginning or end, the concept of time irrelevant. Because now it's forever.

That thing about everything happening for a reason? We decide that the cliché, in this case, is true. We decide that if Marta hadn't died, this killer would never have been detected, would never have stopped. Her death saved the lives of many others. And it brought us back together.

It's not perfect, but it will have to do.

And now, at least, we have each other, free of our earthly constraints, our insecurities and petty differences. Now I have my sister back.

Forever.

Chapter 116

THE LABORED BREATHING of retired special agent Harrison Bookman fills the otherwise quiet room. The door opens with a *whoosh*, and Sophie's perfume wafts in.

"I know this isn't a good time, Books," Sophie says. "But we got confirmation from the old football coach in Allentown. 'Marty' Laney was the starting tailback for the school. A real standout. Then he—I mean she—left school after sophomore year, without warning, and finished high school in Ridgway."

"Probably when Marty, or Mary, hit puberty," says Books. "All the steroids in the world couldn't change nature."

"Right. She didn't play sports when she got to Ridgway. In fact, the reports we have are that Marty was a recluse at her new school. Just went to class and then went home. No school activities. No friends. So it was easier to hide her true gender. Then Marty went to Pitt for college while living at home. Majored in forensic science. After he—I mean she—graduated, she went into the family business. Daddy kept her under his thumb his entire life."

Books lets out a pained sigh. "That father's a real gem. I mean, my mother once told me she'd wanted a girl when I was born. But she didn't make me spend my whole life pretending I *was* one. Did we confirm everything about this asshole?"

"Yes, confirmed. Doctor Donald Laney was a high-school football star who blew out his knee his freshman year at Pitt and never played again. He became a forensic pathologist in Allentown. Mary's mother died in childbirth— the one thing she told us that was true. When the Laneys moved to Ridgway, Doctor Laney opened a funeral home. Mary worked there with her father. And guess what ended up happening at that funeral home?"

"I don't want to know," says Books.

"It was shut down after state regulators received a series of complaints that corpses were being disfigured, mutilated."

"Ah. That would be our Mary," says Books,

"practicing on dead people what she'd later do to the living, once Daddy passed away."

"Yeah, yeah. Well, now she can join her father in hell."

Silence. Then Sophie says, in a softer voice, "Anyway, Books—you hanging in there?"

"Sure, sure. I'm fine, Soph. I'll talk to you soon. Great work on this case, if I didn't say so already."

"You did, actually. But we both know who deserves the most credit for this case."

The room is silent, save for Sophie's retreating footsteps, the whoosh of air as the door opens and closes.

"Yes, we certainly do," Books whispers, choking out the words.

Silence again.

"Oh, Emmy," he says. "Oh, Emmy. Oh, Emmy, please . . ."

I'm not ready, Marta. Not yet. I love you, girl, and I miss you like crazy, but I'm not done here yet.

"Emmy?" Books's breath on my face. His hand taking mine. "Oh, my God—*Emmy?*" he says again, his voice quivering. "You're awake."

I force my eyes open, a flutter at first, and then I see him through fog.

"Emily Jean, I love you so much. I love you with all my heart. You know that, don't you?"

"I . . . do," I whisper. I don't have the strength to even squeeze his hand back.

He runs his fingers gently over my face. "The way we left things . . . I was afraid I'd never get to say those things to you." He presses his lips against my forehead. "You know I didn't mean any of those terrible things I said to you, don't you?"

"I . . . do." I try to smile, but I'm not sure if it forms.

"You lost a lot of blood, but you made it. You did it, Emmy. You caught her. Do you remember what happened?"

"I . . . do." My eyelids flutter and close. I'm not in a hurry to remember that night. I'm not in a hurry to look in a mirror, either. But the scars will heal. They always do.

"I can stay with you while you recuperate," he says. "Just as friends, I mean. No pressure. I can just help however you want. Your mom's here, too. She's downstairs right now getting lunch. She's been here ever since we found you at the cabin."

I adjust myself and feel the stinging pain on my left side, gingerly touch the bandage across my forehead, Mary Laney's parting gifts to me.

Books pats my hand. "You need to rest," he says. "And I need to call the doctor."

"I . . . do."

"You're groggy, Em. Just sleep. I'll be here when you wake up."

He moves away from me. I barely open my eyes. "Books," I manage.

"Yeah? Yes?"

"Come . . . closer."

"Okay." He leans in toward me.

My mouth is pasty, my lips dry and cracked. I barely have the strength to speak.

"Closer," I manage.

Books looks at me funny at first. "Okay, sweetie." He leans in nice and close, his ear nearly touching my lips. "I'm here, Em."

Blessed sleep just moments away, my strength rapidly fading, I lean forward so that my words, barely a whisper, will register.

"I do," I say to him.

ACKNOWLEDGMENTS

A special thanks to everyone who helped with this novel. Pat Layng drew on his experience as a former federal prosecutor in Chicago to give advice and insight into the prosecution of arson cases. Dan Collins, a former federal prosecutor and current partner at Drinker Biddle & Reath LLP in Chicago, provided advice on matters large and small, including the details of securing search warrants and profiling serial killers. And the incomparable Sally McDaniel-Smith, for her tireless attention to the details of forensic pathology and arson—in other words, for explaining how to kill someone and make it look like an accident.

DETECTIVE MICHAEL BENNETT FINALLY RETURNS TO
NEW YORK CITY — AND TO THE MOST
UNSETTLING, HORRIFIC CASE OF HIS CAREER.

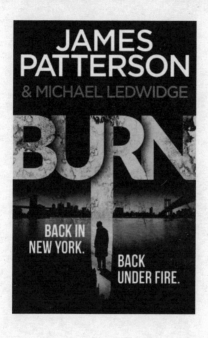

FOR AN EXCERPT, TURN THE PAGE.

LOS ANGELES, CALIFORNIA

THE WORK VAN was a new Mercedes, white and high roofed, with the bloodred words TURNKEY LOCKSMITH hand-painted on its side.

At a little before 7 a.m., it was winding through the Hollywood Hills northwest of LA, the steady drone of its diesel engine briefly rising in pitch as it turned onto the long climb of Kirkwood Drive in Laurel Canyon. Two hundred feet below the intersection of Kirkwood and Oak, the van coasted to a crackling stop on the gravel shoulder of the secluded road and shut off its engine. A minute passed, then two. No one got out.

As the bald Hispanic driver flipped down the visor to get the sun out of his eyes, he spotted a mule deer nosing out through the steep hillside's thick underbrush across the street.

Go for a lung shot, he thought as he imagined

getting a bead on it with the new compound hunting bow his girlfriend had gotten him for his birthday. *Track the blood trail down between the infinity pools and twenty-person funkadelic hot tubs before lashing it to the van's front grille. See how that would go down with Frank Zappa and George Clooney and K. D. Lang and the rest of the Laurel Canyon faithful.*

He was feigning a bow draw when the elegant red deer suddenly noticed him and bolted. The driver sighed, leaned slightly to his right, and depressed the intercom button under the drink holder.

"How's this? Line of sight OK?" he said.

"Yes. Maintain here until the handoff, then head for position two," intercommed back the sharp-featured, amber-haired woman sitting directly behind the driver in the sealed-off back of the high-tech surveillance van.

There was a dull mechanical hum as the woman flicked the joystick for the high-definition video camera concealed in the van's roof. On the console's flat screen in front of her, an off-white stucco bungalow a hundred fifty feet up the canyon slowly came into view.

She panned the camera over the bungalow's short, steep driveway of bishop's hat paver stones, the broken terra-cotta roof tiles above its front door, the live oaks and lemon trees in its side yard. She'd been here several times before and knew the target house as well as her own at this point.

She was halfway through the tea-filled Tervis tumbler from her kit bag when a truck slowed in front of the target house. It was a new Ford Expedition SUV, glossy black with heavily tinted windows. After it reversed up the driveway almost butt-up against the garage, the passenger-side door opened and out stepped a lanky middle-aged white man in a gray business suit. He adjusted his Oakley sport sunglasses for a moment before he reached into the open door and retrieved what appeared to be a military-issue M-16.

Then, up on the porch above him, the bungalow's front door opened and Detective Michael Bennett came out of the house.

The woman almost spilled the tea in her lap as she quickly panned the camera left and zoomed in on Bennett and the crowd of people coming out behind him. His kids were in cartoon-character PJs, their tan and striking blond nanny, Mary Catherine, in a bathrobe, drying her hands with a dish towel. One of the Bennett boys—was Trent his name? Yes, Trent—immediately started climbing out over the stair's cast-iron rail, until Mary Catherine pulled him back by his collar.

The cacophony of the family's calls and laughter rang in her earphone as she turned up the volume on the van's shotgun mike.

"*Arrivederci*," Bennett said playfully to his rambunctious family as he went down the stairs. "*Sayonara, auf Wiedersehen*. And, oh, yeah. Later, guys."

The woman in the van watched silently as Bennett smiled and crossed his eyes and stuck his tongue out at his family. He was pushing forty, but still tall and trim and handsome in his dark-blue suit. Biting at her lower lip, she didn't stop focusing until his dimples and pale blue-gray eyes slid out of the bottom of the frame into the SUV.

As the Ford rocketed out into the street, the amber-haired woman had already put down the joystick and was wheeling the captain's chair around toward the three men in bulky tactical gear sitting and sweating on the steel bench behind her.

If it hadn't been for the glistening snub-barreled Heckler and Koch machine guns in their laps, the large men could have been professional football players. Wide receivers in the huddle waiting for the quarterback to call the next play.

"To repeat one last time," she said calmly as the work van's engine suddenly roared to life and they lurched into the street. "Front door, side door, back door. When the doors pop, you will stay low until you are in position."

The poised woman quickly lifted her own submachine gun from the foam-lined hard case at her feet. Easily and expertly, she worked the H&K MP7's action, slamming the first HK 4.6x30mm cartridge into the gun's chamber with a loud snap.

"This isn't a drill, gentlemen," she said, looking up at the Bennett safe house growing rapidly now on the flat screen.

"Welcome to life and death."

THE WITNESS WAITING room adjacent to the second-floor federal courtroom where I was going to give my statement was a happy surprise after the fireworks show and my unexpected sidewalk rugby match. It had leather furniture and piped-in slow-dance Muzak and a rack of magazines next to the coffee machine.

For twenty minutes, I sat in it alone humming to Michael Bolton as Bob and his guys stood vigilantly in the hallway outside the locked door. The little stunt downstairs had fired them up beyond belief. Even with the tight courthouse security, they weren't taking any chances.

I'd just finished pouring myself a second cup of French vanilla coffee (which I probably didn't need, considering my already frazzled nerves) when the door unlocked and a middle-aged blond female court officer poked her friendly face inside and said it was time.

All eyes were on me as I followed the officer's blond ponytail into the bleached-wood-paneled courtroom. The line of orange-jumpsuited convicts sitting at the two defendants' tables peered at me curiously with "haven't I seen you someplace before" expressions as I made my way to a podium set up beside the witness box.

Alejandro Soto, the highest-ranking of the Tepito cartel members in attendance, seemed especially curious from where he sat closest to the witness box. I recognized his gaunt, ugly features from the video of the Bronx motel where he had brought my friend Tara to rape and kill her.

I stared directly at Soto as the court clerk asked me to state my name for the record.

"My name is Bennett," I said, smiling at Soto. "*Detective* Michael Bennett."

"Bennett!" Soto yelled as he stood and started banging his shackled wrists on the table. "What is this? What is this?"

No wonder he was shocked. His organization was out to get me and suddenly, presto, here I was. *Be careful what you wish for,* I thought as two court officers shoved the skinny middle-aged scumbag back down into his seat.

The violent crack of Judge Kenneth Barnett's gavel at the commotion was a little painful in the low-ceilinged courtroom. Our side could set off some firecrackers, too, apparently. Tall and wide, Barnett had the build of a football player, bright-blue eyes, and a shock of gray hair slicked straight back.

"Detective Bennett," he said as I was about to take my prepared statement from my jacket pocket. "Before you begin, I would just like to gently remind you that the victim impact statement is not an occasion for you to address the defendants directly. It is a way for me, the sentencing judge, to understand what impact the crimes in this case have had on you and society and thereby determine what appropriate punishment to mete out to these convicted men. Do you understand?"

"Perfectly, Your Honor," I said.

Especially the punishment part, I thought, glancing at Soto again.

I took my written statement out of my pocket and flattened it against the podium as I brought the microphone closer to my mouth.

I FLAGGED DOWN a gypsy cab and headed home.

The whole way back up the 101 to Laurel Canyon, I listened to the Mexican driver behind the wheel play a type of music called *narcocorrido*. Having become familiar with it in my recent investigations into the cartels, I knew the traditional-sounding Mexican country music had gangster-rap-style lyrics about moving dope and taking out your enemies with AK-47s.

Though it had a nice, sad sort of rhythm, considering the fact that the story of my life had recently pretty much become a *narcocorrido,* I didn't think I'd be adding it to my iPod playlist anytime soon.

Finally standing in the street out in front of the safe house thirty minutes later, paying the driver, I heard a sudden shriek of rubber. Just south down the curving slope of Kirkwood, I stood and watched as a white Euro-style work van fishtailed off the shoulder and barreled straight toward me.

No, was my weary thought as I watched it come. This couldn't be happening. The van shrieked again as it came around the closest curve and hit its brakes.

Forgetting the cabdriver, I palmed the stippled grip of my Glock and drew as I hit the driveway. I racked the slide, chambering a round, as I ducked my head down and ran up the steps of the house two at a time.

"Mary Catherine! Seamus!" I yelled as I pounded on the screen door with the pistol barrel.

My shocked-looking nanny, Mary Catherine, had just opened the front door when I heard the rattling metal roll of the van door opening from the bottom of the stairs.

"Mike, Mike! It's OK! Stand down! It's OK. It's me!" came a yell.

I turned. Down the stairs, a large bald guy with a gun was standing over my taxi driver, now lying facedown on the street. Also standing now in the open side doors of the white van was a woman. A very pretty woman in blue fatigues with brown—almost red—hair.

"Agent Parker. Long time no see. Are you out of your mind?" I screamed.

I should have known, I thought. It was a friend of mine. Emily Parker, special agent of the FBI. I guess I shouldn't have been surprised. Emily and I had taken down Perrine together less than a month before, and I knew she was still working in LA. I just didn't know *I* was her work.

I racked my weapon to make it safe as I came back down the stairs.

"I mean, Emily, you of all people should understand how paranoid I am these days about things like, I don't know, mysterious vans racing up on me. Is this some kind of practical joke? Why didn't you tell me you and the FBI were watching my house?"

"It was just a precaution for your court appearance today," she said as three drab-fatigue-clad FBI agents with large guns suddenly emerged from the foliage along the side of our house.

"Additional security was ordered," she said. "I kept it low key because you guys have been through enough. I didn't want to get you upset."

"In that case, I guess I'm not having a heart attack," I said.

"Listen, you should be the last one to talk about jokes, Mike," Emily said. "You know how many people are looking for you? Ditching the marshals after that verdict was beyond childish. We thought the bad guys got you. We've been worried sick."

"Ditched? I texted Joe. Besides, I'm a grown

man, Parker," I said. "A grown man who needed some fresh air."

"During a gang riot?"

I shrugged.

"Taking my life back needs to start somewhere. I'm tired, Emily, of the death threats, all the worrying. I came out here because of Perrine, and now he's in the ground, and I'm done hiding. You and I both know the cartels are too busy killing each other for Perrine's turf to bother coming after me. Perrine was a monster. They don't get avenged, last time I checked. Judge Barnett has seen to that. What was it that BP oil spill CEO guy said? 'I want my life back.'"

I walked over and knelt down and finally paid my cabdriver, still facedown on the asphalt.

"What's the quote, Emily? Those who would sacrifice freedom for security deserve neither and will lose both?"

"What's that other quote about a well-balanced Irishman?" Emily said, hopping from the van. "They have a chip on both shoulders?"

Then she surprised me for the second time in two minutes. She walked up and wrapped her arms around me and pressed her face hard against my neck.

"I going to miss you, Mike . . . working with

you. Just working. Don't get the wrong idea," she whispered in my ear.

"Good-bye yourself, Parker. It was fun strictly and platonically working with you as well," I whispered back as she broke it up.

She hopped back into the fed van with the rest of the agents. As they pulled away, I looked up to see Mary Catherine standing at the top of the stairs by the iron railing of the porch.

I immediately gave her my brightest smile. The on-again, off-again relationship I had with Mary Catherine had most definitely become on-again during our close-quarters California exile. She'd actually had to kill a cartel hit woman to protect the kids. We'd talked about it, cried about it. I don't think I'd ever been closer to this incredible young woman. Or more attracted.

I thought her dander might be up a little at seeing me share a hug with Parker, who I'd once or twice almost had a romantic relationship with, but to my happy surprise, Mary Catherine's slim hand slid easily into mine as I got to the top of the stairs.

"Time to go home, Detective Bennett," Mary Catherine said in her musical brogue as she suddenly broke my grip and playfully pushed me toward the door.

OUT NOW

Private Vegas

James Patterson
& Maxine Paetro

Showgirls. Millionaires. Murder.

Jack Morgan, head of Private Investigations, the global PI agency
of the rich and famous, is being pushed to the limit. His car has
been firebombed, his ex is dating someone else, and his twin
brother is still out to destroy him.

But Private doesn't rest, and nor do its clients: not the LAPD
who need Private's help catching two scumbags with diplomatic
immunity, and not the client who has just confessed to murdering
his wife.

Add to that Jack's best friend being held on a trumped-up charge
that could see him locked away for a very long time, and it seems
like all bets are off...

CENTURY

THE *SUNDAY TIMES* BESTSELLER

Unlucky 13

James Patterson
& Maxine Paetro

Two dead bodies are found inside a wrecked car on the Golden Gate Bridge, and the scene is more gruesome than anything Detective Lindsay Boxer has seen before.

There is more to these deaths than a simple traffic accident.

While Lindsay starts to piece this case together, she gets an unexpected call. Sightings of her ex-colleague-turned-ruthless-killer Mackie Morales have been reported.

Wanted for three murders, Mackie has been in hiding. But now she's ready to return to San Francisco and pay a visit to some old friends…

arrow books

Also by James Patterson

ALEX CROSS NOVELS

Along Came a Spider • Kiss the Girls • Jack and Jill •
Cat and Mouse • Pop Goes the Weasel • Roses are Red •
Violets are Blue • Four Blind Mice • The Big Bad Wolf •
London Bridges • Mary, Mary • Cross • Double Cross •
Cross Country • Alex Cross's Trial (*with Richard DiLallo*) •
I, Alex Cross • Cross Fire • Kill Alex Cross •
Merry Christmas, Alex Cross • Alex Cross, Run •
Cross My Heart • Hope to Die

THE WOMEN'S MURDER CLUB SERIES

1st to Die • 2nd Chance (*with Andrew Gross*) •
3rd Degree (*with Andrew Gross*) • 4th of July (*with Maxine Paetro*) •
The 5th Horseman (*with Maxine Paetro*) • The 6th Target (*with
Maxine Paetro*) • 7th Heaven (*with Maxine Paetro*) •
8th Confession (*with Maxine Paetro*) • 9th Judgement (*with
Maxine Paetro*) • 10th Anniversary (*with Maxine Paetro*) •
11th Hour (*with Maxine Paetro*) • 12th of Never (*with Maxine
Paetro*) • Unlucky 13 (*with Maxine Paetro*) •
14th Deadly Sin (*with Maxine Paetro*)

DETECTIVE MICHAEL BENNETT SERIES

Step on a Crack (*with Michael Ledwidge*) •
Run for Your Life (*with Michael Ledwidge*) •
Worst Case (*with Michael Ledwidge*) •
Tick Tock (*with Michael Ledwidge*) •
I, Michael Bennett (*with Michael Ledwidge*) •
Gone (*with Michael Ledwidge*) •
Burn (*with Michael Ledwidge*)

PRIVATE NOVELS

Private (*with Maxine Paetro*) • Private London (*with Mark
Pearson*) • Private Games (*with Mark Sullivan*) • Private:
No. 1 Suspect (*with Maxine Paetro*) • Private Berlin (*with Mark
Sullivan*) • Private Down Under (*with Michael White*) • Private
L.A. (*with Mark Sullivan*) • Private India (*with Ashwin Sanghi*)
Private Vegas (*with Maxine Paetro*)

For more information about James Patterson's novels, visit
www.jamespatterson.co.uk

Or become a fan on Facebook